WILLIAM W. BENNETT

DEADLY RIVERS

Auctorem House
276 5th Ave, Ste 704-2591
New York, NY 10001
www.auctoremhouse.com
1.888.332.7718

Bring It Up Series

Deadly Treasure
Deadly Rivers
Deadly Currents
Deadly Storms
Deadly Darkness
Deadly Cold
Deadly Enemies

To my beloved children and grandchildren

Special thanks to my lovely wife, Cathy.

How blessed is the man who does not walk in the counsel of the wicked, norstand in the path of sinners, nor sit in the seat of scoffers! But his delight is in the law of the Lord, and in His law, he meditates day and night. He will be like a tree firmly planted by streams of water, which yields its fruit in its season, and its leaf does not wither, and in whatever he does, he prospers. The wicked are not so, but they are like chaff which the wind drives away. Therefore, the wicked will not stand in the judgment, nor sinners in the assembly of the righteous. For the Lord knows the way of the righteous, butthe way of the wicked will perish.

—Psalm 1:1–6 *NASB*

CHAPTER 1

DANK, SICKLY LEAVES left unsightly, loathsome smears of a putrid green on sticky skin and drenched fatigues soaked with sweat and grime. Insect repellent kept the blood-sucking and biting insects at bay, but nothing kept the tiny flies from tired eyes or being sucked up nostrils straining for air. The men had learned to keep their mouths closed. Captain Jim Shepherd made a mental note to include some netting to cover their faces and wished fervently he'd thought of it before.

Moving through the bayou in silence, he bore the frustration, just like every man on the team, not even lifting a hand to brush away the persistent pests, concentrating on being as still as possible. At night, movement caught the human eye. Slowly, deliberately, and silently, his men moved toward their objective. Sometimes, they were up to their chest in rancid water, moving at a snail's pace to not disturb the surface. Arms grew tired from holding guns above the surface, but no one offered a word of complaint.

Three months of training in this sweat-hole swamp was nearly at an end. They had their final mission tonight: to surround and capture a light infantry platoon on similar training. Why a light infantry unit was training in the swamp was unknown, but it was a gift, and Shepherd, also known as Jim, appreciated it. The light infantry unit knew that an "enemy" force was in the area and was alert for an attack. Tonight, paintballs and beanbag shots would simulate lethal ammunition; nonetheless, the battle would be quite real.

Whoever commanded the light infantry unit was an intelligent and wily officer with some experience. The spot they chose to defend was difficult to approach, especially with boats. Sentries were well-placed and alert. No fire burned in the camp, stealing night vision from the soldiers who slept there. Later, Jim learned that the captain who led this unit didn't believe anyone could creep up on his unit and surprise them. He had primed and prepared his men for an attack by boat, never dreaming anyone would dare the water on foot.

Special and covert operations were Shep's specialty, and in the Navy, he had become a legend as a SEAL team Captain. His team of twelve had grown to sixteen this year. Four men from Australia's SAS, with the blessings of General James March, joined the *Omega Force* and *Bring It Up* crew, and they were every bit as good as his own men. Tonight, they would prove that against elite troops of similar skill. Quickly, each of the four recruits grasped the training and became one with his old group. That wouldbe evident tonight. At least, he hoped they would be the victors.

A strong believer in dividing his teams into groups that worked well together, Captain Shepherd allowed those four recruits to operate as a separate team of four for this operation. Sean Oxton led the team. A compact man of almost limitless physical resources, his men affectionately called him Ox. His Australian accent and earthy approach to life as a soldier made him an instant hit with the rest of the team. That, coupled with his being an experienced field doctor, made his addition to the team of utmost importance.

With him were Lee Roy Brown, Chance Edwards, and Phillip Eustus. Brown and Edwards were black men, serious soldiers with all the skills and training the SAS offered. Eustus, referred to as PU, pronounced "pew," and was considered Chance Edwards his best mate. The two bunked together.Lee Roy, referred to as Lunch Box by his mates, bunked with Oxton. Bonding with these men happened quickly and easily, often with professional soldiers. It was good to know that, as they approached the enemy position, these men could be trusted and depended upon as an integral part of the team. Each one certainly proved that over the past three months, working harder than the rest to "catch up" to the men with whom they now served.

Oxton's team crept silently out of the water, covering perhaps three feet over the span of ten minutes. Jim listened for any telltale droplets of water that might give them away, the snap of a twig, or the rustle of a disturbed branch. Like the rest of the team, these men could move silently, and they knew the benefits of moving slowly, waiting patiently, and taking every precaution.

Four sentries opened their eyes wide in surprise as wet hands clamped over their mouths and Ontario Navy Knives touched their necks. The blades of the knives were black finished, but the stainless steel gleamed at edges that were razor sharp. They accepted their deaths according to the rules, slumping silently in place to await the end of the operation. Each sentry hoped his man would make the mistake of allowing him to drop. They didn't. Slowly and silently, they were lowered to the ground.

Moments later, the silenced MP5/10s spat out their perfectly aimed three-shot bursts, and startled men grunted in pain as the paintballs slapped against the protective headgear and bulletproof vests the men wore. Hours of creeping through the swamp ended in seconds of perfectly executed military precision. Shouts of "clear" rang out in the sudden silence.

Startled and somewhat chagrined, Captain Ron Kildare shook his head, clearing it from the ringing of the three shots that slammed into the side of his helmet. His smile was rueful.

"Damn! You boys are good!" he said. His men, he saw, were shaken. Every one of them had been "killed" in the exercise, and that hadn't happened to them for several years. The sentries were standing with slumped shoulders and chagrinned faces. One of them shook his head.

"I never heard a thing, Captain," he admitted sullenly. "At least not until this Aussie whispered 'you're dead, mate' in my ear." PU grinned at him. "And I was wearing my night vision goggles and keeping my head moving from side to side, just like we learned. I swear, Captain, I never heard a sound!" he added.

"Anybody who could sneak up on Currillo here is one bad hombre!"Captain Kildare said, indicating the man who had spoken. "He usually takes point for us because he's so good at it. It's been years since anyone was able to sneak up on him! I don't understand how you got your boats close enough to sneak up on us like that."

"We didn't," Dorf informed the captain. Affectionately known as "Dorf" and the tallest of the men in Jim's military unit, Lieutenant Waldorf Bernard smiled down at Kildare.

Captain Kildare looked up at Dorf, who towered over him at six feet nine inches, taking in the hard muscles, broad shoulders, and athletic quickness that was evident and whistled softly. "Now that's a big boy!" Kildare shook his head. "What do you mean you didn't?"

"We didn't use boats. We walked in," Dorf checked his weapon, making sure the safety was on before slinging the gun over his shoulder.

"You took a real chance doing that," Kildare said. "Cottonmouths, gators, and leaches love this blasted swamp."

"Leaches we can live with, and gators don't usually attack a squad of four men moving close together. Fortunately, only one of our team stepped on a Cottonmouth. Our boots are designed to resist snakebite, and the Kevlar leggings and body armor protected him. Just in case, our team doctor has several anti-venom injections and some blood." Jim looked over at Frank Miller, who grinned. It had been he who had stirred up the vicious snake.

"Nasty little critter tried to bite me four or five times. It was a little exciting there for a few seconds," Frank grimaced.

One of the men started a generator, and the camp was fully lit in a few minutes. Jim and his team removed their clothes and burned off the leeches that had managed to find their way through their heavy clothing. There were only three found. Their victims watched, aware that every one of these soldiers was in top physical condition, even the slimmest of them. Just looking at them told the "enemy" soldiers that the opposition had been a SEAL or Marine Force Recon group, and one that was as deadly as imaginable. Kildare called in for transport out of the swamp, and while they waited, the two units drank from their canteens and ate an MRE breakfast.

Captain Kildare knew about Jim and, for a few moments, briefed his men on Jim's history as a SEAL Team Captain. The light infantry looked with respect upon the men serving with Jim and never questioned that they were anything but a SEAL unit in training, much like themselves. Jim didn't bother to enlighten them.

Three transport helicopters picked up the men and supplies and shuttled them to Fort Jackson. There, Jim's team showered, changed into civilian clothing, cleaned, oiled, packed all their gear, and hopped a C-141 Starlifter transport to Bolling Air Force Base. Using military transport wasn't usually allowed for civilians, but Admiral Runion pulled some strings to get them to Washington. Jim thanked the flight crew for the flight. No one asked what unit he was with; everyone assumed his team was bona fide. He didn't bother to correct them.

The men carried their equipment to the gleaming CH-53D Sea Stallion helicopter, sitting majestically alone beside one of the hangars. On the side, near the tail, the company logo shone in the afternoon sun. Although everyone slept on the trip to Washington, they were still dog-tired. Twenty minutes later, the helicopter set down on a helipad just behind the Live Oaks mansion they all called home when they were away from the sea.

Everyone pitched in to help secure the helicopter and carry equipment into the house's basement. One wall hid a secret door, which opened into their weapons and equipment storage room. Even then the men didn't drop equipment and head up for sleep. Anything that needed to go into the washing machines was separated into the appropriate net bags. Guns, knives, and special equipment were checked, cleaned, rechecked, and only then carefully stored. Not until everything was stowed correctly did the men go to their bunkhouse or bedrooms in the mansion for a well-deserved rest. That kind of dedication made Jim proud to lead these men.

Early the following day, Jim skipped down the curving stairs and into the main foyer of the house. Smells from the kitchen told him that breakfast was on the way. Grinning, he opened the front door. Stepping into the muggy late-summer Maryland morning, he gently closed the door behind him. This retreat sat on thirty-six acres of developed wooded land. Crushed limestone paths meandered through the trees and around the property. Choosing one to take him down near the river, he set off on a brisk walk for his morning exercise.

Running was out of the question for this particular morning. Still stiff and sore from their ordeal in the swamplands of the bayou, he rejected his usual five-mile run and settled into a cardiovascular exercise walk. When he returned to the house a half hour later, most of the stiffness was gone, and he felt invigorated. Practically running up the steps, he entered the house and made his way up the steps and into his opulent bathroom for a shower. Five minutes later, he headed down to the dining room.

CHAPTER 2

B ILL F RANKLIN AND Tom Patterson, interesting new additions to the team, helped Wendall March and Bob Stankus set up the breakfast buffet. Wendall, usually called Windy by everyone, and Bob, whose nickname had changed from Stinky to Cuss, were one-year veterans in the company. Bob had graciously allowed the team to pick his new nickname commemorating his first year of service. Abe and Sturdy rescued them both from a life of addiction on the street.

Both were in much better physical shape, and their attitudes and demeanor had changed dramatically since the first days of their service to the crew. Confident now, moving with vigor and purpose, they seemed like, and were, very different men. In many ways, they were like all the rest of the men who served *Omega Force*.

Jim was proud of Abe and Sturdy for their efforts and proud of both men for their improvements. Charles Lincoln, nicknamed "Abe" because of his last name and love for the nation's founding fathers, and Tom Sturdevant, bearing the appropriate moniker of "Sturdy," led the galley crew on the ship. Both men were devout men of God and learned that life on a ship was an excellent place for someone to recover from addictions, providing constant work for men who needed that to realize that they could contribute meaningfully.

Bill Franklin, whom the crew nicknamed Bull, was a heavyset man with flaccid muscles and a pockmarked face. Only twenty-nine, he looked fifty because of the toll drugs and alcohol took on the human body. That would change, Jim knew, once on board the ship. He reminded Jim of Cuss when he first joined the crew, untrusting and antisocial. Although he was six foot two, the same height as Jim, his posture made him seem shorter. Bob was coaching him, carefully instructing him as they worked side by side.

Tom Patterson was another story. Everything about him said Navy, and until the past year, he had been a career Navy man. Five feet nine inches tall and a trim one hundred and fifty pounds, he moved with assurance and purpose. Two years past his wife left him while he was at sea. He began to drink heavily and was eventually discharged from the Navy for medical reasons related to his sudden increase in alcohol consumption. Abe rescued him from self-destruction by inviting him to serve on the kitchen crew.

Clean for nearly four months, Patterson certainly looked healthier, a tribute to Doc Wozniac, Abe, and Sturdy's efforts. Doc Wozniac, the team physician, was closely monitoring his liver problems, and Abe was helping him learn to eat properly to improve his health. Tiring easily, Patterson still worked hard, and the kitchen work was not particularly onerous. He seemed to be doing well and even nodded at Jim when the captain entered the room. As a new recruit, he was fitting in quickly and learning the ropes.

Sturdy came out of the kitchen with his huge arms full of hot dishes perched precariously on hot pads. Petty Officer First Class Tom Sturdevant was a giant, second in command of the kitchen crew. He stood one inch shy of seven feet tall and weighed three hundred and forty-five pounds, all iron-pumping sculptured muscle. Sturdy grinned down at Jim as he set the dishes out carefully, one at a time, balancing each one and dropping none.

"Welcome back, Shep," he greeted, his voice deep and resonant.

"Thanks, Sturdy. It's good to be back!" Jim replied with a smile of his own. He shook hands with Sturdy, his disappearing in that giant paw, feeling the man's strength in his grip.

"How did the team do?" Sturdy looked over the array of hotplates on the buffet, absent-mindedly wiping his hands on his white apron.

"Let's just say that if we ever go to war against the Everglades or Bayou, we'll get our butts kicked big-time by little, tiny irritating bugs!" Jim said with a laugh.

"So, how many of the light infantry survived?" Sturdy's question didn't surprise Jim, and he looked up as their eyes locked.

"None," Jim answered without inflection.

"And was the battle long and hard?" Sturdy shot the question as he began walking back toward the kitchen.

"Getting to the battle took the longest. The battle lasted just over a minute," Jim replied, picking up a warm plate from a fresh stack and lifting the lid off the bacon.

Sturdy shook his head, returning to the kitchen with all four helpers in tow, knowing the deadly abilities hidden behind Jim Shepherd's humility. Jim heaped bacon, sausage, and eggs on his plate, put the plate down at the table, and returned for a chilled red grape juice and a glass of milk.

Before he began, he bowed and thanked the Lord for a delicious breakfast and a great team. Cecilia Merton glided into the room as he lifted his head at the table.

Shining auburn hair framed a lovely tanned oval face with neat features. Huge hazel eyes, more blue than green today because of her blouse, lit up when they settled on Jim. Jim hurriedly put his napkin down at his plate and embraced Cecilia in the center of the room. Lifting her off the floor, he whirled her around, holding her above his head, and then gently set her down, laughing with delight. She reached up with both hands, took his face gently in her grip, and pulled him down for a long and delicious kiss. Anyone witnessing that kiss could see clearly that she was deeply in love with Jim and that he felt the same for her. For another moment, they simply stared into each other's eyes.

"I missed you!" he finally was able to speak, his green eyes suddenly soft. She reached up and rubbed his short black hair. He kept it short, the typical cut of his jarhead days more out of necessity than habit or a statement of style.

"Did we win?" she asked lightly, letting him go and walking over to the buffet.

"Against the enemy man, decisively!" he replied. "The little, tiny bugs routed us. I'm going to have helmets with netting next time!" he announced with feeling.

"Good idea," she agreed, helping herself to a bowl of oatmeal and fruit. Jim carried both to the table for her while she poured hot water into a tea strainer and dropped tea leaves into the steaming liquid. Strolling to the table, she nodded and smiled as he pulled out her chair, sat, and, when she was situated, watched Jim take his seat next to her.

Pouring milk on her oatmeal and cream into her teacup, she added two sugar cubes to the tea and stirred the liquid. Jim was already wolfing down his breakfast. Jim always ate quickly, partly because of his military training and partly because of his genetic wiring. He was a driver in social style, quite the opposite of Cecilia, who identified herself as an amiable, analytical person. She always ate slowly.

Over the months of their relationship, Jim learned to slow down but usually sat beside her while she picked at her food at what he considered a snail's pace. Everything she did was deliberate, and he loved that about her. Already, he was bouncing up for seconds as some of the crew made their way into the dining room for breakfast. He would probably take thirds, and she would still be working on her first and only trip to the breakfast buffet.

Each man greeted Cecilia with enthusiasm and real warmth. Since rescuing her from the clutches of Fezik al' Loudi, she has become an appreciated fixture and an esteemed and respected part of the team. Most of the crew were single men, and a few were widowers. She enjoyed their attentions as much as any girl surrounded by chivalrous men. Everyone on the crew knew she and Jim were working toward a serious relationship. So their attentions were wholesome, not so much because they worried about their relationship with Jim, but because that was the kind of men they were. Knowing they would be wholesome even if she and Jim were not moving toward that relationship made her even more appreciative of these strangely gentle, polite military men. It was an interesting contrast; the men were deadly yet polite and kind.

Walt Rule came in with James Warner. Walter Fitzhugh Rule, whom Jim had introduced as "Inchworm," was another Navy mechanic and on-deck machinist Jim was able to lure away to their crew. Inchworm was a tall, broad-shouldered, thirty-seven-year-old career sailor. He worked at model railroading, his main hobby when he wasn't tinkering with engines or machines. To Jim's relief, he was a lovable guy with a great sense of humor and a well-timed addition to the crew. Until then, Master Chief Petty Officer James

Warner, most often called "TRT," was the sole mechanic and machinist on the crew.

The last new addition came behind them, two inches taller than Inchworm and solidly muscled. Lonnie Johnson insisted that everyone call him Loony, and for the most part, he was just that. An electrician, also stolen from the best the Navy had to offer, was a quiet forty-year-old man. Humor usually came as a surprise from this quiet man and often brought down the house.

Sparks and Zeke, the Kline twins, followed Loony into the room. Sparks was their head electrician, and he had insisted on hiring another of that ilk for the sake of safety and his own sanity. His twin brother Zeke was a true computer nerd and proud of it. If the fact that the FBI and CIA both tried to hire him away from the Navy is any indicator that others thought he was on top of his class, he was indeed. He certainly could do wonders with computers and computer systems.

John Shepherd, known as JR to the crew, and Wade Adams arrived with Dorf and Mark Drumheiser. Mark, or "Mad Mark" because of his "mad" martial arts skills, was the shortest soldier under Jim's command. He stood a diminutive five feet four inches tall and weighed close to 160 pounds. Dorf, his best friend, was the tallest member of the military unit. John and Wade grew up with Jim and were his closest friends.

Shep looked at the crew seated around the tables as they talked, some serious, some joking, and sighed with pleasure. Numbering twenty-nine, his crew was just about complete. Bring It Up could handle a crew of thirty, with bunk beds even more if necessary. He thought that this crew was just about all they needed. Perhaps a secretary would be a good addition in the future.

His uncle Andrea Orvieto, brother to his mother Gwyneth, was seated near the head of the table with the house staff. Andrea was just sixty, a bluff, hearty seaman who doubled as a deck machinist and pilot on the crew. Jack Boswell sat next to Andrea. Jack was known as "Driver," who piloted the submersible. He was also a former SEAL and a deadly member of Jim's military unit. CG and Vince sat together by Wade, former Marines. CG was Clancy Garrett Franklin, and Vince was Vincent Hall.

Should anything be needed, Abe, Sturdy, Windy, Cuss, Bull, TP, or Tom Patterson sat together near the kitchen door. The kitchen or galley crew was a tight-knit group of non-combatants who were deeply appreciated and respected by the rest of the crew. Meals on board the ship and at the house were always an adventure with those six men in charge.

John Smith, or "Smitty," the ship's navigation officer, sat beside Uncle Zeke. Frank Miller, known affectionately as FM by the crew, sat with Smitty. Charles and Millie Wozniac sat with Gwyneth and Andrea, also known as "Papa," on the crew. All these people were at the very top of their fields of expertise, and Captain Shepherd was proud to lead them.

At that moment, his thoughts were interrupted as his secure satellite phone beeped a tune, immediately telling him who was calling. With real pleasure, he picked up the instrument and hit the receive button, connecting with the incoming call.

"Hello, Admiral!" Jim had a smile on his face and in his voice.

"I heard from the light infantry commander!" Admiral Runion began with an emphasis on the last word. "He wants to know if we can loan you to his group for training. His praise of your unit was almost embarrassing, and I believe he used the word impossible three or four times," the Admiral chuckled. "I told him you were already TDY and would not be available."

Admiral Runion, Secretary of the Navy, was one of six men who put *Omega Force* together and set the unit on its mission.

"The Army calling the Navy for help. Who would have thought?" Jim chuckled, noting that the table had become silent out of respect.

"I called because Sir Edward is here, and he wants to meet with you. I do, too. Can we set up a meeting today?" Admiral Runion requested, getting right to the point. Jim thought about the Admiral's request and smiled in anticipation. Sir Edward, Director of Operations of MI6, was a second intelligence community member who decided to break the paradigm and form *Omega Force*.

"Anytime this morning would work," Jim sat forward, his interest peaked.

"It's about the Hess operation in South America. I hear your place is something to see. Can we meet you there?" Admiral Runion asked.

"Wander on over, Admiral," Jim replied. "I can have the whole team ready by 0930."

"See you then," Admiral Runion said abruptly, and the phone went dead.

Jim put the phone back in the pouch sewn on the side of his right leg. He was wearing double-knee jeans that morning, made by Dickies, that included a cell phone pouch, which he thought convenient for his trim satellite phone. He looked over at Wade Adams, who was getting up to leave.

"Wade, please prepare everyone for a meeting with Admiral Runion and Sir Edward at nine-thirty. We'll meet in the library," he requested respectfully.

"Will do, Shep," Wade replied. Nodding to Jim, he turned to leave. Jim paused long enough to think that something was stirring with the ongoing investigations of the Hess family and their empire. He knew some of the history already, but blanks still needed to be filled in. Marta Hess hired the wrong kind of people, which meant there was more than a legitimate pharmaceutical business going on somewhere. They knew about the illicit drug trade, but he guessed there might be even more sinister criminal activity hidden behind the façade.

"Hello?" Cecilia was looking at him with a smile. He came back instantly. "I'm sorry!" he apologized.

"You were somewhere far away, I think," she said, dazzling him with one of her special smiles.

Once again, he thought how pretty this woman was. She wasn't pretty in the way a fashion model was pretty. Her beauty went deeper than that; it was the real and true beauty of godly womanhood, and it was more enticing because of it. More oval than angular, her face had features that made it unique and appealing in a way he couldn't quite understand. Her nose, a Princess Diana nose it would be called today, was markedly English. Her mouth was shaped into an appealing smile, showing teeth that were not perfect but clean and white. She already had smile lines at the sides of her eyes and a character to her face that said volumes about the depth of personality beneath.

Looking into her hazel eyes, he smiled back, took her hand, and brought it to his lips. "I'm truly sorry for ignoring you, even for a moment," he said. "I'm afraid my attention will be divided all too often."

"I can live with that," she said softly. "You wouldn't be who you are if that weren't true."

A woman who understood! He saw that she had finished sometime during his ruminations. Jim smiled, dropped her hand, and stood, pulling her chair away from the table for her to rise with him. They left the dining room to prepare for the morning meeting. Hoping they would often prepare together, he walked at her side with pleasure.

CHAPTER 3

FINDING THE HEADQUARTERS for *Bring It Up* made for an interesting drive into the more affluent homes in the Washington, D.C., and Maryland area. Admiral Runion looked at the sweeping lawns and forested properties with admiration and appreciation. Millions of dollars were spent to ensure that the area's natural beauty remained intact and that most of the trees stayed. Lush properties sporting small streams, scenic drives, and magnificent edifices were evenly spaced.

Captain Shepherd stood ramrod straight on the front steps to welcome the two men, Cecilia beside him. Admiral Runion looked at her with interest and decided that the two of them somehow complimented each other. They looked like they belonged together. He knew Cecilia was a welcome addition to the team, but she was becoming something more. He smiled, shook hands with her, and introduced Sir Edward. Jim shook hands with both men and turned to lead them into the house.

Milky-white marble tiles lined the floor of the substantial two-story foyer, with streaks of gray and light blue-gray accenting the colors. Twin curving stairways wound up either side of the foyer to the second floor, and above them, letting in the morning light was a domed glass enclosure. The steps were smooth marble slabs, and a beautiful ice-blue carpet ran up the center of each stairway. Even the banisters were marble.

"Wow!" Admiral Runion ran his hand over the cool stone. "This is opulent."

"More like ostentatious," Jim replied, turning slightly to look back. "The price was right when Ken Worthington built it, and the location couldn't be better. Mother likes living here," he added with a grin. He and John had asked their mother to move into the mansion and keep it up, hiring staff and living on the premises.

He led them to the library upstairs, which occupied an entire wing. One wall was two stories high, with a balcony to walk on in front of the shelves. The two men, staring in wonder, realized it was the equivalent of a college library. The collection of books was breathtaking, and for a moment, Sir Edward stood looking around him.

"This rivals the libraries of some of our more well-known lords whose families have collected books for centuries," he commented.

"We purchased the libraries of three colleges, closing their doors in three different countries. Other books were purchased at auctions around the world. Our largest collection is naturally focused on archaeology," Cecilia smiled at him as she spoke. "It took a crew of twelve fully qualified librarians to log and place these books."

"Indeed," Sir Edward replied.

The outside wall was interspersed with floor-to-ceiling windows overlooking the languid river scene. Sizeable comfortable leather chairs dotted the spacious floor, and a long glass-topped mahogany conference table stood majestically in the center on a parquet wood floor. There were fifteen chairs on each side of the oval table and a chair at either end, all on wheels, all spacious and comfortably padded in leather matching the lounge chairs.

Fifteen trained and deadly men stood close to the table, and for a moment, Admiral Runion and Sir Edward studied them as Captain Shepherd joined his team. Possessing the insights that only experienced intelligence officers acquire allowed them to assess their impressions quickly. Men who trained constantly and rode the crest of the wave of perfection as soldiers had a certain way about them. These extraordinary soldiers studied the two intelligence officers, exhibiting the demeanor of deadly predators, even at their most relaxed. Admiral Runion experienced that inward shudder he knew so well that told him danger lurked close by but that it was not directed at him. He smiled at Sir Edward, one eyebrow slightly raised.

Picking out the four new faces took a moment. Sir Edward didn't know the team as well as Admiral Runion and took a moment longer. Sean Oxton surprised both. He didn't look at all like a medical officer; perhaps that was understandable. First and foremost, he was a dedicated soldier. With Chance Edwards, Lee Roy Brown, and Phillip Eustace, Admiral Runion could see the four exhibited the same predatory aura as the other soldiers.

Shaking hands with the men, they were introduced to everyone and then adjourned to the conference table. Sir Edward handed a memory card to Zeke, who sat down at his laptop and began to upload the images and send them to each laptop at the table. There was no order to the way they sat down. Ten sat on one side of the table, nine on the other, suddenly focused and attentive to the purpose of this meeting. Sir Edward was surprised when the kitchen and other crew wandered in and took seats. Jim took the time to introduce each one.

"As you can see from these satellite photos and the photos our man inside sent us, Marta Hess is running something other than a Pharmaceutical program at this location," Sir Edward began, watching the photos appear, one after the other, on his laptop monitor. "I took the liberty of sending one of my best men to assess the situation firsthand. These photographs were all taken over a period of three days from a blind in a tree. In his explorations, he discovered that getting to the training facility required extreme caution and skill, traveling mostly under the cover of darkness."

The photographs showed a military camp and about a hundred men in training. All were Latinos, except the men doing the actual training. Sir Edward brought up those pictures individually and carried on his briefing.

"The older gentleman is a former Soviet officer on whom we would very much like to get our hands. He trained a great many terrorists during the days of the Cold War, especially cells that operated in West Germany. These two younger men are Palestinian. Ira Lehman identified them for us. Ira Lehman was the Director of Operations of Israel's Mossad, another member of the intelligence group that founded *Omega Force*. "These two men travel together as assassins, and they are training some of these men in their craft. The other two are your typical mercenary types who train guerrilla forces. Up until now, they were working in Africa. One is of Dutch descent, the other South African," Sir Edward accepted Cecilia's tall, glistening glass of ice water with a nod of thanks.

"I used Marta's name on purpose. She is really the head of this corporation and behind most of the corruption. Through the years, this family has built a dynasty of corruption behind the façade of their pharmaceutical company. That, by the way, is legitimate. They rake in millions in profits from their legal drugs and billions from their illegal drugs. A few of the pharmaceutical plants are used to manufacture strictly illegal drugs that they peddle all over the world. D.E.A. agents that got close to Marta's organization disappeared."

"The D.E.A. helped us with some of that information," Admiral Runion took up the narrative. "They've been watching Hess Pharmaceuticals carefully, especially since the Medálin Cartel began meeting with her grandfather. Legally, they can make medical-grade heroin and cocaine. It's pure stuff, and a little on the street is worth millions. The Cartel has been using the pharmaceutical plants to manufacture their heroin instead of all the little individual operations in the jungle. Once the drug is purified, it's shipped to the cartel with other legal medicines. Three of the cartel leaders have become entrepreneurs in the online medicine business worldwide. That's how they get their orders and ship the stuff now. It's really very clever from an entrepreneurial perspective. We all know how foolish living outside the law is so that I won't give them credit for intelligence."

"Uh, gentlemen," John cleared his throat. "We're not really involved in fighting the drug trade."

"No, I know that," Admiral Runion answered. "Marta Hess has branched out into biological terrorism. We have clear evidence that this particular laboratory is used exclusively for the development of biological weapons. We even know that she has one!" Admiral Runion paused after the last statement, judging the reaction.

"What we don't know is what it is or how or where she plans to deploy it. All we do know, chaps, is that there is a large body of men training in a camp for terrorists," Sir Edward spread his arms in uncertainty. "You boys are good at sorting out such groups."

For a few minutes, the men sat silent, looking at the images on their computer monitors. Five minutes passed before one of them sat back and turned his head to look at Captain Shepherd, signifying they were willing to take on the mission. One by one, they did the same. Jim looked around the table and then nodded his head. The real work was about to begin.

"We don't have a cover for an operation there yet, but I think I know someone who can provide us with one," Jim suggested. "I do have one question for you, Admiral." Admiral Runion nodded, a slight smile playing on his lips. He thought he knew what was coming.

"Did you know about this when you let me know there was an opportunity for us to train in the bayou?" Jim's eyes danced with inward laughter as he posed the question. "This is in the Amazon region, which is very similar to our bayou in heat and water."

"I thought the opportunity might come up," Admiral Runion looked at his fingernails as he replied.

"And you call me a pirate?" Jim replied, laughing.

"Well, I certainly don't live like this!" Admiral Runion shot back, waving his hand to indicate the beautiful house. Everyone laughed.

"Cecilia, would you be so kind as to call Dr. Alistair Gregg, explain that we need an excuse to visit the Amazon region of South America. See what he has to say, will you?" Jim requested quietly, smiling at Cecilia.

Cecilia gave that a moment of thought before smiling at Jim. She looked at her watch to determine the time difference and nodded to Jim as she rose and left the room. Jim watched her go before turning back to the table, saw the smiles on some of the faces, and blushed.

"Why don't you guys just shut up!" He was immediately embarrassed. "What?" John and Wade said together, raising their hands in mock confusion.

"Wade, I need drawings and plans for four riverboats designed for shallow river travel but with enough room to house teams and equipment. They need to be light but armored against attack. Get with Master Chief Warner and see if he thinks Inchworm, Loony, and Sparks would be any help," Jim ordered after sharing in the laugh. "Smitty and Uncle Zeke, you may want to help with the navigation and computer systems."

"We're on it, Shep," Wade said, rising quickly.

"The rest of you guys start looking into what insects, animals, fish, birds, plants, etcetera we might run into traveling along the rivers there. I need detailed maps and everything we can discover about the area. Also, I want ordinance suggestions. We're going to be in a hot, wet climate. What weapons will do well there, and which should we leave on the ship? Let's see if we can find a bona fide cover for our new boats. Doc, will you and Ox get together to determine what inoculations we need for this? Zeke, let's ensure we have all the legal papers to cross borders and enter foreign countries." Jim looked at each man as he made the request, and his eyes followed Wade out of the room.

Sir Edward and Admiral Runion exchanged looks. Smitty was already pulling maps and spreading them at one end of the huge table. Every person was busy all at once, and the air of competence was almost tangible. Both men liked working with professionals, and they smiled in appreciation.

"Well, Captain, we'll leave you to it." Admiral Runion said, rising with Sir Edward.

"I'll see you out, gentlemen," Jim responded, rising quickly. They followed him out of the library and down to the front door.

"Come back alive," Admiral Runion spoke quietly as Jim walked past him to lead the way out. It was something he always said to Jim during his service in the Navy. Jim grinned at the memory, nodded, and accepted the knowledge that the Admiral still cared about him. Thinking about it, he realized that, in a way, he still worked for the Admiral, though now their roles were as equals. Deciding he liked the relationship, he smiled as he led the way out.

Jim stood on the porch and watched as the two men drove away. He thought about the year he'd spent away from the Navy and the missions his team had accomplished. It wasn't much different from his days in military service. The only real difference was the lack of military oversight. Often, bad intelligence could kill good soldiers. Regularly, men making decisions behind the scenes made the worst possible decisions, sending good men to their deaths.

Omega Force gathered its own intelligence. Every crew member was involved in the planning process, and most knew the realities of such missions. Death was a genuine possibility, and regardless of how well one planned, things always were fluid in battle, changing, and a good soldier had to adapt appropriately or die. That, too, they accepted as part of what they did. But it went even deeper. He and his men believed in fighting the new terrorist threat to the world, and they were the best at what they did. Turning back, he began gathering everything he needed to plan a successful mission.

CHAPTER 4

Early the following day, Dr. Alistair Gregg returned Cecilia's call. A curator and teacher, an archaeologist and obtainer of rare objects, he worked for the Cairo Museum of Antiquities. Gregg, a British citizen, was on loan to the government of Egypt and had been at his post for thirty-two years. Now, sixty-one years old, he was as adventurous and exciting as he had been at twenty. All his students loved his courses and were willing to pay for excursions with him. Jim listened to his refined voice from halfway around the world.

"Captain Shepherd!" Alistair said. "Hello, my friend! I am using the phone you gave me, so we are secure. Am I correct?"

"Yes, Alistair. You are correct. It is good to hear your voice," Jim replied.

"Thank you. Now, my young friend, I am on the trail of some Mayan stelae and perhaps just one stela. Stelae is plural, stela is singular," he spelled the words as he spoke them. "They are signposts, much like totempoles, usually carved out of metal, stone, or even wood. I have in my liver splotched, wrinkled, old hands the diary of an explorer who claims to have seen one along the Japurá River. What do you think of that?" Dr. Gregg asked.

"My first question is: What is an expert in Egyptology doing studying Mayan stelae? Second, what is a Mayan Stela doing so far away from Central America?" Jim queried, remembering his history. "Aren't most of the Mayan cities located there?"

"Ah ha! You always were astute and went directly to the heart of the issue on the second question, my friend. What indeed? I have been studying ancient civilizations of all types. As to the Mayan mystery I've unearthed recently, there is the whisper of a rumor, the mere passing of a soft wind through the trees, that a vast treasure was transported south into the Amazon region, to a hidden city, to protect it from the clutches of Spanish conquerors. There is an even more distant whisper of a rumor that, at one time, the Mayan people inhabited that very region, living in a hidden city.

"One of the rumors says they lived there to protect themselves from the cannibals that inhabited the region. I'm very excited about this. I'm so excited, in fact, that I've invited everyone from our last team to join me. I took the liberty of suggesting that you might pay all their expenses," Dr. Gregg stated, his voice filled with excitement and anticipation. "We are all very excited to follow this expedition!"

Jim smiled at the suggestion that his company pick up the tab for their expenses and appreciated the trust shown by his scholarly friend. Bring It Up had indeed paid for the scholars' travel expenses and was willing to do so again. Dr. Gregg had come to understand him well and appreciate his needs.

"Of course, we'll pay the expenses. Let me know all the plans, and we'll make the arrangements. The team can pick up their tickets at the airports."

"Thank you, my friend. I shall email those plans by this afternoon," Dr. Gregg promised. "Until we meet. Uh, where will we meet?" Jim smiled as the professor remembered a critical detail at the last moment.

"Baltimore airport, and then to our home away from the ship, Dr. Gregg. "See you there," Jim replied with a laugh.

He closed his phone and put it in its pouch, fondly thinking of the spry little academic. Immediately, his attention was drawn to the discussion of the riverboats and their manufacture. He looked at the drawings and listened as the men discussed the various aspects of engineering them. What they had already accomplished was amazing, and pride filled him as he thought about leading such men.

Master Chief Warner and Wade Adams were in their element. Warner worked hard to develop a hydraulic propulsion system modeled after a little-known technical institute experiment with hydraulic-powered automobiles. It had been a success, and Master Chief Warner studied the design concept carefully, knowing that he could use it to propel a boat as easily as an automobile. The drawings he presented were detailed and Wade let Jim know the plans were pure genius. Hydraulic propulsion would mean their boats could be propelled in almost complete silence. Such an advantage in research vessels was truly a breakthrough, especially in the Amazon!

Wade Adams shared the Master Chief's excitement and proved once again a genius in engineering. James Warner was not the only man on the team who was amazed at how quickly Adams could go to the heart of a problem, solve it, and then put his ideas on paper so that others could understand it. Everyone who looked at those plans was impressed. The team spent the next twenty-eight days in constant communication with each other and the fabricators as their riverboats took shape and were carefully fabricated and put together.

No one on the team found this twenty-eight-day period boring. Every member, researcher, and crew member was involved in planning the expedition and operations pending. Training continued as usual, and the new crew members fit in. Bull lost almost twenty pounds in those days and put on serious muscle. He found shooting a fascinating hobby and learned everything he could about the weapons he was using, avidly listening to the training he received and learning quickly.

Jim observed him and noted that he was also intrigued with martial arts training. When he was invited to join the training, he accepted. His temper often got the better of him as he struggled to learn, but Mark was a teaching expert and soon had him learning to focus his energy so that his anger worked for him, not against him. In the process, he lost some of that edge he seemed to carry around others, warming to some of the crew. That made Jim feel that praying for his crewmembers was paramount and that Jesus was listening to his prayers.

Daily Bible study continued as usual, and the men met together morning and evening for prayer. During those twenty-eight days, the team's greatest asset was the spiritual bonding. Jim knew this, encouraged it, and enjoyed that Master Chief Warner, Abe, or Sturdy often quoted Founding Fathers to drive home the importance of daily Bible study and prayer to the crew.

Mrs. Shepherd and her staff attended the Bible studies and prayer times by invitation at first and by the end of the twenty-eight days by desire. Gwyneth was amazed at the depth of faith these men and women possessed, and her faith began to grow in what seemed to her leaps and bounds. Even more impressive was the overall effect of those times on her staff and the men and women from *Bring It Up*. They became a close-knit family with all the nuances of being siblings rather than friends or teammates.

Dr. Gregg arrived three days after his call to Jim with his two assistants, Mary Ann Lewis and Barbara Stafford. Shortly after that, members of his expedition began to arrive. Soon, the house was full and busier than ever!

Pretty Heidi Van Haaten from Holland arrived first and basked in the admiration of the team's men. Calvin Beardsley and his crew arrived next from Portsmouth to help with the riverboat building. His crew bunked in the warehouse Jim leased for the work and waited for their tools and equipment, which came over by boat.

Lisle Mirelle, the lovely Belgian, arrived that same day and immediately bonded with Heidi. Dr. Richard Persons, a fifty-two-year-old history professor, arrived soon after. Ferenc Adley, the French archaeologist, was the last to arrive, completing Dr. Gregg's team. Dr. Gregg kept his team busy researching the Amazon basin and discussing the possibilities and problems of following this elusive trail of evidence.

Gwyneth participated in some of the research, bonding almost immediately with Cecilia, Mary Ann, and Barbara. Jim suspected that his mother enjoyed having more women near her age to interact with. She also seemed to love Cecilia as a mother loves a daughter. Alistair seemed quite happy to accept her as part of his team, and as the days passed, she spent many hours each day working in the library. Because Jim loved research and being with Cecilia, he also spent hours each day with those in the library.

Had he known it, he would have been surprised to learn that his presence impressed the scholars working there. He exhibited a gift of keen insight and the ability to connect information sources, providing a quicker and more accurate track in the research. For him, the time was simply delightful. He was doing a task he loved as much as he loved the sea, soaking up knowledge to help his crew succeed in their venture.

Near the end of their research, the team had amassed enough pages of information to fill a dozen six-inch thick 3-ring binders! Each hard copy had already been scanned and put into a single work in the computer system and would one day provide the basis for a notable scholarly work, a sixteen-hundred-page textbook for college students that would not net the co-authors of Gregg and Persons much in financial gains, but a huge success in the world of academics. The fact that every member of the team contributed to the work gave Jim a deep sense of pride in the men and women who served under his command.

Patents for the propulsion system and river houseboats required hours of work, but by the time the prototypes were finished, they were pending and recorded, the fees paid, and papers filed. Of course, the "official" drawings did not show the secret compartments in each boat or the added protection in the walls against outside attack. For all intents and purposes, designed to travel very long distances up rivers little explored, these boats were a safe haven for researchers.

The day of departure arrived, and Bring It Up Coral sat at his berth, gleaming in the morning sun, as final preparations were made. Two reporters showed up to interview Dr. Gregg about his expedition. One of them asked for a tour of the ship and was granted his request. Jim sat in his office, busily filling out the last-minute paperwork necessary for this voyage when the reporter passed his office door. Dr. Gregg introduced them briefly and Jim smiled as the reporter was led away. His cover story was now bona fide by the press. In his line of work, that was always an advantage.

Once the papers were properly filled out, filed, or handed over to the port authorities, Jim made his way to the bridge and found John and Wade already in possession. Since the harbor pilot was on the bridge the two men came to attention as Jim entered.

"Captain on deck!" Wade snapped loudly, saluting Jim.

"As you were," Jim ordered, winking at John when the pilot turned his back. John winked back, the excitement in his face something tangible. "Are we ready to go to sea, Commander?"

"Lieutenant Bernard and Lieutenant Drumheiser are making the last check, sir. At their signal, we can proceed," John pointed to the two men on the rear deck, and then turned to the Pilot. Dorf and Mark gave their signal at that moment.

Jim handed the pilot the proper papers and the man made his way off the bridge and down to the dock. He would monitor the ship out of the harbor. As he walked off the ship he was smiling, having been wished a good day by both Lisle and Heidi. Dr. Gregg had been there too, and the pilot knew that this was an exploration venture into the Amazon. Thinking about the two pretty smiles he'd received, he walked into his office and radioed Bring It Up Coral that he could depart.

John took his place at the wheel and guided the ship out, while Jim and Wade turned to watch as the barge they were towing followed. Sitting sideways on top of the barge were four riverboats, painted in the Bring It Up colors of burgundy, pearl white, and aqua blue. Each boat could be covered with a camouflage skin if necessary, those tucked away in a storage cabinet on board. On the stern of each boat a name had been registered. *Captain Rob, Gwyneth, Warner's Wader,* and *Alistair's Lady.* Dr. Gregg had been deeply honored by the choice of the last name.

Jim solved the problem of naming the boats by letting everyone suggest a name, and then having the crew and teams vote. Those names had been voted the best picks. *Captain Rob* was what they called the automatic pilot on the ship, after Jim and John's father. *Gwyneth* was Jim and John's mother, their hostess at the Live Oak house. Jim Warner and Wade Adams suggested *Warner's Wader* as the builders. Barbara Stafford suggested *Alistair's Lady*, and it was a hit.

Listening as the crew went through the ship and checked everything, Jim watched the barge follow along. It was good to be at sea again. Taking a deep breath of the Atlantic breeze wafting through the open windows and doors of the bridge, Jim smiled with pleasure. They planned to follow the coastline, staying about a mile from shore, making their way slowly toward Belém. Slow progress meant that no one would suspect them of anything else but an archaeological expedition. Still, he suspected that Marta Hess would watch them. Hope for the best, plan for the worst. His thought made him smile. Adaptability was his watchword, and he intended to keep Marta Hess under careful scrutiny.

She knew that Bring It Up was responsible for recovering the biohazard canister, and he thought she might know it had contained something other than the virus her father engineered since no one died when it was opened. Everything was in place to keep her forces ignorant of the mission against her, but that didn't guarantee success. The fact that they had a very good chance of discovering the hidden city was icing on the cake.

The riverboats would help. Technologically advanced as they were, no one would suspect they were anything other than research vessels designed for a specific job. Ken Worthington thought selling their design and prototype might net the company several hundred thousand dollars a year in sales and royalties. Calvin Beardsley would spearhead that new venture. Researchers were always looking for new ideas in river travel, and these boats offered almost everything necessary, especially the lab designs.

Days passed, and they fought the usual mundane battles with sunburn, rust, wear and tear, and the ever-present Atlantic storms. An occasional training injury put a man off the team for a day or two, even longer if he sprained an ankle or bruised some ribs. Recovering quickly, the men were anxious to return to training. Every man on the team knew that his health was paramount to the team's success and bore the time off as best as he could. A day off meant missing the excitement of training and the competition between soldiers.

Doc, Charles Wozniac, M.D., a Navy specialist until he joined the Bring It Up Coral crew, quickly warmed up to young Sean Oxton, the team's field medic. Sean was a fully qualified battlefield doctor and surgeon, and they agreed on most treatments right from the beginning. Sean seemed to like and respect Doc, too. The two consulted often, Sean yielding to the older man's expertise. Jim was proud of the two and frequently thanked God for two such men on his crew.

Lonnie Johnson and Walter Rule, known more popularly as Loony and Inchworm, seemed to fit into the mix easily. Johnson had a guarded attitude toward the team. Jim knew from Sparks that Johnson feared his role as a non-combatant might be held against him, as it had on other ships in his time of service in the Navy. It would take him some time to realize that the Team didn't hold that against any of the crew, all of whom carried his or her weight. He wasn't too worried about Loony and his attitude. So far, the man carried out his responsibilities with expertise.

The rest of the crew was riding the crest of the wave to perfection. Keeping them there was the key. They practiced hostage simulations, shot thousands of rounds of ammunition each week individually with their weapons, and trained in hand-to-hand combat regularly. Not one of the Team resented the hard work, though a few complained more out of joking than anything else or to try to get sympathy from one of the girls. Each man knew the value of constant practice.

Dr. Gregg and his group watched them often with fascination, and they were introduced to Omega Force's secret mission, something Jim knew he would have to reveal this trip. Vowing to keep the secret, they all agreed to sign a non-disclosure agreement, and he thought they would indeed keep the secret. In time, he knew, the secret would be known, but it was still well guarded for now. Knowing the secret helped in the bonding between the academics and the soldiers.

Lisle and Heidi entertained the men, enjoying the attention and flirting with one and all. Andrea seemed to be their favorite, and the men smiled when he reminded them to look after his little girls. Everyone called him Papa, and he didn't seem to mind being a father figure, especially to the men. Jim knew that some of them had used that relationship to seek advice and that Andrea gave good advice.

That happened often in a close-knit military group. You became part of a family because people needed that. Away from your real family and facing terrors and horrors that were very real, the men in your unit became more than fellow soldiers; they became closer even than brothers. The older ones became older brothers; if they were old and wise enough, they became father figures. Occasionally, the men fought like brothers, and because they were a family, their relationship was stronger when it all worked out. Resolution of such problems was essential to each man. Every good soldier understood that most of being a soldier was training.

The daily grind, routine, discipline, all of those became watch-words. Without them, the possibility of being dead was genuine. With them there was a chance your edge would be sharp enough to allow you to return from battle. Those who had tasted battle appreciated the training and discipline. All of Jim's men were experienced, and he was thankful for that. No one appreciated the routine all that much. Such was life.

CHAPTER 5

INCHWORM LEANED OVER the small one-cylinder diesel engine and watched the oil ports individually go about their business of squirting the lubricant up over the crankshaft. Down here, the smell of diesel oil was strong. His booming voice announced that everything was working properly, and the engine stopped turning. With deft fingers used to work, he quickly put the engine back together again, tightening the bolts to specifications with a torque wrench.

They went through this once a week, ensuring the saltwater air and constant motion of the waves did not damage the engines on the riverboats. It was part of the job and routine, and Inchworm understood the need. He was an excellent mechanic. Master Chief Warner appeared above him as he finished up.

On another riverboat, Lonnie Johnson finished checking the electrical circuits. Footsteps sounded behind him, and he turned to see Dorf Bernard ducking through a hatchway to walk through his section. At six feet five inches, Lonnie was used to being taller than most people. Dorf was four inches taller and built like a tank.

A Petty Officer Third Class, Johnson wasn't used to officers like Dorf pausing to talk. Yet Dorf always did. Dorf served as a lieutenant on this crew, unlike any lieutenant Lonnie had ever met. Dorf stopped and watched as Lonnie closed up the electrical panel.

"Hey Loony! Everything working properly?" His manner was always friendly, and it had taken Lonnie some time to realize that the man actually liked and trusted him and needed his expert advice. That was another thing that Lonnie was not used to. In the Navy, officers never treated him this way. On this boat, he was the expert, and what he said went. Anything electrical was referred to the electricians on the vessel.

Initially, he mistrusted the team's friendliness, soldiers, and fighters. In the Navy, they had distanced themselves from the non-combatants. Not here. These men actually realized their dependence on men like him and treated him as an equal. He was as necessary to what happened on this venture as every other man. They treated him as an equal and another combatant when he trained with them. Loony smiled, one of the first Dorf had seen.

"Yes, sir, Lieutenant," Lonnie replied respectfully.

"Hey Loony. You asked us all to call you Loony. Can you just call me Dorf? I know I'm a lieutenant, but everybody else calls me Dorf. Haven't you noticed that most of the crew calls the captain Shep? We're not in the Navy anymore. We're all part of a company that does some pretty cool stuff. I'd appreciate it, man." Dorf's hand landed heavily on Loony's shoulder.

"Okay, Dorf. It takes a bit of getting used to," Loony said with a grin. "This is the first boat I've been on in a while where I feel that what I do is truly appreciated."

"Yeah! The Navy's like that sometimes. People forget that everybody doing his job is what makes the whole thing work. But we're not like that. Rank defines responsibility. You won't find anyone pulling rank here. I've been having a ball since I joined this outfit," Dorf admitted with a laugh. "Here, I get to do everything I really love, so putting up with the rest is fairly easy."

He moved on, and Lonnie Johnson smiled. Mistrusting this crew from the start had been a mistake, but he hadn't known how he could change that. The nice thing was, it didn't seem to matter now. He'd had friends on every ship but none among the officers above him. He felt that Dorf was already a friend, and the feeling filled him with a sense of surprise and no little pride.

Inchworm arrived at that moment, and Loony grinned. Walter Rule was full of fun and laughter. Why they called him Inchworm was still a mystery. The man was a veritable dynamo. He did everything quickly and deftly. Two inches shorter than Lonnie, he was balding, in good physical condition, with a ready smile and a happy nature. As usual, he had a smile on his face when he entered.

"Yo Loony!" he said, happy to greet his roommate. "The Inchworm has arrived! Where's the apple?"

He always said that. Loony grinned back. "Back in the galley on the main boat. Are you finished checking the engines?"

"Of course!" Inchworm replied, spinning a wrench around one strong grease-stained finger on his left hand. "TRT asked me (asked me, mind you) to see if you could give him some advice on the last boat. He thinks there might be a problem with the ignition. I asked him if he wanted to tackle it, and he told me we had an electrician with the right tools and knowledge to take care of those things."

TRT was the nickname the men chose for Master Chief Warner. The letters stood for Thermal Removal Tool. Over the engine room hatch, Master Chief Warner mounted a plaque with a sixteen-pound sledgehammer and the scored end of an acetylene torch. Below them were the words: "Delicate Adjustment

Tools." He often called his torch his thermal removal tool, so the name stuck.

Lonnie climbed into the next boat and walked up to the bridge, where Master Chief Warner waited. When he arrived, TRT smiled and nodded to the open panel.

"I think I've got something wrong here, Mr. Johnson. Could you please check it for me?" Master Chief Warner always called the men Mr. and used their last names. The Navy had ingrained that into him over the years, and he wasn't about to change. He always asked rather than ordered, which was not something the Navy always taught. Lonnie grinned and nodded.

"Sure thing, Master Chief," he said. He'd heard others call the Master Chief "TRT" but wasn't there yet with this older man. Master Chief Warner always called him Mr.; he felt at ease using the man's rank.

Employing his multi-meter, Lonnie checked the wires and discovered the problem almost immediately. After a few minutes of soldering, he rechecked everything and closed the panel.

"The bouncing worked one of those connectors on the wires loose. I soldered it, so that shouldn't happen again. I'll check all the others to make sure they don't have the same problem," he said, putting his tools away.

"Thanks, Mr. Johnson. I'd feel better knowing you checked them all," Master Chief Warner confessed. "Do you think the dampness at the equator will be a problem for our wiring?" he added thoughtfully.

"Not really, chief. Sparks designed the panels to have these seals to keep moisture out. Loony tested the soft rubber seal with his fingers as he spoke. Also, there's a small fan in there to keep everything dry. We may see some corrosion, but nothing to worry about." Lonnie replied. "Sparks and I checked all the specs, and everything should handle the weather without a hitch."

"Well, you and Sparks are two of the best. You would know," Master Chief Warner said. "Thanks," he added.

Lonnie thought about the riverboats as he made his way through each one, checking and soldering the connections, although the others had yet to work loose. These were terrific boats; the electronics were the best, sparing no expense.

On the river, they would draft about four inches and could be propelled over logs or sandbars that were even shallower. The pontoons were amazingly strong despite their lightweight design. Every comfort was considered for the trip, and Lonnie knew about most of them because they involved electronics. The air conditioning system was state of the art. Diesel generators could be used to back up electricity when necessary. Solar power would be the primary energy source, and those systems would be state-of-the-art. All the lighting on the boats was also state of the art. On the bridge, the pilot had all the necessary tools to navigate.

Sparks even designed the boats to repel snakes and other predators. Around the outside of the boat, solid copper wires were charged to shock anything that touched them. The shocks wouldn't kill but would discourage anything biological from touching them again—and anything human wouldn't like it either!

That wasn't the only protection they had. All the windows were bulletproof, and the walls were protected by a layer of Kevlar on each side. The outer shell was made of plastic and used to construct some aircraft. It was considered protection from projectiles as well. Besides that, narrow portions of the wall could be removed, in the walls on the sides, through which one could shoot back at an enemy.

Lonnie knew each riverboat would tow a specially designed rigid raider raft with a powerful outboard engine that could carry sixteen fully armed soldiers up and down the river when needed. Whatever this team tackled, their equipment was impressive, the very best, and he knew and understood why. That, too, was unlike the Navy in some ways.

Some of it was fun, too. Lonnie was becoming quite a marksman with the Heckler & Koch MP5/10SD. He liked the feel of the weapon and its ease of operation. Suddenly, he wondered if he might be called upon to repel borderers while the Team was away. It would be his first chance to use his training.

Later that day, back on the ship, he asked Captain Shepherd if that was possible. Captain Shepherd stood momentarily looking out his office door, past where Lonnie sat in a chair across from his desk. The captain wasn't ignoring him, only thinking. Lonnie waited patiently. Jim smiled.

"I believe that that opportunity may often come your way, Lonnie. If it comes to that, you'll be a good man to have in a fight. In a few weeks, you'll be able to shoot as well as anyone on the team with a pistol, and you are already equal to many of us with the MP5/10. Although you've never worn it, we have a Kevlar suit and vest in your closet in the ready room," Captain Shepherd said, his eyes returning to Lonnie's and looking straight into them. "You may not have been in combat in the Navy, but you will get your chance on this team, probably too often. That's why you have your locker down there. Every crew member has a locker down there for that very reason."

The ready room was the secret armory they had hidden in the hold.

Lonnie knew about the suit. He'd seen it in his locker but never tried it on. "Remember that when the team is gone, those river boats and this boat are your responsibility to defend.   That's one of the reasons we chose you, Lonnie. You're a good soldier with a good service record," Jim added. For a moment, Lonnie sat in shocked silence. These men were the deadliest fighters he had ever encountered, and he was told he was one of them. It filled him with pride and with fear at the same time. Loony was beginning to see why these men were so close and why they gave their all for the captain. At last, he found his voice.

"Thanks, Captain. I wanted to know," he said quietly.

"Most of the men call me Shep when we're not at port or around strangers," Jim said with a smile. "You may too, Loony."

"It takes a little getting used to, uh, Shep," Lonnie said with a sheepish smile. "I'll get it in time," he added with another grin.

"It takes a while to get the Navy out of our system, is what you mean," Jim replied with a grin. "Don't let it worry you. You'll get the hang of it soon enough." Loony smiled as the captain said the last, knowing he was being encouraged.

"I see now why you include us in all the planning sessions and let everyone know what's going on," Lonnie said conversationally. "We all need to know."

"It's more than that!" Jim exclaimed, his voice rising a little with his eyebrows. "We need your input, too. Everyone on this ship can contribute something to our efforts. King Solomon said that where there are many counselors, there is victory or success; however, you want to interpret the sentence. I believe that, and I depend on you to help us succeed. You personally! Every man and woman in this outfit has that responsibility."

"Yes, but I'm a noncombatant!" Lonnie said before he thought to hold that back.

"Just because you haven't held a gun on the front lines doesn't mean you're not a soldier. We couldn't do what we do without you. And you've been trained. You have a keen mind. Don't ever be afraid to offer a suggestion!" Jim said with some heat. "I know there are officers who ignore that their noncombatants are necessary. They sometimes even think of them as unable to enter the battle. They're wrong! The Navy doesn't waste time training men to fight. Good men have trained you, and if the time ever comes, you'll hold your own and do us proud. But you make us proud every day just by doing your job. Never let yourself doubt that."

"Thanks, Shep. I can tell you mean that. I won't let you down in my daily routine or if it comes to fighting," Lonnie said simply. "May I ask you something else?"

"Whatever, whenever," Jim replied with a wave of his hand.

"Why am I part owner of the company when I came on after everyone else?" Lonnie asked.

"Everybody on this ship, except the good Doctor Gregg and his team, are part owners. We share in the profits. It protects us and gives great incentive to everyone. From now on, any profit we make gets divided equally among us, after operating expenses, etcetera. You might like to know that the vote to add you to the crew was unanimous, as it was with all the new guys. We might not have voted that way a year ago for the new guys in the kitchen crew, but after watching Abe work with Cuss and Windy, we knew it was a good thing. By the end of this adventure, we'll all be good friends. Just wait, and you'll see!" Jim finished.

"Cool!" Lonnie exclaimed happily, rising. "Thanks, Shep. I'll get back to work now."

"See you around," Jim replied as Lonnie left the office. At the door, Lonnie stopped, turned, and saluted him. Jim returned the salute smartly with a smile of appreciation. He went back to work feeling better about Lonnie.

CHAPTER 6

BULL WAS ANOTHER matter. Bob Stankus appeared at Jim's door shortly after Lonnie left. He knocked on the doorjamb before entering and sitting in front of Jim's desk.

"May I talk to you for a minute or two, Shep?" he requested.

Jim put the paper he had just signed in the outbox, sat back, and looked at Bob with a smile. "My door's always open, Bob. What can I do for you today?"

"I'm sorry about Bull at breakfast this morning," Bob blurted. Jim could see Cuss was nervous as he continued. "He shouldn't have talked to you that way, and Abe dealt with it. I just feel bad. I should have seen it coming or something. Bull just needs time, like I needed time when I first joined."

Bull forgot to refill the milk pitcher, and when Jim asked for milk a second time, the man became defensive, even asking if Jim didn't realize he was busy! Jim recalled the incident with a smile. Bob had rushed him out to the kitchen to quickly deal with the problem.

"Do you remember what you were like when you first came on this ship?" Jim asked with a grin.

"Oh, God! Let's not go there!" Bob said with real feeling. "How did you put up with me?"

"The same way we put up with Bull," Jim said. "It took you months to come around. It will take Bull the same amount of time, maybe even more. I think he's ashamed of his past and that it bothers him that we know about it. We'll just have to be patient. I think you handled the situation very well, Bob. I'm proud of you. If anyone can help Bull, it's you."

Bob was instantly embarrassed, flushed from blushing, and looked away, his eyes saying he was pleased by the compliment and his body language saying he was uncomfortable receiving it. Jim understood the feeling. He often wrestled with the same conflicts within himself and was pleased that Bob had a strong sense of humility.

"Thanks, Shep. You all have been good to me. I just hope Bull can see that soon."

"He will. Give him time. I leave all the discipline to Abe, as you know, because that's his crew. Let Bull know you talked to me and tell him what you said. It might do him good," Jim suggested.

"I will. Thanks again," Bob stood, saluted, and left the office.

Cecilia appeared at the door, looking around the jam with an amused expression. Jim suspected she had been standing outside the office for a few minutes.

"May I have some of your valuable time, great sage and leader?" she asked impishly, coming into the office.

"Just how am I supposed to get any work done?" Jim asked, throwing up his hands in mock dismay, his eyes shining with delight. Cecilia smiled at him. "And what sage advice can a simple sailor give a lovely woman?" he added as she sat down demurely.

"Good riposte!" she said. "I thought perhaps you might offer a poor lonely soul company at the lunch table," she added.

Jim looked at his watch and realized that it was almost lunchtime. He grinned. Taking Cecilia to lunch was something he wouldn't pass up for anything. "Let me finish one or two more things, and I'll be glad to escort you to lunch," he said. Reaching for the last report he needed to deal with, he smiled at her. "Will you wait?"

"Since you invited me, of course!" she replied. It would allow me to study my great sage and leader in his natural habitat!" she giggled.

For the next ten minutes, he tried to get work done, but every time he looked up, Cecilia smiled at him knowingly. At last, he gave up, shuffled the papers to the side, and rose with a sigh.

"Such a great sigh!" she said. "The weight of your office, I'm sure." "About a hundred and twenty pounds of trouble sitting across from my desk!" he quipped with a smile.

"I shall eat less, then," she responded, rising. She was secretly pleased.

Her weight was actually one hundred and thirty pounds.

"Maybe we'll finish at the same time then," Jim said, stating one of the things he'd noticed about them. He ate quickly while she took her time. It didn't bother him, which she knew, and she smiled.

"I don't have taste buds in my stomach like you and so many of your men," she commented, her lips serious, her eyes dancing with laughter. "Nor have I developed the ability to swallow a steak in one bite!"

"Then, by all means, take your time," Jim replied, taking her hand as they walked down the hall. She liked the feel of his hands, hard, calloused, strong, yet gently holding her own. At five feet eight inches, she was tall for a girl and used to looking most men in the eyes. Jim was half a foot taller, and beside him, she felt tiny.

It was a good feeling. Without thinking about it, her body leaned against his as they walked.

That day, lunch included cold-cut sandwich meats that could be eaten with or without bread, complete with all the fixings. Tempting salad fixings were plentiful, as were several different kinds of cheese. Jim, who stayed away from bread as much as possible, helped himself to several pieces of rare roast beef, spiced mustard to dip it in, several cheeses, and a healthy salad with blue cheese dressing.

Some thinner men made huge sandwiches, which they wolfed down in typical soldier fashion. Most of the Team avoided bread and sugars as much as possible, often causing Doc to worry considerably about their cholesterol levels. He worried needlessly since most of them were between one hundred twenty and one hundred thirty on their charts. They needed more proteins to keep their bodies going and burned calories like lumberjacks.

Bull approached the captain's table, his head down, with shuffling steps. He stood beside Jim and mumbled an apology, to which Jim nodded but said nothing. Still shuffling, the man turned away and returned to the kitchen, mission accomplished. Bull watched from the corner of his eyes to see if anyone was making fun of him. To his surprise, no one was, nor had anyone taken more than a cursory interest in the interchange.

"That was well done," Abe said when Bull entered the kitchen. "Now get back to work and mind your tongue."

Bull almost petulantly returned to work, carrying out refilled pitchers and tidying up the buffet. The man was drug and alcohol-free now, entering his fourth month after detoxification. Abe knew that the man still had difficulty believing he was earning his keep, actually working a job and making a contribution. It would take time with this one, maybe even more than it had with Bob.

Bob was smiling, whistling at times, and enjoying his work. Windy, of course, was also doing well. Both were trying to help Bull, though Bob had the best chance. Abe wondered if Bob ever thought about the fact that he was now helping someone in the same way he had been helped. He was reasonably sure that Bob was doing it for that very reason, but they hadn't talked about it yet. Soon, Abe thought they would, but he was waiting for Bob to make the first move.

Through the porthole windows of the swinging stainless steel kitchen doors, he watched Bob help the man put things just right. Bob did it in a way that didn't threaten Bull. Abe smiled, and Windy looked out beside him.

"Bob's doing wonders with him, isn't he?" he asked.

"Great wonders," Abe replied. "You helped Bob; now he's helping someone else. That feels good, doesn't it?"

"I never really understood why you helped me until Bob came along. Now I know. I'm going to be helping Tom more than Bull, I think," he added thoughtfully. "I know what it is to be betrayed by a loved one."

At that moment, Tom appeared, and the two backed away from the door as he entered, carrying a tray of dishes and flatware to be washed. He grinned as he passed them, talking on the way.

"That Bob is doing miracles with Bull," he said.

"We were just talking about that," Abe said with a smile.

"And how am I coming along?" Tom asked, pausing a moment to look at the two of them.

"Physically, you're doing much better. We need to get you healed up in the emotional department, though," Abe answered honestly. That was one thing Tom loved about Abe. He was candid. And Abe could say things in a way that didn't hurt. Smiling at the two men, he spoke.

"And is Windy going to help me through that since he's gotten over his betrayal?" Tom asked a little too innocently.

"I don't think you ever do get over it completely," Windy admitted, his face serious. "At least, I haven't. It still hurts deeply. But I've learned how to live with it. I think I can help you if you let me."

"Well! That was honest!" Tom said, smiling lopsidedly. "I guess I'll have to try, although I don't feel like it. When I think about it, I still shrivel up inside and either feel totally defeated or a wave of rage, neither of which I want!"

"Actually, you'll probably help me as much as I help you. We've been through it, and we understand, probably better than anyone else," Windy offered.

Tom nodded, his face suddenly filled with sadness as he turned away. Abe sighed, and Windy winked at him. It was a beginning. The two went back to work. Windy knew that, like him, Tom would find it very difficult to trust any woman ever again. Yet deep in his heart, he had hope.

Sturdy, who witnessed the whole thing, looked down from his great height and smiled at them both. "God will provide all that we need. If we stay focused on Him and His word, it will all come together for good in the end." Sturdy often said things like that to remind them where their true help and wisdom came from.

Later that night, they encountered their first tropical storm. Before the water became too rough, four men went back to the barge to keep an eye on their precious cargo. Dorf, Mark, Phil Eustus, and Inchworm volunteered for the storm watch. Once they were safely on the barge, the HSB was carefully stored on board. Lashings were checked, and hatches were sealed as the men prepared for the growing storm.

The storm raged all through the night. The men constantly watched the barge, checking and rechecking the ties, straps, and chains that held everything in place. Dorf stood in one of the river-boats, his legs braced against the roll, watching the tow cable to be sure they didn't fall too far behind or begin to snap forward, which might cause them to collide with the rear of the tug. His eyes were focused, and he kept his mind focused on his job.

Wade, then Andrea, and finally Jim took the helm of Bring It Up Coral, while Driver, Vince, and FM maintained the rear watch on the tug. Winds whipped up to force three on the scale, but the ship plowed through the rising waves and weather as though the sea were calm. Jim loved the feel of the power beneath his feet as nature blew her fury against them. Bring It Up Coral was designed to tow a crippled oil tanker through anything Mother Nature could throw at her.

Some of Dr. Gregg's team were seasick and spent the night in the hospital wing under the tender care of Doc and Aunt Millie. Bull, however, facing his first real storm at sea, found the experience exciting and spent part of his evening moving around the ship to see how the men handled such a storm.

Having never been on the bridge itself when anyone was there, he crept in sheepishly while Andrea was at the helm and Vince was at watch. Both men welcomed him, and neither asked him to fetch them anything from the kitchen. He stayed on the bridge, intrigued by all the high-tech instruments and gear, the computer center, and the compass deck, learning about his ship and crew. Every question he asked was answered without rancor or reprimand, which pleased him.

When Jim came on duty, Bull left the bridge to get some sleep before his early rise for breakfast. Jim spoke with him briefly and smiled as the man walked out the door and down the steps. Bull was hooked on the sea. He never knew what he had missed all these years, and Jim knew the look. From now on, the man would only be happy on the sea. Always challenging and constantly changing, the sea was as fickle as the weather that drove it. That was true. But ultimately, the sea was a fantastic challenge, an exciting entity.

Much the same thing happened to Jim at a very young age. The thrill of a storm was all it took, and the sea became his love. He wondered if it was the danger he craved, the challenge, or just not knowing what was coming from one moment until the next. The sea was like that—dangerous one moment, easy the next. Deadly one moment, it was enticing the next. He would never get enough of the sea as long as he lived.

Riding out the storm, they churned into calmer seas and kinder weather early the next morning. Jim gave up the watch to John at eight hundred hours, his hands and calves aching from the strain of the storm, feeling somehow more alive for the adventure. John, who knew exactly what his brother was feeling, smiled at him as they exchanged places.

"Master Chief Warner says everything is ship-shape in the engine room.

C.G. just came in from checking things on the deck and says everything is fine. One strap broke during the night, and he replaced it. It was on the crane, but nothing came loose," John reported quietly. "Cecilia says she's saving a place for you at breakfast," he added, a knowing smile on his face.

"I should just go to bed and spoil her fun," Jim teased.

"I'd go to bed dressed. Knowing her, she'd walk in your bedroom, haul you out by your ear, and down to the dining room," John replied with a wink and a laugh.

"Good point. I'll go have breakfast," Jim agreed with a laugh. On the way down, he toyed with the idea of going to bed and having Cecilia storm in on him. He quickly discarded that idea and went down to the dining room, tired and hungry. He was among the last to eat that morning and was glad Cecilia had already enjoyed her breakfast.

Bull seemed to have an extra spring in his step as he worked around the breakfast buffet. He even greeted Jim properly as the captain came to the buffet to fill a plate. Jim smiled.

"Great storm, eh?" he spoke with a smile of understanding. "Best time I've ever had, Captain!" Bull responded.

"We'll make a sailor out of you yet," Jim replied, turning away with a full plate. "Bull, you may call me Shep when we're at sea. You're not an employee but a partner and a friend."

He didn't see the flush set in Bull's face or the pleased look on his face. Bob did, understood it for what it was, and silently gave thanks.

CHAPTER 7

AFTER FOUR HOURS of much-needed rest, Jim got up, showered, and dressed in his work coveralls. He visited the men, cleaning everything on deck and the engine room. FM was down there with Inchworm, and Master Chief Warner was still asleep in his quarters. The two men greeted the captain with respect.

"He's a great ship, isn't he?" Jim asked as he entered the glass-enclosed control center of the engine room. It was the only place one could talk without raising one's voice.

"He's got the power to spare, that's for sure," Inchworm agreed. "Doing what he's designed to do with panache! This baby is designed to eat storms like that for breakfast!"

"Enthusiast!" FM said sourly, not meaning it, of course.

"I'd like to see the fuel consumption ratio comparisons between running over calm seas and running through the storm," Jim said with interest.

"On your desk, Shep," FM said. "Master Chief asked me to run them for you. He figured you'd like to know. They were about the same as last time. We used a little more fuel because we were quartering the storm this time."

"Thanks, FM. If I don't see him before you, tell Master Chief thanks for me," Jim replied.

He finally returned to his office to deal with the ever-present paperwork that plagues every Captain. Bull appeared a short time later, bearing a tall glass of iced tea with two slices of lemon perched on the edge. Jim thanked him, and the man retreated, less morose and inhibited than before.

This was, Jim knew, only the beginning. When things went well, one tended to forget the dangers that lay ahead. He reminded himself of the danger and got back to work, sipping the tea with pleasure when he had squeezed his lemon wedges, dropped them into the liquid, and stirred the lot. Like everything on a ship, his desk was bolted to the floor, and a cup holder attached to the right-hand edge of the desk held his cup in place, keeping it from spilling onto anything on the desk surface itself. When it was empty, he left it there until he finished the work, getting up just in time to go down for dinner. He took his empty glass with him.

Following the shoreline, as planned, those without duty often stood on the observation deck studying the land and boats with interest through powerful binoculars. It was not a boring trip, and they arrived in Brazil, heading into the port of Belém in mid-morning, surrounded by ships, yachts, and boats of all kinds. Here, a harbor pilot came on board the ship to guide them. Bring It Up Coral was ordered to drop anchor and await the arrival of the harbor pilot. Every crewmember on board followed Jim's lead, putting on his or her dress uniform that morning so that when the pilot did come aboard, he would see the crew at their very best.

An hour passed as they floated at the end of the anchor chains, the ship rising and falling with the gentle morning swell. An official-looking boat pulled alongside, and two men were ushered on board. One was the harbor pilot, and the other was supposedly a government official checking their papers.

This was unusual enough for Jim to raise his eyebrows at John and Wade. Both nodded back. The whole situation smelled wrong. Warned by his instincts, Jim went through the process with just the right amount of wariness and cooperation.

Senior Jesus Manuel looked over the records, his eyes scanning them carefully. His name wasn't really Jesus Manuel. It was Jorge Stefan di'Ondonas, attorney for the Hess Pharmaceutical Corporation. Bribing his way to becoming an official inspector of papers and ships was child's play to one so versed in South American politics. Senorita Hess was not satisfied with the arrival of this boat and its crew. She wanted to know if they had traced her from the Mediterranean. It was his job to discover the truth.

Jorge determined that Dr. Alistair Gregg, through a research grant, hired *Bring It Up* to explore the entire Japurá River. They were looking for Stela or Stelae from the Mayans. Somewhere, he had heard stories of markers left by the Mayans along one of those rivers. Dr. Gregg was legitimate, his papers all in order, and a respected member of the Museum of Antiquities in Cairo of all places. Another tie to the Mediterranean!

Senior Jorge asked to see the contents of the hold and was granted his request. Whatever crates he asked to be opened were laid bare for him to see. Asking to see the rest of the ship brought raised eyebrows again, but the men acquiesced and gave him the tour. He looked in closets and drawers and found no weapons and nothing to suggest that this was a military unit of any kind. His probing questions unearthed no connection to Senora Hess and the Mediterranean.

Previous searches and research came to the same conclusion. Jorge was not satisfied, so he asked to see the barge's contents.

Politely, an Ensign took him to the barge in the highspeed boat with a very tall Lieutenant. Searching the riverboats took almost an hour, and again, he came up empty. The barge was used to transport the boats and held nothing else except the four rubber rafts that were obviously lifeboats for the riverboats.

Frustrated at finding nothing, he retreated to the ship and announced to the River Pilot that all was as it should be and that the ship could be berthed. He warned Captain Shepherd that his ship might be searched again from stem to stern because of the threat of terrorism. Jim simply stared at him through stormy green eyes that somehow made the attorney very nervous.

Thinking about it, he realized the idea that the crew of Bring It Up Coral might be involved in a terrorist attack was abhorrent to the captain and the crew. He didn't care about offending them, but he knew how to read people, and this man and his crew represented the kind of people he disliked the most. They were honest, hard-working men and women who believed in a highly moral standard of living. The very demeanor of every man and woman on the crew told him these were also dangerous people. If pushed, they would not bend but would, in turn, retaliate.

Once berthed and with all the bills paid, the crew went about launching and supplying the riverboats. Jorge stayed close by and watched, noting that the officers were no longer in dress uniform but now wore simple work uniforms without insignia and were working as hard as any of the crew. Sweat stains grew on their tan coveralls under the arms, down the chest, between the legs, and behind the knees. They worked hard, like a crew earning its keep by sticking to a schedule.

Later that evening, an official search of the ship and riverboats took place, and again, nothing suspicious turned up. Dr. Gregg, traveling alone into the city, visited the museums there by appointment while his assistants, also traveling alone, did research at the library, university library, and then at the museum libraries. That they were allowed to enter the latter's most sacred inner sanctum was mute testimony that they were who they said they were. Jorge also noted that a contingent of retired Navy personnel hired to secure the ship arrived and met the captain, each carrying a duffel bag onto the ship.

With relief, Jorge lifted his car phone and dialed the compound. Marta Hess had two secretaries, and the phone was answered quite professionally on the first ring. "Hess Pharmaceuticals," a soft Spanish voice said in idiomatic English. Secretaries always spoke in English first because, as Marta once explained, English was the language of the world.

"This is Jorge. Please put me through to Ms. Hess," Jorge said quietly. It pleased him to be powerful enough to reach such an august person quickly. After only a moment of silence, Marta Hess picked up the phone.

"Well?" her well-bred, somewhat petulant voice spoke.

"Twice, the ship and riverboats were searched. I searched them myself. All is legitimate. There are no weapons anywhere to be found other than a shotgun on the bridge, where one would expect to find such a thing. It is in plain sight, locked away, and only the Captain and Commander have the keys. Hunting rifles are also locked away. The boat has been hired by Dr. Alistair Gregg for an exploration to find Mayan Stela or Stelae on the Japurá River."

"That fairytale?" Marta Hess's voice sounded surprised. "Very well. Let them come, but keep them under surveillance for the first two legs of their journey," she added after a moment of thought. "Have Tupi take care of it. Pay him well enough to discourage them from going forward."

"Si," Jorge agreed with an evil smile. Tupi was an idiot, a savage idiot, and no one would ever connect with Hess Pharmaceuticals. He was a known river pirate. Jorge made the call, negotiated a fair price, and added a bonus if the exploration team was handled correctly. Tupi, of course, asked for payment upfront. Jorge agreed with a sigh.

Jorge had no way of knowing that the *Bring It Up Coral* monitored every word he spoke into his phone and the numbers he had just called. Zeke whistled softly, labeled the thumb drive, and then asked Cecilia to take it to Jim. As soon as she was out of her seat, he looked for information on one Tupi, the river pirate. Accessing the computer records of this backwater law enforcement agency was easy, and within moments, Zeke had pictures, the name of the pirate's boat, and his rap sheet.

Jim, after listening to the tape, smiled grimly. Cecilia recognized that look in his eyes and smiled herself. Whoever this Tupi was, he was in for a rude awakening when he crossed swords with Jim Shepherd and his crew. She took the labeled drive to the safe and locked it up for evidence after putting it in an envelope with a code written in one corner. Jim watched her movements with some puzzlement, studying her face carefully to read her emotions. Surely, she knew he was going into danger, yet she seemed to think this was logical and proper. Again, he found himself amazed by this surprising young woman.

Long after darkness, the weapons and military supplies were carried onto the riverboats and hidden in their specially designed spaces. Each man had his own weapons and suit storage beneath the floor of his berth. When all was ready, the men climbed into their new beds and slept through the remainder of the night until the predawn darkness of early morning. Dr. Gregg and his team slept on *Alistair's Lady* with the kitchen crew. Their boat would be used for meetings, eating, and as a base of operations for his studies. It was the only vessel with a full galley, designed with Sturdy's great size and height in mind.

Captain Rob would take point with Six Team One. Jim was in command of this team. Driver, Zeke, FM, Ox, and Smitty were with him as the fighting unit. Cecilia and Master Chief Warner traveled in this vessel.

Warner's Wader would follow with Six Team Three in residence. Wade Adams had command of this team. Lunch Box, Mad Mark, Chance, PU, and Sparks were his fighting unit. Loony and Inchworm bunked with them.

Alistair's Lady took third position, with Andrea at the wheel. *Gwyneth*, under John's command, brought up the rear with Four Team Two. Dorf, C.G., and Vince were the rear guard. Their boat had the heaviest load of equipment and storage because they had the smallest crew.

Towing the rigid raider-style rubber rafts behind them, the four riverboats started their small diesel engines and began the long and challenging journey through the Amazon region. Leaving Belém behind in the darkness, Jim thought about the ship now guarded by a private security firm that had flown down for that purpose. Admiral Runion was responsible for its presence, though in such a roundabout way that no one would make the connection. They seemed to be capable men; all retired Navy, a skeleton crew of six men to keep the boat ship shape.

No one could operate the ship anyway. Zeke made sure of that. The ship's computer systems were locked securely behind bulletproof glass walls, operating in sync with the computers on board the riverboats. Anyone attempting to steal the ship was in for some nasty surprises. The guards were instructed to allow the ship to be searched at any time by any official for any reason. The security system on board would keep a digital record of all who boarded the ship.

Once away from the city, Master Chief Warner began giving instructions on starting the hydraulic system that would propel the boats up the river. Experimental though the system was, Master Chief Warner was excited about this phase of the journey. Jim watched him with respect as the slender man walked them all through the process of starting everything.

Four propellers were located in a shaft running the length of each pontoon, each designed to work perfectly with the others, using the water pushing through to propel the boat and increase the hydraulic pressure. Once the pressure reached a certain point, it would continue to build without needing the diesel engine. Master Chief Warner watched the gauges carefully and commanded the four pilots to disengage the diesel engine.

CHAPTER 8

Silence reigned, sudden and startling. The hydraulic system worked without noise, propelling them forward with more power than the engine, faster and faster until they were skimming across the water at a speed of twenty-five knots! Jim eased back on the controls, no longer using the fuel-feeding controls of the engine but another set just to the right until they settled into a mile-eating eight knots.

At first, the silence was eerie, but after an hour or so, they got used to the lack of engine noise. All the electrical equipment was up and running as the generator, powered by the hydraulics, worked as it was designed, keeping the batteries fully charged and helping the solar system operate efficiently. After an hour of running silently along the riverbanks, the crew gave Master Chief Warner and Wade Adams a resounding cheer. Silent running would make these boats awesome research tools. Plus, they could travel night and day without using a drop of diesel fuel!

Their first run was along the Amazon River to the town of Macapá, where they planned to stop and buy fresh fruits and veg-etables for the kitchen crew. It was there, Jim was sure, they would find more agents from Hess Pharmaceuticals and, after that, the Pirate Tupi.

Rain began to fall early that first evening and would continue for many days. Traveling along the Amazon River and any of its tributaries was considered hazardous, and regular traffic along the river came to a complete stop. Between Belém and Macapá, travel risks were considered marginally safe, but only for experienced river pilots who knew the terrain and the dangers. Most took advantage of the rainy season and spent their days in local bars or merely living on their boats.

Zeke opened the last laptop computer inside one of the air-conditioned rooms, now looking at six different monitors. One monitor showed an enhanced satellite picture of the four boats on the river. Another showed the river on a GPS program Smitty developed that continually cross-checked the GPS signal with the E6-B computer on *Bring It Up, Coral.* It also monitored the position through two satellites Zeke had somehow linked to his computer system.

Smitty sat beside Zeke, watching that particular monitor and ensuring that the feed went up to the bridge so Jim could pilot them accurately through the tricky river currents. Another monitor portrayed a mock-up of the river bottom in front of the lead riverboat, showing any debris, depth, sunken vessels, or other obstructions.

Zeke checked the fourth monitor carefully. It showed groups of people as blips on the screen. At the moment, the satellite sending that image was looking down at the target terrorist camp. Each blip was elongated where people were moving, while others were perfectly round, indicating a stationary human being.

Monitors five and six were used to keep track of the systems on the riverboats and keep an eye on the weather. Cecilia came into the room with two cups of coffee and put one at the elbow of each of the men. Zeke thanked her without looking up, his fingers dancing over the keyboard as he entered commands. Smitty grinned, shook his head, and raised his cup in thanks.

A few minutes later, she walked onto the bridge, open to the dampness and heat of the Amazon, a combination that seemed to envelop her instantly, almost suffocating her. She drew a breath and stepped over to place a thirty-two-ounce insulated cup of iced tea beside Jim. He looked down at her and smiled.

Sweat poured down his face and turned his arms slick. His T-shirt was soaked through and dripping. The sweatband on his forehead seemed soaked as well. Wearing tan shorts, his exposed muscular legs were slicked with sweat, too. It would hit everyone like that for a while until their bodies adjusted. If all the sweat bothered him it certainly didn't show.

Without conscious thought, she picked up a damp terrycloth towel and wiped Jim's face and head. He smiled in thanks and kissed her forehead without taking his eyes from the river in front of them. Reaching up, she pulled his head down sideways and kissed his neck.

"I'm going up front with the rest," she said quietly, turning after hanging the towel and walking back into the air-conditioned comfort. Goosebumps rose on her arms and shoulders as the cold hit her like a sudden slap. Hurrying through the corridor, she made her way to the observation deck at the front of the riverboat. Like the bridge, it was open to the elements.

Jack Boswell, Frank Miller, and Sean Oxton were seated at a bamboo table, almost draped over their folding chairs, drinking from sweating soda bottles. Master Chief Warner was leaning on the railing overlooking the brown water, a half-empty cup of coffee dangling dangerously from his finger. An electric refrigerator sat against the inside wall. Every forward deck had one of those refrigerators, and the kitchen crew kept it stocked with water and soda. Cecilia went to it and took out an ice-cold Diet Coke and a slice of lime. She poured the drink into a plastic glass, added ice and lime, and then joined the three men at the table.

"Doc says it will take nearly two weeks for our bodies to adjust to this heat," Sean complained, sipping from his bottle. He was drinking Cherry Coke. The other men were drinking regular Coke.

"It will seem like an eternity!" Cecilia sighed, wiping sweat from her face and looking at the sweat already forming on her arms. "And we're all going to smell so nice," she added.

"Smell, with this natural shower going on all the time?" Ox announced, waving at the pouring rain.

Cecilia smiled, opened the gate, walked out to the very bow of the boat, and stood in the rain until she was soaked. When completely soaked with the rain, she returned to her chair. She caught FM checking to see if he could see through her tan blouse, and she kicked at him.

"I don't think the shower will help much," she said. "I think I sweat as much in the rain as I did sitting here."

They sat silently for a while until the call came to stop the boats, tie up to the shore, and head back to *Alistair's Lady* for dinner. Abe, who understood the dietary needs of men living on the equator, provided a salad bar with lettuce, spinach, fruit, fresh vegetables, and slices of ham or turkey. Knowing the men and their preferences, he grated four cheeses and mixed several dressings. There was something on the table that every single person liked, and the men and women appreciated the effort that took, pausing to thank him or members of his crew often.

Temperatures inside the dining room were a comfortable seventy-six degrees and seemed cold to those who had been sitting out in the weather and warm to those who had been in the computer center. Andrea and Jim were the last to arrive. Both decided to check the moorings once again and make sure the electrical systems were all working properly.

Drained from the day as they were, everyone spent a lively time at the tables. Dr. Gregg's team shared what they discovered in their research with anyone who was interested, which included just about everyone. Master Chief Warner talked mechanics with Inchworm and Sparks, and Loony sat with them, talking about the electrical and battery backup systems. Tom Patterson saw how close Cecilia sat to the captain and frowned.

When he mentioned it to Abe, the jovial cook explained their relationship. Because of his own experience, Patterson still had difficulty believing that any woman could be trusted, and Abe warned him against judging her unfairly. As Tom moved away, Abe looked at Sturdy, and the two shook their heads at the same time. This could be trouble.

Nothing came of it that night or for the next two weeks as they made their way steadily toward Macapá. Abe and Sturdy worried about the problem and finally came to Jim. They were concerned about his reaction to such an accusation against Cecilia. Jim was no fool. Having seen Paterson's looks directed at the two, Jim had already interpreted the situation correctly. He smiled at the two giants standing before him.

"I promise not to retaliate," he promised with a grin. "I know you're worried, but he hasn't said anything so far. If he does, it's still your responsibility. I leave all that discipline to you. But don't be too hard on him. His wife's betrayal hurt him deeply, I think.

"I understand a little of that betrayal, which is why I'm going so slow with Cecilia. Someone betrayed my love a long time ago, and the scars are still very tender. I never would have said that to another man a year ago, but you can see that God is softening my heart and opening it to both receive and give love again. So don't worry about it. You're doing a good job with him."

Both men raised their eyebrows and beamed at him. Abe was nearly as wide as he was tall, his arms, chest, and legs swelling with huge free-weight lifting muscles. Sturdy, nearly seven feet tall, was also a weightlifter. Neither was built for the kind of warfare Jim's team was involved in, but he wouldn't pit any of his men against either of them, with or without a weapon. Because they were so strong, they were also very gentle and careful, but not with the men. He grinned.

"A year ago, you would have torn his head off!" Abe grinned in response. "You've changed some since then."

"I might feel like tearing his head off, but I won't. I guess I have changed. At least toward our own crewmen, I've changed," Jim added, his eyes suddenly hard. He couldn't afford to grow soft toward his enemies.

Early the next morning they arrived at Macapá, finding the docks crowded with boats moored until the rainy season was over. After paying some local workers, some boats were moved so that all four of theirs could tie up in a line. Next, Abe and Sturdy caused a stir in the town as they wandered through, buying fresh fruit and vegetables for the journey.

Workers were hired to carry the goods to the boats. An official appeared, wearing a tattered suit, asking to inspect the boats. He looked at their documents, inspected the boats, and engaged Dr. Gregg in a conversation about his expedition. He looked almost crestfallen when he left the boats. Zeke, seated at the computer, put his headphones on and checked to determine if any cell phones were in use. Sure enough, a cell phone was activated minutes after the man left. Tapping into the signal, Zeke listened with a smile as the man reported to Marta Hess that there were no weapons on board any of the boats other than the shotguns and hunting rifles, one of each on each bridge. Ongoing research demonstrated they were on an archaeological expedition. Dr. Gregg and his team had many maps and papers to demonstrate this.

He had seen no soldiers, though some of the crew looked tough enough to be soldiers, and no uniforms. Dr. Gregg seemed to be in charge of the expedition, and everything seemed above board and straightforward. Marta Hess listened without comment, thanked the man, and hung up.

Her next call was to someone in Manaus named Miguel Santos. Zeke listened in as she gave her directions. Logging the number used to contact the man, he sent an email message to someone named Claire in London. That message would be on Sir Edward's desk minutes after being received. Hopefully, by the time they reached Manaus they would have a picture of Miguel Santos.

CHAPTER 9

Underway quickly the following morning, the four riverboats pulled away from the docks. Jim was at the wheel in the lead boat, and as soon as they were away, he picked up the radio microphone.

"Captain Rob to Warner's Raider," he said.

Wade's voice came back immediately. "Warner's Wader, over."

"Please see if Master Chief is ready to test the stealth mode. I want silent running at fifteen knots. I'm going to notify Uncle Zeke that we want GPS pilot system engaged in five, repeat five minutes after we go silent. Over," Jim ordered. "Please respond, Alistair's Lady and Gwyneth, over."

"Alistair's Lady understood, over," Andrea's voice responded first. "Gwyneth is ready, over," John said immediately following.

"Warner's Wader standing by. Master Chief Warner is ready," Wade's voice came over the radio.

"Roger that. Go to stealth in five, four, three, two, one." Jim engaged four toggle switches on his control panel, and everything went dark for a moment. The hydraulics began working, the lights came back on almost immediately, and they ran silent. From here on, they would run with the hydraulics at a steady fifteen knots.

"Zeke, perhaps you would be good enough to engage that fancy system you and Smitty dreamed up," Jim smiled as he spoke, using the radio again after five minutes had passed. "We're holding steady at 15 knots," he added, checking the gauges.

"Going online now," Zeke's voice responded.

Zeke and Smitty watched the computers as the system was engaged. All four boats came online instantly. Connected through the computers on the ship and using the available satellite systems, they could pilot the riverboats using computer systems. When they were satisfied that the system was working correctly, showing everything pertaining to safe piloting. Zeke picked up the radio microphone.

"Pilots, prepare to release in five, four, three, two, one," he ordered. He nodded to himself as his computer system took over.

All four pilots released the wheel, watched as the boats maintained fifteen knots, and continued on course. Ten minutes went by, then twenty. At twenty-three minutes into the experiment, an underwater obstruction appeared on the screen. This was a critical test. All four boats adjusted properly, and moved around the object, returning to their original course. Jim watched it all with interest.

"Uncle Zeke reports that the system is up and running properly. You pilots are now obsolete," he added facetiously.

"As long as there is no power failure," Cecilia said softly, sitting behind the two men. "That's some system!" she added.

"Even if the power fails, we have time to recover. The battery backup systems are redundant," Smitty said, looking through the computer monitors with satisfaction. Obviously, both men thought about that eventuality and were prepared for it. Cecilia nodded.

The navigation program was Smitty's design, though Zeke had written it. Both men talked their way through the entire thing, and when it was finished, Zeke decided that it was not going to be offered to the public or the military—not, at least, until it had been tested completely. Even though there was a risk in testing the system in real-time, he was confident it was minimal.

Released from the bridge, Jim stretched and stepped away from the wheel. Immediately, a three-dimensional figure appeared, as if by magic, where he had been standing. It was a hologram from a system recording his every move over the past few days. With a grin, he made his way down to the front of the boat and looked up at an image of himself on the bridge. It was almost unnerving to see himself standing up there behind the wheel, his head moving, his body swaying with the motion of the boat.

"Oooh! Cecilia might like that one better!" Ox teased from his seat at the table. His grin was wide as Jim turned to him, a smile on his face.

"He looks like the strong, silent type. No problems with that one either," Ox continued. "At least he won't smell from sweat!"

"That's really good!" FM said, looking up at the image.

"Wait until you see the whole show," Jim replied. "Zeke's been taping us moving around at night. Daytime movements when we're not moving have also been added to the program. If we leave these boats, it will look like everyone is still here! He even recorded our night sounds!"

"I thought the cameras were for security!" Jack said, looking up at the camera pointing down toward them. As he looked closely, he saw that it was indeed a multiple system. "Clever bugger, our Zeke," he said.

"Uncle Zeke is beyond clever. He is a genius!" Zeke said, coming out to the bow platform to join them as Jack spoke.

"And modest, too," Ox added with a wink.

"A genius never worries about what others think of him. He knows his value," Zeke said haughtily. He was grinning as he pulled a cold water bottle out of the refrigerator. "Recording your sleeping sounds made me wonder why you don't set off the methane gas alarms in your cabins!" he added.

"May I see this mastermind program at work?" Jim asked through the laughter.

"Yeah, Shep. Come on back," Zeke invited with a nod of his head in the direction he was heading.

Jim followed, pausing only long enough to pull a bottle of water for himself. Unscrewing the cap, he took a long drink as he walked down the corridor and crowded into the tiny computer room. Cecilia looked up as he stood behind her, reaching back to touch his hand as he laid it gently on her shoulder.

She was sitting on a stool with wheels, her long tan legs crossed, one foot swaying up and down slowly. This morning, her eyes were lovely blue against the aqua sleeveless blouse she wore above her tan shorts. The matching socks only accentuated the tan on her legs, and Jim could see her cleavage from where he was standing. He tore his eyes away instantly and blushed, catching Zeke watching him with humor. Cecilia saw the interaction and laughed.

"I knew you men were bottle-fed," she teased, standing up gracefully. "You, at least, are a gentleman," she said, pointing a finger at Jim. "I caught one of your crew checking to see if he could see through my blouse yesterday when I stood in the rain," she said with a grin. Working around a crew of men, especially soldiers, gave her some interesting insights into their minds. Jim's cheeks burned even redder, and she moved back to allow him better access with satisfaction.

"Oh! You checked too?" she asked, too innocently. "Oh, she's good!" Smitty said, grinning at Jim.

"Devastating!" Jim agreed, recovering somewhat. Cecilia's smile was secretive. "Why don't you explain all this to me?" Jim added, trying to get away from the embarrassing situation.

"Well," Zeke began, "girls have mammary glands to produce milk so they can feed babies. That's why they have breasts. Milk is produced there to nourish infants, providing all the nutrients necessary for their tiny bodies." Jim's face turned crimson again, and he waved his hands.

"Explain the computer system, please!" he begged as Cecilia and Smitty burst out laughing.

"Oh!" Zeke said innocently. "Basically, using the E6-B computer on the ship and the satellite systems available to us, we can track our positions exactly, plot any river changes taking place, and head for our objective through the best possible channels. The depth-finder equipment and sonar trace the bottom front and rear. If you'll note, the boats are now running about six feet apart. If you wanted to, we could close that up to four feet so you could jump from boat to boat, but that would look too suspicious. I'm going to lengthen the distance now to twelve feet."

Smitty punched a command into the computer, and the three following boats slowed slightly until they were twelve feet apart, then maintained that distance.

"That's better than we can do!" Jim said.

"Not really," Zeke announced, causing Jim to raise his eyebrows. "It may be a little more accurate, but the actions of these boats have been monitored throughout the trip, and the computer is merely copying the type of maneuvers you and the other pilots are capable of."

"I obviously have some good pilots in my crew," Jim said, nodding.

"Look at this!" Zeke said suddenly, pointing to one of the screens. "Here are six boats and a group of men setting up an ambush for us!"

Jim looked, saw the blips on the monitor, and watched the boats spread out on either side of the river as it passed close to an island. There were none on the other side of the island, and Jim wondered why.

"Can we go on the other side of that island?" he asked.

Zeke typed some commands into his laptop, bringing up a detailed map of the river that had been done by a surveying crew less than two years before. A European group did the research on the waterways, and their work seemed competent. He looked at the island, and the river details carefully, studying the depths and shifting sandbars mentioned in the report, and then grinned.

"Using the hydraulics to propel us and the draft we're experiencing, all four boats could make it through. There's a sandbar there, but I think we can clear it. That's why they're not paying attention to that side," Zeke replied.

Jim reached for the radio. "Gwyneth, this is Shep. Do you copy?" "Go ahead, Shep," John replied.

"We have pirates setting up an ambush up the river. I'm going to take the front three boats around the other side. Six team three will deploy across the island to ambush the boats on that side. Six-team one will swing around and return downriver, flanking the enemy while you spring their trap. Hold one minute," Jim said, noting that Zeke had a finger up.

"I can program all that into the computer so that John is hands-free and can fight with his team," Zeke said.

"J.R., Zeke says the system can handle all the maneuvers, so you are hands-free to take part. Over," Jim said.

"Roger that, Shep. We'll wait for your signal to spring the trap. Good hunting," John replied.

"Captain Rob, this is Alistair's Lady, over," Andrea's voice came over the radio.

"Go ahead, Papa O.!" Jim replied. "What do you want my crew to do?"

"You have watch on the six team three boat. Please have Abe take his crew on board once the two boats are moored, over," Jim instructed.

"Roger that, Shep," Andrea said. "Over and out."

Jim remained in the room watching the boats separate, three of them moving out to the south side of the river, all of them slowing down. Running silent in the rain, it didn't take long before the boats disappeared from each other in the mist. Nodding, Jim went out to get his team ready for the attack. "Okay, boys, we've got a pirate named Tupi setting up a little diversion for us. Let's get ready to party," he said to the men lounging on the bow.

Instantly, they were on their feet and heading to their rooms to get their gear. Jim went to his own room and, unlocked and pulled up the floor section that hid his gear. Carefully, he unpacked everything, checked his weapons, and dressed for the battle. Training over the last two weeks had acclimated their bodies to the heat, but the suits were still hot. Shep made sure that each man had an extra quart of water when he checked the men. Staying hydrated was essential.

Ox crouched at one of the gun ports in the front. It seemed odd to see his form sitting at the table in front of him, sipping from a very real-looking bottle of Cherry Coke. They were staying in the air-conditioning as long as possible. He winced as one of the pontoons scraped across the sand bar, but the boat hardly slowed. He heard six-team three moving through the island's brush through his headset, cutting their way toward the three boats hiding on the opposite side. He couldn't hear their steps, but listened to their whispered conversations with interest.

At last, they were in place, able to see the enemy through the thick brush, and the signal came to spring the trap. John's riverboat crept up the river in the appointed channel, and the three boats on the north shore moved away. None noticed that the three on the island shore did not move.

Six-team three crept aboard the three boats, two on each one, taking care of the threat. Each boat had six men in it, and all six were watching downriver for the appearance of the riverboats they were about to attack. They felt the rocking as the two men came aboard, turned in surprise, and slowly raised their hands, dropping their weapons.

One pirate was foolish, whipping out a knife as his gun fell. The silenced three-round blast from Brown's MP5/10SD sent his body over the side. The other soldiers swallowed nervously as it disappeared in the brown water and did not move. Restraint zip ties were used to secure their hands behind their backs. Six team three put them on the shore and fastened each to a tree before talking to the three teams operating and moving out onto the river. His team was now separated into pairs and operating the stolen boats.

As John's boat closed with the first pirate boat, shots rang out. Two of the pirates carried shotguns, and one an old Uzi. Bullets sprayed across the bow where three men sat playing cards. Their forms disappeared as Zeke cut the cameras. That instant of surprise was all that John's crew needed. All four fired through the gun ports, taking down four pirates immediately. The other two dove for cover.

John pumped a grenade into his launcher and blew the boat out of the water. He could hear the screams of the men as they went down with the boat. The second boat was coming into view, even as Jim's boat came out of the mist. He would take care of the third boat.

"John, the three boats coming from the other side have six-team three on board!" Wade warned.

John grinned. These pirates were in for a big surprise. He kept the second boat at bay with gunfire until the three pirate boats joined. Suddenly, the second boat was surrounded by three of their boats firing on them. Cursing and screaming in rage, the pirates tried to fight. Their weapons were no match for the weapons of six team three. Four-team two kept them pinned down, so they couldn't get off good shots anyway. Three were taken alive, but three others died in the battle. The men of *Bring It Up* were not impressed with the machismo of the pirates or their useless deaths fighting against obviously superior forces. There had been no discipline in the battle, only brutality.

Captain Tupi, the pirate, was in the third boat. When he saw what had happened and the riverboat bearing down on his smaller craft, he ordered his men to raise their weapons over their heads as though in surrender. He planned to bring them down and fire once the enemy was in range.

Jim guessed his plan, seeing the guns in the air, and ordered his men to destroy the weapons. Two of the men were so surprised as shots hit their weapons that they fell backward over the side. The others brought their weapons down to see them rendered useless. Screaming with rage, Tupi pulled out his pistol and began firing at the riverboat bearing down on him.

"I want him alive!" Jim snapped. Aiming carefully, he knee-capped one of the pirates. Taking their cue from their Captain, the other team members did the same, and suddenly, screaming men, bleeding from horrific wounds, surrounded Tupi. When his clip was empty, he threw aside the weapon and, pulling his knife, leaped upon the riverboat's bow. A maniacal look of rage twisted his face into a mask of hatred and evil. In his mind, he was going to find whoever was responsible for this outrage and gut him like a pig!

Ox met him there, quickly disarming the man and subduing him in seconds. Gasping, weeping now in frustration, Tupi fell weakly to the floor after another blow from the Australian nearly took off his head. Five men silently appeared around him, and he stared up into the stormy green eyes of their leader. Suddenly, for the first time in his life, Tupi understood the meaning of fear. His hands were secured behind his back, the backs of them pressed cruelly together, the wrists bound tightly with restraint ties.

Until this moment, Tupi had been the one to take prisoners, dole out punishment, and put fear into people. He simply refused to believe that this was happening, but looking into those hard green eyes, he knew beyond the shadow of a doubt that he was in deep trouble. Fear mushroomed inside him at the silence of the men around him. Trying to hide it came second nature to him, and he blustered, despite the pain in his head and jaw, threatening with empty threats.

CHAPTER 10

Unceremoniously, the pirate was hauled painfully to his feet and forced to stand before Captain Jim Shepherd. He tried bluster but found himself shivering under that steady gaze. Working saliva into his mouth, he tried to spit in his captor's face, but someone cuffed his head from behind, and he ended up spitting down the front of his naked chest. Another cuff rang in his ears, straightening him back out and causing the edges of his vision to grow dark momentarily. Who are these men?

"We'll have none of that! You're a proper wally, and that's a fact," a hard Australian voice said in his ear. "You make one wrong move, and I'll nail your testicles to a piece of driftwood and dump you in the river, mate. I'll make sure it's one of those branches full of thorns so you can twist and scream a little before you die!"

Jim almost choked on that one. He managed to keep his features unchanged, though his mind revolted at the thought of what Ox had suggested. Watching Tupi's face pale told him the man was thinking the same thoughts. It was an ancient torture, and since World War II Jim only came across one man who had practiced it.

"Master Chief!" Jim's voice rang out in the silence that followed.

"Sir," Jim Warner said, coming to attention.

"Why don't you find a proper piece of driftwood, a hammer, and some nails for us? I don't think this would-be pirate believes us. Also, find a supple branch with thorns to wrap around it before we nail it to this man's testicles!"

"On my way, sir!" Jim Warner said, keeping his face straight. Talk about manipulating a prisoner! He went in search of what was requested, returning four minutes later with a piece of driftwood, a branch of long thorns, two deck screws, and a screw gun. "I couldn't find nails, sir, but I did find two deck screws and my screw gun. It ain't as quick and easy, and it hurts a sight more. Most of the men we've done that to lost consciousness with the screws. But then, so did the ones we used the nails on," Warner bounced the screws in his hand, dropping the driftwood on the deck at the same time, and spun the screw gun once. Tupi's eyes nearly burst from his skull in panic. Just seeing the objects of torture unmanned him completely, and he jabbered fearfully, barely able to produce words, and since he spoke in Spanish, some of the men didn't understand.

"¡No! ¡Por favor! ¡No puedes hacerme esto!" he screamed in Spanish. He felt weak, as if he might vomit, and hated himself for showing such weakness in the presence of enemies.

"Oh, for heaven's sake. He's going to grovel and beg. I hate these cowardly little pukes!" Dorf said, getting into the game.

"A woman hired me. Actually, it was her agent, an attorney from Belém." the man blubbered, trying to give them information.

"We know about Jorge and his call to you, and we know about Marta Hess. This is useless! Let's just get this over with," Jim said with disgust. "Strip his clothes off."

In seconds, he stood before them naked. Unlike many natives along the river, this one was corpulent and unfit. He lived among starving and poor people, but it was obvious he took good care of himself, often feasting gluttonously and drinking himself into a drunken stupor. He stood shamed among the men who captured him, his head hung, his heart filled with rage and hatred, but over-all that crippling fear glued his tongue to the roof of his mouth.

"You know, Captain. I'll bet if we stripped all our captives like this and left them on the island over there, they might just find it difficult to recover quickly from that," Mark said quietly, looking at Tupi like a butcher looks at a piece of meat, deciding how to slice it. Tupi didn't like that look at all. "We could entice some bugs to make his life miserable!" Mark added.

"Yeah! Why waste two good deck screws on this scum?" John added.

"Make it so," Jim said softly.

Struggling and begging for mercy Tupi was escorted to the island, where his remaining pirates were stripped of their clothing and weapons. Each was stripped naked and sprinkled liberally with sugar water to attract ants. They were sitting in a circle, each tied to a separate tree, facing outward, when the riverboats pulled away. One of the men on the last boat waved at them as they passed.

"Bye now. Be sure to write!" Vince said from the bow of the boat.

Tupi couldn't believe that these men knew so much or that the remains of his pirate crew were now sitting naked in the pounding rain on an island. Swimming to the other shore was out of the question. There were pythons, crocodiles, and piranha in these waters. If an Anaconda or Python did not discover they were help-less and kill one or more of them, and they survived, there was still the problem of getting off the island. They would have to construct a raft; to do that, they needed sharp objects. None had any to offer. Getting free would be a long and difficult, and he hoped the crocodiles would not decide to come up on shore. Humiliated and defeated, Tupi watched the boats disappear silently into the mist.

No longer was he even able to curse them. His boats had been destroyed while they watched, their last hope gone.

"It will take some time to get those restraint ties off, won't it?" Wade asked with a nasty grin.

"Ten to fifteen hours, I'd imagine. I saw you pouring liquid on them.

What was that for?" Jim asked, looking at Wade.

"Sugar water, boss," Wade said with a laugh. "Bugs love sugar water," he added. "Ants, too!"

"They may just brave the water!" Jim burst out laughing with the rest of the men. "A fitting punishment," he added soberly. "How many innocent people have those pirates looted, raped, and killed?" he shook his head.

"He'll tell about the guns and military precision," John said when he had finally stopped laughing.

"Perhaps," Jim mused, his mind churning the likelihood of that. "He was paid in advance. If he survives, he may just disappear for a while, ashamed of his failure. That would be more in keeping with his character, I think."

"He did seem afraid of the Hess outfit," Ox said in the silence that followed. His face took on a thoughtful look. "I concur with Jim. I don't think he'll show his face for a long time."

CHAPTER 11

SANTARÉM MAY HAVE been included on a map as a place to stop along the way, but it turned out to be a filthy mud hole filled with poor peasants and dirty, bedraggled shopkeepers and a leaky clapboard tavern filled with undesirables of all kinds.

It boasted a military outpost run by a greedy officer and weary soldiers who spent most of their time at the cantina drinking. The expedition passed the town early in the morning before most of the people were up, seeing it for what it was and glad they didn't need to stop there. Most craft would need to stop for fuel and supplies if such could be found.

Sitting in the computer center, Zeke counted the number of people in the town as they passed by, letting his machines do the work. There were six hundred humans, a hundred and eight pigs, twenty-three goats, sixty donkeys, and a vast number of birds, some of them domestic chickens, wandering the empty morning streets. The military compound consisted of twenty men in two dilapidated barracks and an officer in private quarters. All were present, asleep, and unaware of the passing of the expedition.

Bored with the town, Zeke switched to the terrorist camp and saw that people were already up and training. Two groups, thirty men each, were running. Zeke wished he was with them. His running was done on treadmills, which was effective but much more boring than running outside. At least on the ship, they had run the length of the ship, up and down steps, seeing the sky and being aware of the sea around them. Here, they stared at a wall and ran until the mill indicated a distance of five miles.

Six treadmills in the room meant you could at least talk to the others as you ran. Idly, he watched them run, tracing the distance to only one mile. Wimps! A mile barely warmed you up. It took them nine minutes to run the mile. Good. That meant these men were not in top condition. Most didn't shower after the run; they just headed into what looked like a dining hall for a long breakfast. Not in top condition and lazy about hygiene! Ha!

Again, good! These were lazy men, probably not fully motivated. That was the thing about the new breed of terrorists in the world. They tended to be lazy, vicious, and cowardly.

Blowing up women and children was their thing. Actual combat was something most of them feared and hated, especially if it was against soldiers. Zeke had met many terrorists in his day and found them, for the most part, very disappointing as combatants. Although he hated combat, he did appreciate an opponent that at least challenged him.

One hundred and twenty men occupied the various barracks in the compound. Others came from another compound to work in the labs. About twenty-five all together, and they avoided the terrorists. They were probably afraid of them. Zeke thought of them as fools and then quickly changed his mind. These were the engineers of whatever biohazard they were cooking up in there. None were fools, and it was unwise to underestimate an enemy.

Officers were easy to count. During the day, three of them lectured the men, and three more trained them in weapons use and combat techniques. These seemed as lazy as the troops and spent time with them about once a week. They were probably teaching them how to strap an explosive pack or a hand grenade to a child so that the maximum number of innocents could be killed.

Six officers and one hundred and twenty men were a large force to reckon with, even for seasoned soldiers like Zeke. He didn't like the odds, but Captain Shepherd was a genius when it came to strategy, and Zeke had been part of a SEAL team once that had faced even greater odds. Jim took them out of that situation without a scratch. Yet each man knew that the more enemies you faced, the higher your chances of being wounded became. Here, in South America, machismo was important to these men. They would not easily give up.

Dr. Gregg was having a very good morning. Macapá proved to be one more place to gather a piece of his puzzle. Up early, he sat at a drafting table and filled in the last bit of information, then sat back and looked at a map that was nearly complete. With this information, and the information they would gather from any Stela they found he was confident they could find the hidden city. Obviously, the city existed, of that he was certain, and he was determined to find it!

Why did they journey this far south? What were they looking for, and why choose to settle where they did, in a nearly inaccessible location hundreds of miles away from their homes? There were no answers for these questions yet, but he planned to search until he discovered the reason.

Barbara Stafford came in, carrying an extra cup of tea, which she put down at Dr. Gregg's elbow. He looked up at her with a smile and thanked her. She moved around to look at the map. It was finally complete, and she drew in a deep breath as she looked.

"So, you've completed what we have!" she said, surprised. Her eyes studied the work critically and approvingly.

"Yes. I think we have enough now that the Stelae themselves will tell the rest," Alistair said, leaning back and sipping the tea.

"Isn't it interesting how we meet just the right people to make all this possible?" Barbara asked, seating herself at a small desk. "We help them by providing a legitimate cover, and they help us by taking us directly to our objective. Neat!"

"Yes, quite. These chaps are serious treasure hunters, but I think they could be serious archaeologists as well," Alistair mused quietly.

"One or two of them certainly show promise," Barbara agreed.

"One or two?" Mary Ann Lewis entered with a cup of tea of her own. "Every one of these men is filled with promise. I'm having difficulty choosing which one will be my husband!" Mary Ann grinned impishly.

"We were discussing their promise as archaeologists," Barbara said, her own eyes twinkling as her best friend entered the room.

"Heavens, dear! I just got out of bed! All I can think of is all those males around me and I'm sleeping alone!" Mary Ann quipped. "They're all such gentlemen. Too bad, really!" she sat at her desk and laughed at Dr. Gregg's expression.

"Well, it would be nice if one or two of them were cads enough to offer a romantic interlude!" Barbara said, laughing at her friend as Mary Ann gave her an outrageous wink.

"I think they're actually afraid of us!" Mary Ann said.

"Probably because you keep pulling such outrageous pranks on them!" Alistair said with a grin of his own.

He liked his two assistants. They were serious students but also women, and they spiced up his life in amazing ways. He went back to studying his map as the two talked quietly together. Whatever prank they were thinking up would come out soon enough.

At breakfast that morning, the team from the last boat appeared at his table. Formally, they bowed to the two ladies, their faces splitting with huge grins, their cheeks and necks suffused with color. Then John turned to the crowded dining room and spoke, his face crimson, his grin wide.

"We'd like to thank these two ladies for an entertaining morning. This morning, we discovered that the fly of every pair of underwear we owned had been sewn shut!" he announced. "We discovered this at a most inopportune moment, as you can imagine."

There was a moment of silence, followed by minutes of laughter as the men pictured their companions discovering that fact. Jokes flew across the room, some ribald until John raised his hands for silence. He looked at Barbara and Mary Ann with a mischievous grin.

"Hazing is against the rules, ladies," he said. Everyone laughed again as the four men took their seats. All during the day funny stories of the discovery went around the boats. Jim, who knew his brother, knew that Barbara and Mary Ann were in for a rough time. He would respond with a similar prank, probably involving their underwear. That his brother would indeed carry out such a prank, he did not doubt, merely wondered what he would do and how he would do it.

Later that week, the girls came into breakfast in their bathrobes, faces as red as beets, demanding to know where their clothing and underwear were. Both had their arms crossed and stared around the room with a fierce gaze. Amidst the laughter, Abe and Sturdy brought their clothing to them on silver trays, the garments soaked first and then frozen solid. Both girls shivered as they took the clothing and headed to the laundry to wash and dry them.

"You shall rue the day!" Mary Ann threatened as they left the room with their frozen underwear. Jim thought that perhaps John and his crew would.

CHAPTER 12

IT WAS UPON such lighthearted fun that they came to Manaus. Jim was not surprised that Miguel, of whom he now had pictures and a dossier, was one of the first to greet them. Posing as an official, he asked to see their paperwork and to inspect the boats. This he did with a thoroughness that Jim watched with amusement. As before, he retired with little to report to Marta Hess.

Miguel was not a man to be stumped. He offered expert guide services beyond the Japurá fork. Jim took him to the computer room, which showed only detailed maps of the river system on the computer monitors. Miguel saw that such services would not be needed. Dr. Gregg assured him that he was a competent explorer and archaeologist and would hire help if he felt it was necessary. At the moment, it was not, he regretted.

Miguel returned later to suggest that dealing with the natives might be difficult and that he could offer interpretation services. Dr. Gregg pointed out that during the rainy season, most tribes moved away from the river because of flooding. To whom would they talk?

At last, desperate to somehow delay this expedition, he devised a plan to attack their crewmembers in the town, gathering supplies of fresh fruits and vegetables. The dozen men he sent came face to face with Abe and Sturdy and had second thoughts. They returned to Miguel to suggest he try something else. Miguel took them back into the town and decided the two men were very large indeed.

He suggested a knife, and one of his men pulled one and advanced threateningly at Sturdy. Looking at the knife and then over at the group of men, he growled deep in his throat. He handed his basket to Bob while Abe handed his to Tom. Both men put the baskets on the ground and grinned. Then Sturdy slapped Abe in the chest, and the two of them roared and attacked the group of twelve.

Jim, who was leading his group, began to move up to cut off any escape. He left most of the fighting to the cooks. Abe didn't want to hurt anyone, so he picked them up and threw them about like rag dolls, while Sturdy did the same. Anyone who pulled weapons found one of Jim's team at their elbow, carefully removing the offending tool and sending them back into the fray. Miguel flew through the air, nearly fifteen feet, and crashed through one of the walls of the opposite store. That seemed to be the final act in this little comedy as the fighting stopped. As suddenly as it had begun, the fight was over.

Zeke recorded his broken call to Marta Hess, and the men listened to it several times with glee. It was funny.

"I wish to report that I have failed you, great lady. There are two on that boat. I thought they were mere cooks, but they are devils! Devils! One is a giant! He must be eight feet tall! I saw him pick up two of my men, one in each hand, lifting them as easily as I would lift a babe. Then he threw them across the street! They are devils!

"The other cook is not so tall but stronger than our largest bull! He threw me through a wall, great lady, clear across the street! His strength was awesome, and I was helpless in his hands!" Miguel whined. "I am badly injured!"

"Did the cooks hit any of your men?" Marta asked.

"No, great lady. They only threw us about. When we pulled weapons to defend ourselves, the other devils took them away," Miguel said petulantly.

"Took them away?" she asked.

"Yes! I pulled a pistol from my belt, and suddenly, my arm went numb, and the pistol fell from my hand. One of those devils picked it up, shook his head, and threw it away in the mud, shoving me back into the fight. I tell you, all of us were seriously injured!"

"And did you search their boats before this fight?" Marta Hess asked quietly.

"Oh yes, great lady. It is as all have said before. They carry no weapons or uniforms. They do not need them! They are devils!"

"I'm sorry your men were hurt, Miguel. I'll send someone to take care of the damage to your town. Thank you for helping me," Marta said, keeping the disgust she felt for this incompetent man from her voice.

"Please, great lady. Do not trouble yourself over these devils. Let them find their hidden city and be gone from our midst," Miguel suggested. "They are terrifying men, giants, many with great muscles, and they are fearless! Absolutely fearless!" as soon as he spoke, he knew he'd said more than he should. Remembering the kind of people Marta Hess hired, perhaps a little late, he broke off the conversation with a hasty goodbye.

Marta Hess hung up the phone and tapped the glass top of her desk with her fingernails for a few minutes. Every search had come up negative, so she decided they were not carrying weapons. What happened with Tupi? The bloody pirate had not checked in or called her for weeks. Had he taken her money and done nothing? Perhaps. Perhaps this crew was able to overpower him. She knew the two cooks. One was nearly seven feet tall, and the other was powerful in build. Perhaps they did all the fighting for this group. Could they overpower Tupi's pirates?

The answer was obvious. Somehow, they had either slipped past the pirates or overpowered them. Well, there were more pirates to hire along the river, and between Manaus and the Japurá fork, there were many islands from which to launch an attack. She made two calls from her office, both tapped and recorded by Zeke. One was to alert the pirates that boats were coming up the river with goods and equipment worth stealing. She mentioned that Cecilia and other women were on board and could be sold for a tidy profit as slaves. The other was to one of the Cali drug cartel bosses. Zeke passed on the call recording and the cell phone number used to the DEA. Then, putting his report together, he passed it to Cecilia with a wink and asked her to take it to Jim. She looked at him for a moment with a knowing smile.

"You just don't want to go out on the bow in the heat!" she said as she rose.

"And you want to steal a kiss or two from that man of yours," he retorted with a grin.

"Indeed, I do!" she said. "I'll tell him one of them is from you," she laughed as she skipped out of the room.

"I get it from you if he returns it!" Zeke yelled through the closing door. Smitty laughed as the door swung closed. John Allen Smith looked at his long-time friend and fellow soldier with exasperation. The man was almost too serious regarding computers, yet his funny moments could be surprising. That last interchange had been one of those moments. The two men grinned at each other.

Jim received the report and a kiss from Cecilia on the forward deck. Cecilia sat down with a bottle of water and listened to the noises of the surrounding jungle. Bird calls, monkeys, and other jungle sounds all seemed loud out here initially. It was still raining heavily, and she was tired of the steady drumming beat on the boat's roof and the water's surface.

Jim read through the report rather than listening to the tape. Zeke's cryptic style of recording dialog and interspersing comments was better than the tape itself. Pirates would be a threat. After reading the report, he went to the computer center. As he entered the room, Zeke looked up.

"I told Cecilia I get your kiss from her!" he said, his expression deadpan. He looked so earnest that Jim was momentarily caught off guard. Smitty choked and coughed, laughing so hard his face turned beet red. For a moment, Jim stared at the two men, perplexed.

"What?" Jim was surprised. He had no idea what Zeke was talking about, and after looking from Zeke to Smitty, he did not immediately get an answer.

"Never mind," Zeke said with a wave of the hand. Jim looked over at Smitty, who was spilling his coffee as he shook with silent laughter.

"Am I missing something?" Jim asked, his face breaking into a grin.

Smitty explained the interchange between Cecilia and Zeke, and Jim threw his head back and laughed. Then, his face suddenly serious, he looked down at Zeke. The room became silent as he stared at his friend, his eyes crinkling with laughter.

"That's all I need. If I start handing out kisses every time I discipline one of you clowns, you'll need another," he teased. All three men laughed. "If you want to kiss a girl, I'm sure Mary Ann or Barbara would be more than willing!" he added. "I'll mention to them that some of you are missing having a girl around to kiss."

"I had to open my mouth!" Zeke said, the anguish in his voice and sudden worry lines on his forehead telling Jim that his barb hit home.

Jim made a mental note to mention it to Barbara and Mary Ann. It would be fun to see what the two of them would do. He asked Zeke to keep a sharp eye on any movement on the river in front or behind them and then used his radio to warn the other boats of the impending danger.

"Be ready to move inside as soon as you hear a warning," he added unnecessarily on the radio. The men understood the warning for what it was.

At the moment, the boats were traveling about four feet apart, so he went to the rear, leaped across to the second boat, and then made his way through that one to the third. Stopping to talk to his men along the way took only a few minutes, and soon, he was in Dr. Gregg's spacious workroom.

"Hi folks!" he greeted them.

"How in the world did you get here?" Barbara asked, surprised.

"I jumped from boat to boat. We're traveling about four feet apart right now, so it was easy," Jim admitted.

"Oh, easy! We're on a river with piranha in the water, probably crocodiles and big snakes, and you just leisurely jump across! Boys!" she added, holding up a finger and shaking her head dramatically.

"I'm sure the captain had a good reason for paying us this visit," Mary Ann interjected with a smile at her friend's antics.

"As a matter of fact, I came to talk to the two of you about kissing one of my men," Jim replied with a wide grin.

"Shall I demonstrate our ability?" Mary Ann said, jumping out of her seat. "Uh, Cecilia might get jealous," Jim said, backing away quickly. Mary Ann laughed. "Actually, Uncle Zeke was mentioning that he didn't have anyone to kiss. Do you two think you could dream something up for him? Something appropriately comical, I think."

"Captain!" Dr. Gregg sounded scandalized. "This is like providing a lethal weapon and asking an unruly juvenile delinquent to go mugging!" He looked at the two women who were rubbing their hands in anticipation.

"Dastardly, isn't it?" Jim said, his grin infectious.

"We'll do our best, Captain," Barbara said. Jim laughed.

They talked about the discoveries Dr. Gregg and his team made for a while. While they talked, the other team members wandered in until the room was quite full. Jim watched Barbara rope in Heidi Van Haaten and pretty little Lisle Mirelle into her corner for a heated discussion. He talked to Adley and Dick as they joined the professor.

Jim listened as the three men detailed the information, leading them to believe that the rumors of a hidden Mayan city were true. He knew these men were not treasure hunters. They were archaeologists and scholars, but their excitement certainly left nothing to be desired. The artifacts and history they would uncover were their treasure. He listened intently and learned since he loved that part of what he did as much as finding treasure.

Dr. Gregg commented on it when Jim left, going aft to jump to the last boat and visit with his brother and his team. "That man would have made a fine historian. Bloody unlucky, the sea stole his love first, what?" The statement surprised his two assistants since Dr. Gregg wasn't given to cursing. It meant that he really felt strongly about that. Shaking his head, he wondered what kind of a student Jim might have become had he decided to follow that career.

"Hi, guys!" Jim laughed as he leaped easily onto the bow and then over the railing. John, Dorf, C.G., and Vince sat at the table together. Maps of the river region were spread out, especially of the islands they were approaching. Jim saw that and grinned.

"We were discussing the most likely places to meet an ambush," John revealed. He tossed a pen on the table and grinned at his brother, and the two grabbed hands and bumped shoulders. He exchanged similar greetings with the other three men, and they sat again while he turned to the refrigerator. Moving from boat to boat in this heat sapped a man of energy!

Jim grabbed a diet Coke with lime from the refrigerator and sat with the men. He popped the top and drank deeply before speaking. Putting the can down on the bamboo tabletop, he looked around at the four men.

"You are the most vulnerable, and I think they'll probably wait for us to pass and try to take your boat first," Jim suggested.

"That's what we figured, Shep," Dorf agreed, sipping from a water bottle that was still cold enough to sweat.

"We're going to use the holographs to give them the idea of trying to sneak up behind us," John explained.

"Two men can take them from the rear deck," C.G. added.

The rear deck was on the second level. It offered the advantages of a raised platform from which to fire and good visibility. After listening to the idea, Jim decided he liked it and said so.

"We'll deploy two on the bottom deck to mop up," Vince said. "Makes for a little excitement!" he added with an evil grin.

"Argh, matey!" Dorf said, imitating the typical Disney pirate accent and mannerisms. "I'll be sure to wear me eye patch and wave me saber about in a truly menacing manner, I will, Cap'n!" he added comically.

"That ought to give several a heart attack!" Jim had to laugh. The others joined, and Jim spent the rest of the hour visiting with his brother and friends. At last, he needed to return to his boat, and he leaped the railing again, leaped to the next boat, and made his way forward. It was exhilarating and dangerous to jump from boat to boat, he thought with a grin. I guess I've still got some growing up to do!

CHAPTER 13

N OTHING MUCH HAPPENED at lunchtime, but the hilarity at supper was worth his efforts. As Zeke entered the dining room, Heidi, Lisle, Barbara, and Mary Ann screamed like he was a rock star, fell upon him, and covered his face in lip prints from kissing him. Blushing a deep red, he took his place at one of the tables amidst the laughter.

As expected, FM piped up that Zeke got all the fun, and he was next. Mary Ann gave him an exceptionally long kiss on the lips, and when she drew away, he pulled her onto his lap and yelled. "Oh, baby! Where have you been all my life?" To her surprise and secret delight, he kissed her thoroughly. Amidst the catcalls and whistles, she emerged, her face flushed, her eyes bright, and FM laughed.

Cecilia looked at Jim quietly as he enjoyed the antics of his crew. He looked back at her, his eyes baleful. "What?" he asked, feigning innocence, seeing the look in her eyes. She burst out laughing, and he joined her.

The girls descended on Lonnie Johnson next and then moved on to Sean and the Australians, who bore it all with stoic faces.

All four girls stood, gave an irritated toss of their hair to the four Australians, and announced that Americans were just more fun. That sent everyone into gales of laughter again. Jim was glad that Bob Stankus was not left out of the fun as they descended on him next. He blushed more than any of the other men.

"Shucks, Cuss!" FM said, looking at him critically. "Maybe you better go have Doc take your temperature or something!" Bob couldn't help laughing, and he retorted.

"It's my blood pressure I'm worried about!" he said. "My heart's beating way too fast!"

"Such a nice man!" Barbara said, patting his cheek. He blushed again.

Jim knew that moments like this were important to the crew and to the morale of everyone involved in this expedition. He was learning to display emotion, or at least Cecilia said he was. His social style did not include this type of horseplay, yet he had to admit it was fun. The problem was he rarely thought about it or gave it much credence. His humor tended toward sarcasm, and he learned early that an officer has to be careful about that sort of thing regarding morale. He realized that the fun was deeply appreciated and, therefore, necessary. Quick to notice that the girls stayed away from Bull and Tom, He nodded with appreciation.

Those two were not ready for such frivolity yet, and the girls were aware of that. They kept their fun to the men they knew could deal with it appropriately.

His thoughts returned to sarcasm. It took effort to learn to recognize sarcasm for what it was and to stay away from it. Once he gave his life to Christ, some of that changed, and it became easier to avoid it. He pondered that for a moment while the laughter went on around him. Had the change in his heart really infiltrated his personality so profoundly? It appeared so.

Sturdy came out in the middle of all the fun. Since none of the girls could reach his face, Mary Ann went into the kitchen and retrieved a three-foot stepladder Abe kept there. The girls used that to climb up and kiss the giant. Sturdy seemed to be enjoying the attention. He would gently lift each woman off the ladder after his kiss and set her on the floor. They seemed to enjoy the journey from the ladder to the floor as they all went back for seconds.

Jim knew that the crew would remember moments like this with a fondness he didn't understand yet. Even the men of the team would talk about times like this while resting or before going to sleep at night. He tended to want less talk and more action or sleep, as the case may be. But that was his nature, and it wasn't the nature of all the men. John was the opposite: expressive, loving to talk, even small talk. Jim hated small talk. Yet he had to admit that John was a happy soul, and the men and women seemed to enjoy his company.

They came to the fork of the river where going north would take them onto the Japurá River, and going south would keep them on the Amazon. Stopping for the night, they tied up to some trees and to each other to keep the boats from drifting back down the river or onto a submerged log or sandbar. The ground was higher here, and not far from where they were tied, the jungle animals prowled through the dusk. For the first time, they could hear the grunts of Puma, several different types of monkeys, and other mammals that lived in this region. It all seemed very close and very real.

Abe hatched the plan of putting Alistair's Lady and Gwyneth side by side and using the two front decks for dinner. Beef and chicken Fajitas were served with large slices of grilled onions, red and green peppers, guacamole, sour cream, cheese, tomatoes, and lettuce. Hot soft flour tortillas, chips, and mild and hot salsa were provided. The meal lanterns were hung around the perimeter of the decks to spice things up, adding extra light. Three different kinds of melon were also included.

Mosquito netting stretched tight around the outer portion of the boat, allowing people to pass through the front railing gate out onto the bow. An arched passage was made between the boats with duct tape and extra netting to keep the bugs at a minimum. Everyone wore their bug spray, something they rarely thought about anymore. This crew used an unscented spray that no one could smell, but one could feel it in his or her hair, especially if someone forgot and rubbed an eye. That always sent one of them looking for water to rinse away the irritating substance.

Perhaps it was the extra light, the smell of the food, or the noise; no one was sure. For the first time, the outer defense repelled a giant Anaconda that got curious. Sparks flew as fifty thousand volts of electricity came into contact with the giant snake. Flinging about in the tree half its body was still attached to, the snake made quite a splash for a few minutes.

"I'm glad that works!" Phil Eustus said with feeling. "That was a bloody big snake."

"They come even bigger down here," Alistair commented, watching the snake drop into the water and swim away. "This one is only about sixteen or seventeen feet long. Twenty-five footers have been captured, and there are stories of larger ones."

"What you want to do if one comes after you is lie down with your feet facing it. If it tries to swallow you, wait until you're up to your knees, sit up, and ram your knife into its brain," Mark instructed, quite serious as he spoke.

"Oh, right! Of course!" Ox said sarcastically. "I'll just lie down and let it start eating me! That sounds like a completely reasonable thing to do! Here snaky-snaky! Dinner is served!"

"If it wraps around you, it will crush you before trying to eat you," Mark said. "Once it starts crushing you, either you die from all the crushed bones or asphyxiation. Either way, it's an excruciating way to die."

"Could we just not talk about these snakes!" Chance Edwards said. "I don't want to think about that when creeping through this bloody jungle."

"The good thing is, with that big of a fellow in this part of the jungle, there probably won't be any more," Mark added, not listening. "They're not really social reptiles. They tend to hunt huge areas and to avoid other Anacondas."

"I wonder why!" Ox said. "Who'd want to get cozy with something that ugly?"

"Only a female, and only when she's ready to mate. Then you could run into several males simultaneously," Mark replied.

"Oh, thanks!" Chance said. "I feel much better now!"

Jim listened to the interchange with a smile on his face. Snakes, the occasional hunting cat like a Puma, and other natural enemies didn't really cause him any fear. They, at least, were predictable. Human enemies were far different. He looked over at Cecilia and saw a worried frown on her face.

"Did that snake scare you?" he asked quietly, leaning close to her ear.

"A little, yes," she admitted. "Promise me that you won't leave me on this boat alone!" she added with a shiver.

"You have my word," Jim assured her. To his delight, that was all the assurance she needed. Sighing, he took her hand and held it.

As is often the case upon such an expedition, things changed dramatically instantly. Early the following day, Jim lay in the bow of a rigid raider. FM was at the wheel, and Ox was stretched out next to Jim, in a prone position, his MP5/10SD ready and a

Heckler and Koch G-36 prepared at his side. All three men wore their combat armor suits and full battle gear. At the moment, they trailed the last boat by about one hundred yards. Jim guessed the first attack would come against the last boat because it was the most vulnerable.

When it came to military tactics, it made sense. It would take time for the lead boats to turn around and come to the aid of the last boat. Rain poured out of the sky in torrents, pounding the Kevlar sides of the raider in a steady thunder. Water poured off the edges of their cabbage patch hats, but their vision was clear.

From the mist ahead, the unmistakable sound of an outboard engine roared to life. Watching his computer monitors carefully, Zeke warned the last boat of the pending attack. Jim raised his hand, waved it forward, and FM pushed the throttle forward. The Rigid Raider sprang out of the water, reaching a speed of almost fifty knots before they had covered a hundred yards. Out of the mist, they came upon the pirates. None of the pirates noticed the rigid raider until it was too late.

John, Vince, and C.G. suddenly appeared on the second deck at the rear and opened fire, while Jim and Ox fired from their prone position, both now on the starboard side. Five pirates went down in the first burst of fire, confusing the remaining four. Then three more went down as John and his men fired almost directly below them, taking everyone but the driver. He already had his hands over his head in surrender as Dorf appeared on the lower rear deck, weapon at ready.

Dorf took the man prisoner, used the plastic restraint ties to bind his hands behind his back, and then he bent down and, with an adjustable wrench he produced from his tool belt, unscrewed the drain plug from the bottom of the boat. It began to fill with water as it floated away. Before Jim could order his men out to interrogate the prisoner, Zeke called.

"I have another target two hundred yards forward from our position. Sixteen men in two, repeat two boats. The boats are pontoon boats with outboard motors," Zeke reported over the headsets.

"Roger that. Rigid Raider Team will engage in a strafe and run. We need to know when we are on them, Zeke. I can't see more than ten feet in front of me. Give us regular positions, please," Jim replied.

"Go, raider team. I'll guide you in," Zeke said into his microphone.

FM pushed the throttle forward, and the rigid raider shot upstream again. Following Zeke's directions, they came out of the fog on the first of two pontoons while the pirates were looking intently for sight of them. Jim and Ox were ready and opened fire quickly, spraying the boats at 800 rounds per minute.

Flashing by the first boat, they kept up the fire into the second boat as they sped by, and then they were hidden in the mist again. FM didn't wait for the order but spun the boat and cut the engine, holding them now by reversing slowly enough to keep them almost stationary.

"Good shooting!" Zeke said. "Five down on the first boat, six on the second. Seven men remain alive, three on the second boat and four on the first. Pontoons are in pursuit, repeat, in pursuit. They are running side by side. Run on bearing two four one degrees, and you'll shoot between them." Zeke ordered.

FM watched his compass setting and kept it at two hundred and forty-one degrees. Jim moved to the port side, aiming his Heckler & Koch G36 with a 40-mm grenade launcher beneath the barrel. As they sped between the boats, both men fired two grenades, both on target. The inside pontoons were destroyed, and the boats capsized almost immediately, hurling the men into the water. Screams of fear and pain sounded over the surface of the water.

"We have two more boats coming downriver from about a mile away, Shep," Zeke's voice sounded over his earpiece. "These look like actual patrol boats, much like the ones used in Vietnam. Both could have machine guns mounted on the bow." Zeke's voice was calm as if announcing guests at the door. Jim appreciated that.

"Copy. Six Team Three. Take two raiders and flank them. Engage from behind. We will engage from the front, going between them."

"Roger, Shep. We're leaving now," Wade's voice replied calmly.

Jim heard the roar of their engines, and at the same time, FM punched theirs into motion again. Zeke guided them between the two patrol boats. One was slightly in the lead, on the north side of the river. Ox would take that one. Jim would take the one on the south side. FM crouched behind the bulletproof windscreen before him, hoping the mist would keep the enemy from getting accurate shots.

Death was a reality every soldier faced every day. One could die in training, by accident, in an accident, in many different ways. In battle, FM rarely thought about the reality of death. He was aware that a stray shot could take him or any of the men and even more aware that a well-aimed shot or grenade could destroy their boat and them in an instant. But that awareness was overshadowed by the adrenalin rush of battle, of doing his job with expertise and panache, and the thrill of the moment. A rebel yell formed inside, but he didn't voice it aloud.

Ox timed his shot perfectly, launching a grenade right into the center of the patrol boat. Jim didn't have time to see it because he was timing his shot. It, too, was perfectly aimed and did maximum damage. Before the pirates could recover, the two rigid raiders came up from behind and launched more grenades into the boats.

Then, the men climbed over the sides, using their side arms to mop up. Once the pirates were accounted for, the drain plugs were pulled, and the boats were allowed to sink. All three rigid raiders returned, side by side, moving slowly in case there were any more pirates. Zeke reported that the river before them was now clear.

Jim spoke with each of his men once weapons were cleaned and stowed and showers were finished. Doc and Ox reported that none of the men had received wounds other than the usual scrapes and bruises when moving about from boat to boat. The captain's journey took him through the research vessels, and he ensured each man knew he was pleased as a commander.

This was part of the job he enjoyed. Each man received him in a soldier-to-soldier contact that could include a handshake, shoulder bump, or just touching the knuckles of a closed fist. Each man straightened as he came to congratulate him on a job well done and ask what each thought of the strategy and mission. Every soldier had something to contribute, and Jim listened carefully. Soldiers are trained to assess every situation, and these were among the finest soldiers in the world. What they had to say would be important, so Jim listened carefully, often writing in his pocket notebook.

For their part, the men found his undivided attention and careful concentration a mark of respect. He wrote it down if they made a suggestion, and they knew that he would remember. PU noticed that a lot of shells went into the water and wondered if they might damage the propellers of the rigid raiders. Jim wrote that down and later, out of genuine concern, had Master Chief Warner and Inchworm check each propeller.

Small details like that could be of significant importance. None of the shells in the water had damaged any of the props. Jim asked the mechanics if they would, and both men thought it was possible. After each mission, they checked them and devised a protective cover to keep shells from reaching the propellers. PU noticed the interchange and felt pride. He knew his opinions were respected, and his estimation of Jim Shepherd went up another notch.

CHAPTER 14

Back on the riverboats, the team cleaned and oiled their weapons and put them in their cases beneath the floor of their rooms. Their battle armor and bulletproof vests were carefully dried before being folded neatly and stored away with the weapons. After showers, the Team gathered to evaluate.

Cecilia met Jim as he came out of his cabin, her eyes looking him over, showing relief that he was whole and unharmed. She didn't say anything, just took his hand and walked with him as they made their way to Alistair's Lady, now moored to some trees. If her grip was a little tighter than usual, Jim understood.

Jim walked around the dining room, shaking hands with his Team, and telling them again personally and publicly what a good job they'd done. His praise included the men who stayed behind and guarded the boats and science crew, and that fact was not missed. When he finally sat down after talking to them all he saw that they were at a good place emotionally and mentally. That was of utmost importance because they would need every advantage and edge he could give them in the days to come.

"We did a good job neutralizing the enemy. Any problems you want to talk about or something you noticed?" he began.

"Shooting from the raider takes a little timing. This design doesn't bounce as much as the last one, though," Wade commented. "The front end stays close to the water, too," he added.

"Good tactics on the takedown, Shep. Those patrol boats were a little dicey, climbing aboard in the rain. Lunch Box and C.G. both sustained slight injuries from slipping. If a bad guy had been up and ready, they might have taken a bullet in the armor, or worse," Ox mentioned. "GSG9 uses a softer sole on their boot. That might work."

Jim nodded and wrote a note on his computer to check that out. Dorf was next to speak.

"The barrel plugs we're using need to be replaced regularly. This climate is hard on rubber; I noticed mine was slightly cracked. It hadn't reached the point where moisture could get into the barrel, but it was cracked. That happens in hot, dry climates at a quicker pace, though we never use the plugs in that climate."

"Are the replacements in the same shape?" Jim asked.

"No. They're still wrapped, which seems to protect them some," he replied. "I checked."

"Thanks, Dorf," Jim said simply. He made another note for himself on his computer, noting that all the men were doing the same. Keeping weapons at maximum operating capacity was essential to a soldier.

"Did anyone have problems with their weapons in the wet?" Jim asked next.

"I noticed that my clips were wet, but the oil should keep everything working properly," John replied. "I dried everything and oiled it again last night. So did everyone else that I saw," he added.

Jim nodded. He'd taken note of that himself. "What about the enemy? How would you rate their skills, weapons, and motivation?"

"The one still alive still thinks he's one bad dude. This morning, he told me what he was going to do to my family, my woman, and me. They seem to be highly motivated but poorly skilled. Their weapons are in a bad way. They don't take care of them like they should. Each one we examined was rusted and dirty. This machismo thing is strong in these buggers, Shep. We ever get into a firefight with a large body of them, I doubt they'll give up, even if we wipe them out to a man. Our captive is certainly keeping his machismo working at high voltage! He's afraid, but he's trying not to show it! I wonder if he thinks that because we're Americans, we won't do anything to him," Vince offered.

"Proper wallies, these blighters!" Phil Eustus said, shaking his head. "Ol' PU put a nine in one's knee, and he still tried to draw on me! I was tryin' to give the poor fool a chance, what?"

"That's a good thing to remember. We're dealing with pride here, an unreasoning pride. Don't turn your back on one of these men or underestimate his desire to keep coming," Jim stated after a moment of thought.

Standing at the group's outer edge, Windy saw the men take this obvious reminder with solemn nods. He'd learned that they didn't resent the obvious being stated. If it related to their work, they listened. Repeating information made it stick. It used to irritate him when people repeated the obvious, but he'd learned to appreciate it in the last year. If men like this were willing to hear it, he realized he needed to be willing to listen. Thinking about the concept, he listened as the conversation continued.

"How about the riverboats and our rear guard?" Jim asked, looking over at the kitchen crew.

"One or two mosquitoes wandered in, but Cuss pointed his gun at them, and they left," Sturdy said with a grin at Bob. "Actually, I was proud of my boys. They followed the drill."

"TP has good ears and knows how to handle that MP5/10," Zeke added when the laughter died over Sturdy's mosquito story. "He heard Smitty getting water for me from his post at the rear deck and came to check on us. His feet were very quiet as he moved, too. I was impressed."

"I didn't know you saw me!" Tom Patterson said, shaking his head. "Uncle Zeke sees all!" Zeke replied. "Uncle Zeke is watching you!"

All the men said it with him that time, and they laughed at Zeke's famous line. Jim noted that TP seemed very pleased by the praise and knew that coming from former SEAL team members, it would be taken seriously.

"Good," Jim said when the laughter died. "Now! What do we do with our prisoner?"

"He knows about us, Shep," John commented, his face suddenly sad. "So do Tupi and his boys," Jim replied.

"Strip him naked and leave him on one of the islands," Sturdy suggested. "That's what we did to Tupi and his men. I don't think they'll brave the water. They are probably still on that island!" he added. "This man will probably be in the same fix."

"We may very well have sentenced Tupi and his men to death, doing that," Ox said softly. "But he would gladly have killed any of us. I say we at least gave them a chance."

"I agree with Ox. This pirate would kill any of us, given a chance," Dorf said. "At least he'll have a chance of survival. That's more than he would have given any of us."

Jim waited as the room grew silent and finally looked around. "Anyone who disagrees with leaving him on an island should speak now." No one spoke, and finally, he sighed. He felt that he was condemning the man to death, but he agreed with Dorf. It was more of a chance than the pirate would have given any of them.

"JR, your team can handle that," Jim said quietly. John sadly nodded, and his team left. Everyone listened to the rigid raider's outboard motor as it made the trip to one of the islands. Twenty minutes later, the boat returned, and the men rejoined the others, who had not moved. This was serious business, and everyone wanted a report.

"He says to tell you that he will find us once he gets free, and he will kill all of us," JR said after drinking down half a fresh bottle of water. "I hogtied him to a small sapling with plastic restraint ties, and we covered him with sugar water. The rain would wash it away in time, but the ants in the area seemed very interested. They are those red stinging ants, too!" he nodded once with a grin of anticipation.

"May I suggest a time of prayer?" Jim said, looking at Abe. His friend nodded. "Abe, will you lead us, please?" Abe nodded. Everyone bowed, and Abe thanked the Lord that none of them were injured and prayed for the prisoners, not that they would escape, but that they would find in this trial the need for God. After that, he prayed for the continued journey and that the men and women on the boats would keep their eyes focused on Him and trust Him through every situation. As a prayer, it did a lot to settle everyone down. Jim looked around and finally nodded his head before giving his next order.

"I think we're ready to move on. Thanks, everyone. Take your posts."

Tupi and his men had, indeed, finally freed themselves from their bonds. It had been the sugar water that sealed their fate. Three days after being bound to the trees, the first of them broke free, but by then, Malaria had taken its toll on his body. Mosquitoes, drawn by the sugar water, fed off all the men and injected them with the deadly disease. Dizzy and disoriented, he worked to free the others, finally settling upon a sharp rock as the best tool for the job. Tupi was already burning with fever.

None dared brave the water, and they huddled together in the pouring rain until the flooding finally covered the island. By then, two of them died of fever, and the rest of them were so ill they could barely move. Too weak to climb into the trees and bleeding into the water from the many bites as bugs fed voraciously on their extremities, it wasn't long before the predators found and devoured them. Tupi was alive when the Anaconda took him, too weak even to scream.

The remaining pirate fared no better once John and his team left him hogtied on the ground, ants swarming over his body. His entire skin was eaten away, and in three days, he died in agony, still bound, screaming as the insects continued their grizzly feast. It would be years before the bones were discovered. The evidence of restraint ties was washed away in the flooding, and as the bones were scattered in the flood, no one would ever piece together what happened to those men.

CHAPTER 15

Death. Its stench filled their nostrils as they came upon the little village of Japurá. Cloying and overpowering, it hung in the damp air and drifted downriver to warn them. No one should have been in the village along the river. They had a village on higher ground that they moved to during the rainy season. When the town appeared out of the mist, Jim studied it through his binoculars before ordering them forward.

There were bloated, rotting bodies in the streets, and the levy had been sandbagged to prevent the waters from coming into the streets. Dead animals lay everywhere, and the sounds of people in agony could be heard from one of the buildings near the water. Inland, some way from the village itself, an open-sided tent had been erected, and under its protection, a large group of people stood or sat, facing the building from which the moans came. If anything could be said about their faces, it was that they had suffered everything imaginable and now waited for whatever would come.

"Medical team, please come up front pronto. Wear your hazard suits. I need an assessment fast!" Jim said into his radio.

Ten minutes later, the three medical team members stepped on shore and entered the building. Dead and living were crowded together on the floor, cots, and furniture. Two old women were trying to help the suffering, their faces drawn and tired, blank from having suffered so much loss, exhaustion from serving so many with so little.

Jack Boswell appeared a few minutes later to ask questions and translate. After about ten minutes of conversation with the two women, he keyed his headset.

"Shep, this is Driver," he said.

"Go ahead, Driver," Jim replied, hearing the tension in his friend's voice. "We have some kind of epidemic here. Coming in, I noticed that the river is about to eat this town. Doc and Ox say we've got to work fast, or all these people are going to die. Boss…" he paused to find the words. "There are babies in here. God help us!" he cried. Jim heard the agony in his voice and could feel tears well in his own eyes.

"Hazard suits, now," Jim said into his headset. Picking up the radio microphone before him, he cued the announce switch to go over the intercom. "Hazard emergency. Lock everything down and get into your suits now! Dock and meet me on Captain Rob," he ordered. "We've got to move fast, men, and save this town. This one will challenge us, men!" he put the microphone down and sighed deeply.

Cecilia appeared at his elbow, already in her hazard suit. She looked through the clear plastic faceplate, her eyes wide and anxious. "What can I do?" she asked.

"Give Millie a hand, please," Jim answered.

Cecilia nodded and headed onto the shore. Jim put on his hazard suit and met his men on the bow, assigning them duties as they came up. He put Wade to work on the sandbags to save the town and gave him the kitchen crew, Master Chief Warner, and Inchworm. He watched the medical team plow through the mud to the tent outside the village while he assigned his men other duties.

At Doc's orders, he carried dead bodies into one of the structures, probably someone's home, across the street. It was the village chief who appeared to identify the bodies for him. Once all the dead were identified and recorded, he poured gasoline all over the floor of the structure, walked out into the street, and tossed a match. The house went up in flames.

Bone-weary from carrying the bodies, he joined Wade, helping lift bags filled with wet sand and place them on a growing dam curving around the town on both sides. No one talked about the deaths, the bodies, the burning building, now just smoldering ashes hissing as raindrops hit them. If any of the men thought they needed a break, none suggested it. This was a race against time and against the power of the elements, and none were willing to yield an inch. Jim had never been prouder of his men than in those hours they grunted and heaved and lifted sandbags until they could barely move.

After dark, the men ate on board Alistair's Lady and fell into their hammocks, exhausted. Jim searched for the medical team and found them in the makeshift lab adjoining the room Doc, and Millie used to treat people on their assigned riverboat. None of them were wearing their hazard suits anymore.

Cecilia sat with Millie, the two embracing each other and quietly shedding tears. Doc and Sean sat with their heads down, hands dangling between their knees, faces drawn, lips hard, straight lines. Jim walked over to the two men and put a hand on each shoulder, standing behind them.

"What do we know?" he asked quietly.

"Half the village is dead. The disease began a week ago and claimed the first lives within forty-eight hours. We set up what hospital facilities we could, and I'm pumping them full of liquids and antibiotics. We radioed for help, but the government can't get anything here within the next two weeks. Red Cross said they'll dispatch a team and hospital supplies today," Doc reported, not raising his head to speak. "Even then, they're a few days away, Jim. We've got to figure out what this is and how to treat it and give these people some kind of hope," tears fell down the doctor's face as he spoke.

"Zeke talked with the Navy. They're going to fly in some help, too. We can expect the first drops in the morning," Sean added, lifting his head and looking at Jim through troubled eyes.

"Get what rest you can. Use anyone you need to for help. I'm at your call, guys," Jim said, patting them both and leaving the room.

Half the village! No wonder these people look so defeated. He went to the kitchen for a snack and then to his hammock. Sleep overtook him quickly, and he felt worse when he rose again in four hours. Groggy and hurting, he went to the shower, visited the bathroom, and finally went for some early breakfast.

As soon as he had some food, he went out to find Wade. Abe told him that Wade had left just moments before. He found him standing at the sandbag dam, looking out over the water as rain poured down relentlessly.

"If we're going to stay here, on the river, we're going to have to put these buildings on stilts," Wade announced when he noticed Jim standing quietly at his side. Jim turned and looked back at the few buildings and the adequate supplies around the village.

"Just tell us what to do, Wade. This is your area of expertise," Jim replied. "If anyone can save this village, it's you!"

"I'm a marine engineer, Jim," Wade reminded him.

"Is that a river out there?" Jim asked, pointing at the rising waters. "So be a marine engineer and engineer a town that stays put when the river comes in for a visit!" Jim was grinning as he spoke, and Wade shook his head, pleased and surprised by Jim's faith in him.

"Okay," he responded. "I'll give it my best shot. I've got some drawings to do. While I work on them, do you think you could get a crew together to cut down about fifty trees?"

"We have four chainsaws. I think we can do something," Jim said.

Later, when everyone had eaten breakfast, Jim took twelve men into the jungle and began falling trees. Four men worked the saws, while others used axes and two-man handsaws provided by the locals. Some of the healthier men of the village helped. No one asked to break for lunch. This was a race against time, and every man knew it. If anyone paused, it was to stretch out muscles sore and cramped from constant use and then to bend again to the task or visit the hastily erected outhouse.

Half the trees were down by evening and had been trimmed and cut to specifications. A tired crew slogged through the mud to the riverboats, showered, and ate a huge supper before returning to their berths for a night's rest.

The next day, breakfast found the stainless-steel containers empty by the time the men left for their work in the jungle. Every ounce of food was consumed. Once Abe and his crew were finished, they joined the work in the village. Wade was a realist. He didn't try to save the huts. Instead, he tore them apart, stacked the good lumber where he could use it, and directed the men in setting poles upon which to erect new huts and walkways. Surprising even himself, he'd designed a village that could literally sit in the middle of the river without suffering damage.

They didn't have to do this. In fact, if Jim had still been under the umbrella of the Navy, he would have been ordered to move on. Somehow, doing what they were doing became of utmost importance to everyone on the crew. Even those who were cynical at first came on board by the third day of work. A new town was taking form, one that would survive floods.

Doc, Sean, Millie, and Cecilia worked as hard, caring for the sick and educating those who were well. Through it all, they kept trying to find the cause of this illness. A week passed, and on the seventh day, no one died. It was the first day since their arrival that no bodies needed to be burned. Grateful though they were that the grizzly task needn't be performed, no one celebrated. There were still answers to be found.

Three completed log houses now proudly stood, complete with thatched roofs and shuttered windows. Two rolls of window screen, somewhat rusted, turned up from the one store, which had closed for the rainy season. All the windows and a door were protected now from insects. Doc thought the local mosquitoes might be carrying this virus, but so far, he had been unable to find any proof. Desperate to find the cause of the disease, he soldiered on.

He and Ox found the answer in the least-expected place. It was perhaps near midnight when Doc and Ox came into Jim's quarters without knocking, waking him from a tired sleep. Jim sat up and looked at the two men. If anything, Doc seemed angry.

"It's in the water!" he said without preamble. "Someone is putting this virus in the water. This isn't a powerful virus; it only lasts about twenty-four hours. So, whoever is doing this returned to give the village a second dose. It showed up this morning, very strong, and by ten o'clock tonight, it was gone."

"This is a man-made virus?" Jim asked for clarification.

"Yes! It combines a virus and e-coli, linked somehow biologically in a laboratory! No guesses whose lab we're talking about!" he added, hitting the heel of his hand against the wall.

Jim got up, shrugged into a T-shirt, and, in bare feet, stepped down the corridor to Zeke's room. He pounded the door, and half dragged Zeke from his hammock. Confused and tired, Zeke rubbed sleep from his eyes.

"Come on. We need to check something on the satellite feed," he explained.

"The boat that came downriver this morning?" Zeke asked as he padded toward the computer room in his bare feet.

"You knew about it?" Jim asked. There was no accusation in his voice, merely curiosity.

"It came down the river but stopped two miles from the village. No one got out of the boat or came downriver any further. They sat there for a while, then turned around and returned." Zeke replied, looking back at Doc with curiosity. "I guessed they might be putting something in the water, though."

"They dumped this virus in the water!" Doc said by way of explanation.

Zeke went to the Apple PowerBook G4, hooked to the satellite, and played back the trip. The boat came from a small camp upriver about ten miles. Another boat had arrived there the night before from the terrorist camp.

"I never thought about a biological weapon being used against these simple people," Zeke said softly. "What kind of threat could they be?" he added with anger now touching his voice.

"No threat. These people were lab rats!" Jim snorted, his fists tightening. "They need to see how it works; how fast, how lethal it is!"

"It's not your fault. I would have thought they were fishing or something, probably what you thought." Doc spoke to both men, watching the replay of everything again.

"Can we kill the virus?" Jim asked.

"Yes. I've already isolated what is needed to immunize the village and care for the sick. The antibiotics we've been using have done the job there already. We can teach them how to purify their water and avoid further incidents," Doc replied. "Other animals that drink from the water will die. Monkeys, cats, and any animal that can contract the virus will die. We have to warn them not to eat dead animals and to burn their bodies." For a long moment, he paused, looking inward, and then he looked Jim in the eye.

"Jim, I'm glad we do what we do!" Doc said into the silence that followed as everyone watched the replay on the computer screen again. "These people are amoral. They have to be stopped. Some of them should die. Putting them behind bars is not the answer! There were babies burned in that house, little helpless innocent babies! God damn!" Doc looked shocked by his language for a moment but didn't apologize.

Jim understood. Doc had watched so many die, feeling the helplessness and horror deeply. But he was asking Jim to kill a woman, and Jim wasn't sure he could do that. Putting her behind bars might not be the best solution, but he knew he couldn't just kill her like he killed terrorists who were at least carrying weapons.

"I thought the virus would be more lethal," Jim said after a moment of thought. "Any comments?" he inquired.

"It kills fast," Doc replied. Ox nodded in agreement. "A simple vaccination would protect others."

"Keep your notes," Jim said, patting both men on the shoulder.

A Red Cross team arrived the next day, and the Navy dropped much-needed supplies. Later that same day, three missionaries arrived in a dilapidated old riverboat with a heavily smoking diesel engine banging away loud enough to be heard several hundred yards away. Japurá was not a scheduled stop for them, but the activity drew their curiosity, and when they heard what happened to the village, they stayed on. One was a doctor, another a trained nurse, and the third a linguist. All three were surprised when they suggested prayer, and every one of Jim's crew bowed heads, ready to pray. Looking at the crew, they judged most of them military people.

Suddenly Japurá was bursting with people! If anyone thought that perhaps the *Bring It Up* venture should continue, no one suggested it. Saving this town had become an accepted mission that took precedence over all other criteria. Dr. Gregg, whom Jim thought might be chafing at the bit to move on, couldn't be dragged away. Now that people who could speak the dialect of these villagers had arrived, he was anxious to use them as interpreters to learn more, which was true, but his first concern was for the well-being of these simple folks. He had been very active in helping clear the branches from the cut timber, his aged hands bleeding from his efforts.

All of them had held suffering infants, and Jim watched his hardest soldiers break and weep when one died. Little children tended to be carefully held and cuddled by the soldiers, and not one of them resented the tears shed or was ashamed of them. Over the past days Jim's eyes had been red and swollen from his own tears. Children and the elderly had been hardest hit, suffering the most.

Red Cross volunteers realized that Wade was doing fantastic work rebuilding the town and pitched in with their tools and strength in a most satisfying way. The hospital hut was transformed into a real medical clinic within a day. Red Cross and Mission doctors fell in under Doc Wozniac, bowing to his experience and established presence as the head doctor. Though Cecilia could easily have turned her attention elsewhere, she remained with the clinic. Because of her forensic training, she was able to follow directions, think things through, and make decisions so that no one ever suspected she was anything but a competent nurse.

CHAPTER 16

TOM PATTERSON WATCHED Captain Shepherd working among the men and women building the huts. It seemed odd somehow that Jim wasn't in charge. He deferred to Wade's expertise and faded into the background as part of the team. Commenting on it to Abe while they prepared a huge lunch spread for everyone helped open his eyes further to what he had become a part.

"Shep doesn't need to be in charge," Abe said quietly, looking at the man as he spoke. "Here, there are others who know more about what needs to be done. I saw this last year when we raised one of the treasure ships. He let the experts take charge. Even here in the kitchen, he defers to me because I am the expert. But do not be fooled by this. In a way, he is in charge, and every man on this crew will do exactly what he tells them to do. Each man knows that his captain respects him, and as a result, every man gives his very best. Jim knows this. He is a wise leader."

"So, we all pull our weight and do what needs to be done, truly as a team!" Tom said, finally understanding what he'd been seeing and wanting for the past weeks.

"Yes, Tom. And now, I think you are truly a part of this amazing team," Sturdy said, laying a giant hand on his shoulder.

Tom Patterson was suddenly filled with pride, a pride he had not felt for a long time. This was something every man who served in America's armed forces understood. He or she was part of something, and when they did what they'd been trained to do, what they were part of was invincible. Battles could be lost, people and equipment could be lost, but none in vain. Such spirit could not be defeated. Ultimately, that spirit would lead them to victory.

Five more days passed, and the town buildings were finally completed. Every family had a new house to live in. A floating dock provided access to the river and river traffic. Each house was joined by a raised wooden walkway complete with rope railings. The village would no longer need to move to higher ground during the rainy season.

Every house roof extended out to protect the walkways from the falling rain, and every walkway connected to a wraparound porch with wood railings. A second Navy drop with supplies purchased by the *Bring It Up* corporation supplied every house with enough canned food and dry goods to keep them going for a year.

Overwhelmed with gratitude, the village's people celebrated their village's rebirth and the providence of a good God by treating all the volunteers with a grand feast. Two younger men entered the jungle and brought wild boar back for the feast. Abe, who had been feeding everyone, found himself surrounded by village women who refused to let him raise a finger to prepare food. His kitchen crew was treated with the same respect. Bemused, they allowed themselves to be herded away from preparations.

For a time, the deep grief over the deaths of so many was forgotten. Laughter and music filled the evening. Jim and Cecilia sat together in bamboo chairs, holding hands and smiling as the children capered about the room. The women gracefully served food on broad leaves from one of the jungle trees.

Water from the rain was now collected in barrels, and any taken from the river was boiled. The people understood that the sickness had come in the water and how to protect against it. For this celebration, they used bottled water for drinking and rainwater for cooking. It was a sumptuous meal.

After the celebration, Jim called his crew to *Alistair's Lady* riverboat dining room. As they came in by twos and threes, he saw how tired they were, though most were smiling. Fatigue was evident in slumped shoulders, moving joints that hurt to test how badly they might be injured, and a general air of exhaustion. It was to be expected. When everyone was seated, he stood, and the room became silent.

"We accomplished something significant these past weeks. I want to thank every one of you for pitching in and wearing yourselves out to help save this village. I don't know exactly when it became the thing we had to do, but it did. Doc, please give us an assessment of your thoughts on the health and future of the village," he said.

"The disease will not be fatal again unless the virus is genetically altered. That should be simple enough for someone bent on destroying people, and I wouldn't be surprised to find a new strain in the water very soon, Jim," Doc revealed, his voice carrying to everyone in the room. "I spoke to the mission doctor, and he and his two colleagues will stay on for a few months. This makes an excellent base for them to work from. They'll live and work out of the clinic."

"Wade, what about the village and the rising waters?" Jim asked, turning to his lieutenant commander.

"We set the pilings deep so the village will be safe. If they regularly treat the pilings with creosote during the dry season, this village should last a long time. That mission linguist helped me explain that to the leaders of the village. I'm pretty sure they understand," Wade replied. "I'm glad we built living quarters onto the clinic. That was a great suggestion, Cecilia!" Wade smiled tiredly at her.

"I designed the ladders and steps leading to the walkways to be retractable so they have some defense against brigands and pirates. They understood that concept very quickly, so I imagine the pirates have been here before. A determined force can still reach the buildings, but it will cost them. It also protects them from predators that come from the jungle," he added.

"Dr. Gregg, you've been spending a lot of time with the mission linguist.

What have you learned?" Jim asked that worthy scholar.

"One of the villagers has seen our stela!" Dr. Gregg said, mustering up a smile from his exhaustion. "He was on a fishing trip up the Mapari River."

Jim nodded in thought for a moment. "Okay, team. Here is what we're going to do," he said. Everyone looked at him expectantly, trusting him to lead them now, sure of his abilities, confident that whatever he decided would be the best course of action. Tom Patterson saw it and turned his attention to the captain.

"We're going to take seven days of R&R here." There were relieved sighs and cheers from the crew. When they quieted, he continued, "I'm sure by then Marta Hess will know we're here and be watching to see what we do. So, we're going to do exactly what we're expected to do. In seven days, we pull up anchor, head up the Mapari, and follow the Stela to the hidden city."

Jim looked at them again before continuing. "Once we've discovered the hidden city, and all the activity is going on regarding the artifacts, the strike team will deploy upriver and take care of the terrorist threat there."

"Brilliant!" Sean Oxton breathed, sitting next to Tom Patterson. "The man's a bloody genius! Hess will surely ask what we were doing here, and she'll discover the discussion about the Stela. She will never expect us to come after her.

Discussion followed as they hashed out the plan. It was lively and exciting as ideas came one after the other. Several noted that Jim wrote everything down in his neat block letters, causing them to feel no little pride in being a part of this amazing unit and sharing in its plans. Jim added one more thought before they broke up for the evening.

"We need to appear to be anything but a military outfit," he warned. "During the next seven days, we rise no earlier than seven and breakfast between eight and nine-thirty in the morning. Work on the boats will be done by noon, and we'll spend the afternoons and evenings with the village folks or sitting around on the boats. We've got to look like a satisfied crew, getting ready for our next stage, and put what comes after way in the back of our minds. We'll be watched, so please take this rest seriously!

"I have never been prouder of my crew than I am at this moment. What you did here was amazing, extraordinary, and worthy of the highest encomiums. As a disaster relief team, you stand second to none! Now, get to bed! You've all earned this rest," he ended.

No one argued that. Most of them took a shower before falling into their hammocks. Everyone slept late the following day. Keeping up a boat or ship was a constant necessity, but the crew did nothing that day but rest. Late in the afternoon, Zeke called Jim down to the computer room.

"Our terrorist friends are leaving their base camp up the river. Most of them are heading west, but a boatload is heading this way," he said when Jim entered.

"Okay, thanks," Jim said. "How long until they arrive?" "An hour, maybe ten minutes less," Zeke shrugged.

"Dorf, Abe, Sturdy, Wade, and John, meet me on the dock, please, in forty-five minutes," he added into his headset as he prepared to head that way.

Some of the men were fishing on the dock. The captain whispered a word, and they left their poles and headed back to the riverboats. Jim asked Lonnie Johnson to stay. No sooner were they in position with poles in their hands than the boat appeared around a bend in the river.

On board the riverboat, several of the terrorists were laughing and joking about what they would find. That stopped as they rounded the bend to find an entirely new village, a floating dock, and upon that dock, seven men, several of them seeming giants. The captain of the riverboat eyed them critically as they approached. The tallest one looked like an oak tree, all tough gnarled muscle bulging through his T-shirt. He seemed to be wearing some sort of heavy sportsman's vest. There was another one, slightly shorter, muscled differently, and perhaps more dangerous because of it. *Who are these men?*

Then, the Captain saw the Red Cross banner and their boats. He could also see the *Bring It Up* riverboats. These men must be from that crew. Rumor had reached them of giants on board. The captain of this band of terrorists spoke fluent English. As his boat drifted toward the floating dock, he spoke with arrogance.

"Where is the leader of this village? We would speak with him!" he demanded aggressively.

"Were you invited?" Sturdy inquired, putting down his pole and putting a foot on the bow of their boat as it came into contact with the dock.

"What do you mean?" the captain snapped.

"Senior Juan Pedro Carella is the elder of this village. He decides who visits his village. Did he invite you here?" Sturdy asked again, keeping his colossal size sixteen boot on the boat's bow.

"He knows who I am!" the captain snapped. "I will speak with him."

"And who are you?" Sturdy inquired, his voice still even though his eyes were growing dangerous. Some of the men on the boat were touching their weapons.

"I am Captain Louis Martin Sirello!" the captain said with a brave show of machismo.

"Senior Carella does not wish to speak with you, Louis. Why don't you take your little band of ruffians somewhere else?" Sturdy suggested.

Captain Sirello stared at him with his mouth open in amazement for a moment and then drew an old Smith and Wesson.38 caliber snub-nosed pistol. In his experience, the appearance of a gun was all it usually took to get his way.

"This is aimed at your heart, senior. Step aside, or I will shoot you!" Captain Sirello snarled.

"Oh, don't shoot him!" Abe warned, stepping up beside Sturdy. "You'll just make him angry! That would be very unwise. Now, be wise and leave the dock before something bad happens."

Over that stretched T-shirt, Sturdy was wearing his bulletproof vest. It didn't look like a bulletproof vest because of the outer covering of pockets and straps for military gear. Abe knew that the bullet would hurt his friend but would be unable to penetrate the vest. He was enjoying himself until the captain actually fired the gun. Sturdy grunted in pain, and his eyes turned as hard as granite as he put a giant hand over the spot where the bullet struck. He winced a little, and if anything, his face became an even fiercer mask.

Abe and Sturdy looked at each other, then grabbed the boat's bow and lifted it, tipped it sideways, spilling the surprised terrorists to one side, two of them falling into the water. Jim, John, Wade, and Dorf were on the boat as it came back down. There were sharp blows, howls of pain, and splashes as the men were disarmed and their weapons thrown into the river. Jim's men noted that those in the water kept their mouths tightly closed and fought to keep their noses above the surface.

Abe and Sturdy pulled the two who had fallen into the water out, lifting them so their feet did not touch the dock, and quickly snatched their weapons. Sturdy tossed his man into the boat, the poor man landing in a bone-breaking heap halfway onto a seat, and Abe, less angry than his friend, gently lowered the man and then used his foot to help him on board. Falling into the boat would hurt, but Abe didn't want to break any bones.

"I told you not to shoot him!" Abe said, once again enjoying himself. "That was a very foolish thing to do."

Jim hustled the captain out of his boat and onto the dock while a crowd gathered to watch the fun. Shaking with rage and shame, the man stared at Sturdy. Then, to Jim's amusement, Sturdy pulled his pocket Bible out of his outside vest pocket. The bullet had penetrated about halfway through the thick little book. Sturdy worked it out with concentration, his face growing angrier.

"And you shot my Bible!" Sturdy suddenly roared. He grabbed the hapless captain by the front of his shirt and hauled him face to face. Captain Sirello was terrified. He was staring into the biggest face he had ever seen, held in the clutches of the biggest man he had ever seen. He tried to keep the terror from his face, but Sturdy grinned.

Sturdy suffered from severe burns on his face and neck from a fire. His face became a mask of cruelty when he smiled a certain way. He'd learned early to be careful but used it now as a weapon of fear. As he predicted, the captain began to shake, and suddenly, the front of his pants grew wet. A moment of stunned silence followed. It was a moment Jim would remember for years to come.

Sturdy looked down and returned to that evil grin. "Whoops!" he quipped. "You seem to have had a little accident in your pants there. All that tough talk and the first thing you do is wet your pants. Whuss!" Sturdy released him, and the man landed on his feet, shamed beyond thought. Some of his men were snickering.

"Do any of you think you could do better?" Sturdy asked, ducking his huge head to look into the boat at all of them. He turned on the grin, and the men involuntarily stepped back. "I didn't think so!" he said. "Pussy-pants river pirates!" he uttered, withdrawing his head. The remark stung the men he saw.

"None of you are worth spit!" Abe said softly, flexing his muscles and staring at them.

Senior Juan Pedro walked out onto the dock, his hair white with age, his old face wrinkled by the sun. Most of his teeth were gone, but that didn't stop his huge grin. To the pirates' surprise, he was accompanied by three younger tribesmen, all carrying M16A Assault rifles. At his nod, the three young men turned and fired three shots, and on posts some distance away, three empty tin cans leaped into the air and fell. Jim's team worked with them for several days, and their aim was dead accurate.

"These men have come before, always to torment us and to threaten us." Juan Pedro said in Spanish.

"These men will not always be here, old man. We will come back!" Louis snarled. The three young men behind Juan turned as one, and their guns were now held professionally, pointed at the crew in the boat.

Abe took the captain's arm in a grip that threatened to meet in the middle somewhere, causing the man to grimace in pain as he was jerked to his toes. The strength of this man frightened him, too. The man was almost as wide as he was tall, his arms like tree trunks, his neck a solid mass of muscle, at the moment showing veins and stretched muscle in his anger.

"You will speak respectfully to Senior Juan Pedro!" Abe said, shaking the man like a rag doll. Jim and the others watched this with grins as the poor man shook.

Jim remembered a threat Ox had given once before and leaned over, whispering in fluent Spanish. His voice was just loud enough for the man alone to hear. "If you are not respectful, we will nail your testicles to the side of your boat and your feet to the bottom and send you home that way!"

All the bluster went out of the terrorist. He sagged in Abe's grip and spoke words of apology that stumbled over each other in his haste to get them out. Abe looked at Jim with his eyebrows up, and Jim smiled and motioned he would tell him later. They listened to the man apologize, and finally, Abe released some of the pressure on the man's arm.

"If you come back here, we will hear of it," Jim stated, his eyes now boring into the eyes of the terrorist. Flinching back under that gaze, he listened. "If we hear that you returned, we will find you. You are a fool if you think we will not find you! Come here, and when we find you, you and all your men will die. Do you understand this?"

"Si Senior! I understand. I understand!" Abe released him, and the man rubbed his arm, his eyes darting about, and his face suffused with color. His life had been served bullying people like this, not being bullied, and the experience left him confused and angry, but above that all and seeping deep into his psyche was fear. Somehow, he knew beyond a doubt that Jim Shepherd would keep his word, that he would hunt him down and all of his men, and he knew if that happened, he and his men would die. Swallowing with difficulty, he nodded his head.

In the depths of his mind, he thought that if he came back and surprised these men, his men might have the victory. He doubted it, but the more he thought upon it, the more it appealed to him. Vengeance would be sweet if he killed Juan Pedro while this arrogant Captain watched. The captain had no idea that Jim could see the thought forming in his head. He spoke again.

"The Red Cross will be here for a time, and the missionaries will be here longer. Do not come back, or I will carry out my threat," Jim promised softly. "Now get back on your boat and get out of here!"

It was clear to Jim that the captain didn't want to get back on his boat and face the ride back with his men, remembering the scene on the dock. He shoved the man onto the boat, and Sturdy kicked it away from the pier.

"Bye now. Don't come back, you filthy cowards!" Sturdy bellowed.

The men sat in the boat, heads hanging in shame, while the captain started the engine and headed back upriver. Abe stepped over to Jim.

"What did you threaten him with?" Abe asked.

When Jim told them, they all laughed. That was the last thing the terrorists heard as they chugged upriver, the laughter of the men on the dock. Later, they would remember it. It would spur them to attempt to redeem their machismo. Such attempts are always empty and always fail, though those who make them never seem to be able to learn the truth.

No matter how hard they tried, they could not gain what they were trying to recover. They thought they would regain respect, never realizing that the people they bullied never respected them. Fear was not respect. But they didn't realize that and never would.

CHAPTER 17

AFTER SEVEN DAYS of R&R, the crew was ready to leave Japurá behind. Everything on all four boats was restored to pristine condition. Inchworm and Master Chief Warner even fixed the missionary's diesel engine, rebuilding it so that it was running perfectly. Sparks and Loony repaired all the electrical on the boat as well. When the missionaries offered to pay for the parts, Jim Warner smiled and shook his head.

"This one was for the Lord, my friends. We know you'll use the boat for His glory."

"Surely the Lord was in this meeting, my friends," the missionary doctor said quietly, his eyes misting with tears of joy. "We met men of honor and valor who love the Lord supremely. That has encouraged and inspired us. I want you to know that. Your faith, prayers, and comments during Bible study have stirred anew the urgency within us to share His love. Thank you."

During the third night of their stay, the pirates did indeed return. Warned by Zeke, the men were ready, waiting until all the men were off the boat. Retracted steps and ladders confronted them, and they could not reach the village. They saw nothing to alarm them when they turned around to sneak on board the Bring It Up boats tied to the dock. Quietly, they set foot on two boats, dividing into two teams. From behind them, the ominous sounds of weapons being taken off safety alerted them to danger from behind. Before they could turn their bodies, men rose from behind the railing of the boats, their guns pointed.

Foolishly, the captain of the river pirates screamed in rage and brought his revolver up. His men were confused, some turning to face the threat from behind, others facing the men on the boats, but all brought up their weapons. Three-round bursts from the MP5/10s put them all down before one shot could be fired from the pirate's weapons. All the shots were kill shots.

With no little disgust, the bodies of the pirates were thrown back on the boat upon which they arrived, and a few shots through the bottom began the sinking process. The boat was pushed out onto the river, where it slowly sank out of sight, taking the bodies down with it to a watery grave.

"Stupid macho thugs!" Wade spat as the boat disappeared. "We did learn something." He looked at Jim and John, and both nodded in return.

"Well, we got to feed the fish and crayfish," FM nodded at his large friend and saw the smile form on Wade's face. "Maybe even a few crocks!" he added as a large one broke the surface just above where the boat went down, a body in its mouth as it moved upriver.

"They don't have any way of seeing what is happening here other than sending people," Jim said quietly. "We would have spotters to watch or cameras in the trees if it was too dangerous for human occupation. Marta Hess probably knows her biological weapon works but not how well. That will make her doubly cautious." His men nodded soberly.

After that, things were quiet, and the men and women of the crew rested, visited with the natives, Red Cross, and missionaries, or just sat quietly and read or relaxed. Twice during the following days, boats passed by, and they could see men studying them, but none landed. So it was that the last day passed without incident, and Jim prepared his crew to leave the following morning. They were resupplied the day before by helicopter. Quietly, in the early morning, long before anyone in the village stirred, Captain Rob pulled away from the dock. Behind the lead riverboat, three more left as quietly.

Three kilometers' upriver, they opened up the diesels until they had enough hydraulic pressure to run the stealth system, and then they were pulsing up the river at a steady fifteen knots in silence. Holographic cameras projected the image of a pilot at the wheel while the computer system ran the boats. Jim was sitting in the dining room with the crew when the first light of dawn touched the jungle.

Beyond the border of Columbia, the Japurá was called the Caquetä River. Around this part of the river, the locals called it the River of Death. No one who fished those waters returned. From Araracuara to La Pedrera, this was known to be true. River patrols from the terrorist camp abounded in those areas, which explained the disappearance of anyone fishing those waters. Jim figured they must have patrol boats and men on shore to ensure the compound's safety.

That worry was for later. In two days, they would turn south up the Mapari River, which they could make in the riverboats. After that, they would modify the rigid raiders, turning them into airfoils to traverse the dangerous waters. Jim wanted everyone to understand the rigors and dangers of the journey.

"Eagerness can get you killed in the jungle!" he cautioned as he closed his briefing. "Remember that. Caution is what will keep us all alive. Keep your eyes moving and watch for snakes and venomous insects in the branches. Never touch a branch that you haven't looked at carefully. No one leaves the group alone, and no one pushes ahead of whomever I assign as point man. Is that understood?"

Dr. Gregg's team nodded in agreement, but he knew they lacked the discipline and training his men had. One or more would forget their discipline and need to be rescued. Jim hoped the events would not be too harsh a lesson. None of them had been through boot camp and training like his men, except Dr. Persons, and they did not know the risks or understand that obedience to orders was paramount to success. Nor were they familiar with moving through a jungle, which was equally deadly. Predators heard as well as they caught scents in the jungle, and he knew that his people would be in constant danger, regardless of the precautions.

Each of the male students was issued a Remington.306 bolt-action rifle. Instructions followed, along with target practice and further help, until they could put three rounds inside the space of a quarter at a hundred yards. None of the men complained about this since it was fun and challenging. When they graduated to moving targets, the challenge grew, but they were up to it and learned to time their shots and hit what they were aiming at with accuracy. Jim understood that this training might very well mean the difference between life and death.

Sean took the time to teach them primary field dressings and emergency medical treatment. He also instructed them on using their odorless bug repellant, water purification tablets, and proper hydration on a forced march. Most of the students were amazed at how much water was required to keep them healthy and safe and that they would be eating salt and other supplements as a daily routine. They listened, not only because they were good students but because they all wanted to learn this type of material for future use in the field.

Along the Mapari River, they moved at a steady five knots, barely rippling the water, the boats so close to each other that it was easy to step from the stern of one to the bow of the other. About every three or four days, an Anaconda, curious about the boats on his or her turf, would encounter their perimeter defense shield. After nine days, the sightings and encounters with the giant snakes ceased until six days passed. The Anaconda that encountered their defenses that night was at least twice the size of the others they'd seen, perhaps as long as twenty-five feet. Everyone got a good look at it on the computer screen after the fact. For some, it was a sobering moment.

"What was it doing?" Pretty Lisle asked no one in particular, watching the screen with eyes stretched wide in fear. Everyone could see the snake's immense size and felt its power as it thrashed in the water.

"He just dropped in for a bite," John quipped.

"Oh, very good, J.R.!" Chance Edwards moaned, aware of what John was doing and playing along. "The bloody thing was big enough to swallow our boat, and you must make jokes!"

"Would it have eaten one of us?" Lisle asked, her voice almost breathless, quivering with fear. John looked down at her and grinned, touching her arm gently.

"Don't hold that against him!" John said lightly. "I've thought about it a time or two myself." He grinned down at her and enjoyed watching her blush as the truth of what he had just said sank in.

"She would have been nothing more than an appetizer to him!" Chance retorted.

"Very appetizing!" Smitty said with a grin.

Suddenly, everyone was laughing, and the spell was broken. Lisle thought that if these men could joke, the danger would not be as great as it seemed, precisely what they wanted her to think. Jim nodded his thanks to John and Smitty with a nod for both of them. Chance grinned at him, showing that he understood what they'd been doing and had been playing his part for their benefit.

This was not the first time Jim worried about the added responsibility of having civilians along with his troops in the jungle. Getting them in and out safely was his main concern, and he agonized over it every night in prayer. Somehow, even though he understood the concept of God's sovereignty, he couldn't quite put the worries out of his mind. He realized that trusting God was a process, but he wanted his trust to grow.

The Psalmist said that even walking through the valley of the shadow of death held no fear for him. Jim fervently hoped and prayed that they wouldn't pass near such valleys on their trek through the jungle. The feeling that they would face grave dangers grew as the days wore on. This part of the rainforest seemed to teem with deadly hazards. In fact, he knew that every river they traveled was a deadly river in this part of the world.

Days were filled with exciting discoveries, making the trip much more palatable. Rain fell in a steady rhythmic pattern. Becoming accustomed to the humidity and constant rain, Jim came to appreciate his more outgoing friends and their ability to bring laughter at unexpected moments. Working together like a well-oiled machine, the crew kept the riverboats in tip-top condition despite the constant wetness and monotony of the rain. It was the discovery of beautiful birds and incredible vistas of flowers blooming that broke the monotony. Startlingly colorful butterflies fluttered about happily, despite the rain, visiting those flowers that graced the landscape.

Because they were running almost entirely silent, they would often surprise some animal that came to the river to drink or hunt. Puma's, black as night, stalked prey on silent pads, their sleek bodies heavily muscled and bunched like a coiled spring, ready to bound into a ferocious slashing tooth and claw attack that brought succulent morsels of food to a satisfying quick end. Various kinds of deer and other animals were plentiful, too.

Amazing birds of brilliant hue flitted through the branches along the river, occasionally swooping to the water's surface to pick off some unsuspecting insect. Snakes seemed to be everywhere. Some were bright colors, while others blended into their environment. Larger anacondas were spaced out and very territorial regarding their hunting grounds. They were also the only snakes that actually investigated the riverboats.

Reptiles and amphibians constantly amazed the crew. Chameleons were abundant, clinging to branch and leaf, some with half their body one color, blending with a leaf or plant, the other half the color of the stem or branch. Their odd eyes stuck out so they could see in a one-hundred-and-eighty-degree arch, detecting food and predators around them.

Salamanders and newts were abundant, usually hiding beneath deadfall, half of which lay in the water. When the riverboats scraped across these, they often moved, revealing the creatures where they lived. The variations in color and amazing markings made them beautiful and fascinating to record. Photos were taken and carefully cataloged as part of the journey. Frogs of amazing color were everywhere, some poisonous, handled only by those trained and wearing rubber gloves.

Insects were both a nuisance and a fascination. Mosquito netting kept most of the mosquitoes away. Everyone carefully applied the odorless repellent to keep the insects from biting them. These mosquitoes carried Malaria and other diseases they wanted to avoid. Doc kept a close eye on everyone, and although he had made sure they had their shots before the trip, he was still worried. In the jungle, there were so many things man had yet to understand. Some insects in this part of the world were beautiful yet incredibly deadly. He sighed.

Sean and Doc also kept a constant eye on the purity of the water on the riverboats. River water, pumped through a series of filters and then treated with chemicals to ensure purity, was used for showers, laundry, and washing dishes. Daily, the two of them tested the water with Dorf and Mark. Filters were changed at regular intervals, and the chemicals were carefully monitored. Nothing was left to chance, and everyone on the crew understood the need for and importance of vigilance.

A troop of orange Tamarins found the boats fascinating and followed along through the jungle growth for almost an entire day. Another troop of red-bellied titi hooted their odd call of warning and retreated into the underbrush. Cecilia was especially interested in the simian life in the trees and brush and photographed and identified several of the Pitheciidae family. The white-eared titi made her laugh, leaping about through the branches and scolding them as they passed.

Meanwhile, Master Chief Warner and Inchworm were busy converting the rigid raiders into airfoils. Making the conversions was a simple matter of removing the outboard motors and fixing a lightweight platform to house the rear fan and gas-powered motor to get the fan moving, along with the solar unit to keep it going. Changing the controls required a series of cables and wires to replace those for the outboard engines. Last, they attached the steering rudders, three on each foil, allowing the boats to be steered by directing the airflow.

Once the two were satisfied that everything worked properly, they tested each boat, thrilling to speeds up to ninety knots over the flat surface of the river! They discovered quickly that eye protection was imperative, as the stinging rain made visibility impossible at high speeds. Learning to maneuver these ungainly crafts took practice, and those assigned to driving them practiced daily until they could operate them at maximum performance levels despite the difference in steering and maneuvering required.

As often happens, it was early one morning, and many of the crew were still asleep in their hammocks when the first stela was sighted. In the lead boat, two men stood on the bridge with binoculars, carefully scanning every inch of the shore on both sides of the river. Jack Boswell was first to notice the unusual shape and call a halt. It was not their first stop by any means, and no one had high expectations.

Several times, the boats came to a stop only to discover a wooden totem pole or natural stone formation. No one had heightened expectations. This was a routine stop to check out the possibility. Zeke guided the boats to shore while Jim, Frank, and Sean prepared to disembark. Armed with Mossberg 590 Tactical 12-gauge shotguns, they carefully scanned the trees around the object for Anacondas and other predators or poisonous snakes, frogs, and spiders.

Once they declared the area safe, Dr. Gregg, Cecilia, and the students stepped on shore to examine the find. As they pulled moss and growth away from the stone, wearing heavy rubber gloves, Dr. Gregg began to feel the first stirrings of excitement. It was a stone with markings, and the markings, though faded, were Mayan! After photographing one of those poisonous colorful frogs discovered in the grass around the stone, he used a stick to push it out of the way and encourage it into the water.

"We found it!" he breathed softly, his eyes roaming the stone with critical scrutiny. "This is the first stela!"

Ferenc Adley let out a whoop of joy, and the other students began congratulating each other and talking in excited voices. Sternly, Jim silenced them. Perhaps the sudden silence around them was equally powerful as Jim's order for silence. They looked about nervously, aware they had broken one of the crucial rules in the jungle. More than anything else, that eerie silence brought caution.

Brown, Eustus, and Edwards broke the spell, approaching with shovels, and began to dig carefully around the stone so that it could be studied. While they worked, Mark, C.G., and Vince cleared the ground with flamethrowers to erect a tarp rain cover under which the team could work. They did this using a flame-thrower first, then raking away all the burnt vegetation. Poisonous frogs could not hide in what was left, and a snake would be easily visible. It was hot and demanding work, but the men doing it did not complain, and they stopped only to hydrate when necessary or use the latrine.

Dorf, John, and Wade worked with the tarp poles, and in a short period of time, a sixteen-foot square was cleared and roofed to protect the team from the rain. Tables, a generator, and bright lights were being set up. Electronic insect-repelling devices were plugged in and put into use. Quickly, the area was ready, and Dr. Gregg and Cecilia began carefully treating the stone with a mild formula of acid cleaner to enhance the markings.

Jim, Frank, and Sean remained on guard at the edges of the tarp, watching the jungle on three sides against danger. Several men watched on the boats to ensure no snakes or crocodiles approached from the water. Shotguns were slung over their shoulders as they studied the river, jungle, and trees through binoculars. Switching between natural sight and enhanced vision, the men kept a constant vigil, ready at the first sign of danger to protect everyone long enough to get them on the boats.

Although no one expected danger of any kind, it didn't lessen the men's vigilance. They didn't even allow themselves to think about levels of danger. There was a job, and it was theirs to do it correctly. Other team members remained ready to leap into action should they be needed. Although they stood and watched the two experts work at the stone, there was an air of readiness and the ability to leap into instant lethal action.

Some men might consider such duty boring. Here, in the depths of the Amazonas region, it was anything but boring. Brightly colored birds flitted about in the trees, and amazing butterflies fluttered about, landing delicately upon some bright flower, their bright wings wildly painted by the Creator in beautiful intricate design patterns. Snakes, lizards, and animals fascinated everyone. Each man watching saw all this while watching for danger, his eyes constantly busy and filled with wonder.

Because of this knowledge, Dr. Gregg could put his total concentration on the stone. Barbara and Mary Ann were already taking pictures while Zeke, still on the boat in the computer center, enhanced and filed them. Seated next to him, Dr. Persons, comfortably sipping a Cherry Coke and giving directions to Zeke, spoke clearly as his comments were being recorded. Zeke didn't mind the company of this exciting professor because the man treated him as an equal and a serious student and often shared tidbits of information that Zeke would have to look long and hard to find in books.

By nightfall, everything had settled into predictable patterns. Under the intense brilliance of the searchlights, Cecilia and Dr. Gregg worked slowly down the stone, clearing away hundreds of years of collected dirt and grime and the tiny indentions where lichen attached itself to the rock and ate away at the hard surface. Mary Ann and Barbara took photos of the work and took copious notes when they weren't snapping pictures. Ferenc, Lisle, and Heidi set up their laptops and, by satellite, accessed the main computer on Bring It Up Coral, where Zeke had already stored an entire bank of information from the Museum.

Most of the soldiers were sitting on the forward lower deck of Captain Rob, sipping their favorite drinks and waiting, as only soldiers had learned how to wait. After a watch of two hours, John, C.G., and Vince relieved Jim, Frank, and Sean at guard duty. Sparks and Loony worked on a perimeter to protect the researchers from predators and dangerous snakes. Insect foggers set at points on the perimeter sent their noxious cloud of insecticide into the air, keeping at bay those pests that infested jungles. At the same time, the electronic repellant devices protected everyone under the canopy.

CHAPTER 18

DINNER THAT EVENING was an event. Abe and Sturdy put the kitchen crew through their paces and provided a sumptuous meal to celebrate the discovery of the stelae. Dr. Gregg and his team worked far into the night, too excited to pause for much-needed rest. Jim allowed them this digression from normal routine but put his foot down the following night.

"People work better when they have a good night of sleep behind them," he urged reasonably when he announced that the lights would be extinguished in half an hour. "I know you don't want to stop; you're too excited, but you need your rest. You may not like it now but will appreciate the distinction in a few days. Ladies and gentlemen, I'm not asking; I'm telling you how it will be!" he added sternly.

Since he was the captain, everyone grudgingly obeyed his commands. To keep everyone safe, each night, the boats moved away from the shore twelve feet, dropped anchor, and tied ropes to trees that grew right out in the water. Nor were they unprotected, for armed guards kept vigilant watch through the night. What passed through the shore camp after dark was not discussed with the research team. Jim kept those reports to himself and worried about any extended trek through this particular jungle in search of further stela.

Using the converted rigid raider airfoils, Jim sent Six Team Three on a trek up the tributary, marked on the map as the Juami River. When the men returned that evening, they announced that the riverboats could traverse the Juami River only a few miles before being abandoned for the airfoils.

Jim met with John and Wade and decided to leave the riverboats anchored where they were with the kitchen crew, Master Chief Warner, Inchworm, and Loony to keep everything going. Doc and Millie would stay behind as well. Andrea, however, would accompany them as one of the airfoil pilots. Jim looked at those staying behind for a moment and then spoke.

"Doc is in charge while we're gone. Keep Master Chief Warner close, Doc. He'll be able to help you make the right decisions. We've chosen a spot we can close off with trees and branches, making you invisible from the shore but not from the air. If a helicopter or plane flies over, expect trouble. I don't think any will, but be prepared. Stay cool and keep in touch," Jim sighed when he finished.

No one questioned his orders of who was in charge, and he knew the men respected the doctor and would do everything they could to help him. His Navy training would serve him well as he led those left behind.

Dr. Gregg and Cecilia were making headway with half the stone deciphered. The next stela lay up the Juami River. Its precise location was on the stone, and they were working hard to determine where it was so that Zeke could enter it into the GPS system, taking them directly to the next one.

It never ceased to amaze Jim how much knowledge ancient civilizations possessed, and he wondered where they got it. If, as the Bible taught, they all came from the same stock and location, much of that information could have been brought with them when they were scattered or traveled. That meant that knowledge, the sum total of human knowledge about the celestial system, was familiar to ancient civilizations. And there was ample proof of that.

Excitement ran high one night after nearly two weeks of study. Dr. Gregg called everyone together in the dining room after dinner to explain what he had discovered in his research. Everyone had been anticipating this moment, and the air was almost alive with expectation. He was practically walking four inches off the deck in his excitement. The crew waited expectantly as soon as the dining room was cleared after dinner to hear the report.

"This is the last of three stelae, and it is part of an ancient map leading to their most sacred city. The Mayans recorded their purpose in moving these treasures from their cities to the north and into this part of the world. They aimed to protect their most valued sacred relics and treasures from the Spanish conquerors and enemies. Some of those enemies are named, and some are not. I can guess at a few. Yet, the very words 'most sacred city' are unusual. Religion, in this case, motivated this project.

"Each stela will hold the secret to the next stone, ultimately leading to the hidden city. That is, of course, contingent if they are still there. It is quite possible one of them could be trampled in the ground, but we know where to look. We have deciphered this stone and pinpointed the position of the next stela. Zeke has entered the coordinates into his GPS system, and we should be able to take our boats directly to the next stone.

"Mayan culture was surprisingly advanced, and we were able to match their symbols with others that correspond to latitude and longitude.

Hopefully, if our calculations are correct, we will find the next stone by evening tomorrow. I'm going to ask Captain Shepherd to step in here and tell us about that part of the trip." Dr. Gregg sat down, beaming a smile at everyone, pleased with himself and his team. He had every right to be pleased.

"We have four airfoils ready for river travel. They're fast and sturdy, virtually indestructible. That doesn't mean we couldn't meet with disaster on the river. Team One will take the lead in Captain Rob's Voyager." Voyager was the name they had given the rigid raiders. "Driver will be at the wheel. Dorf is in command of this boat with Mark and Sparks. Dr. Gregg and Barbara will go with them," he continued. "Team Two will take the Warner's Wader Voyager. FM will be at the wheel, and I will command that boat. With me will be Zeke and Smitty. Cecilia and Lisle will travel with our boat." his eyes swept the crew as he spoke.

"Team Three will take the Alistair's Lady Voyager. Wade Adams will be at the wheel, and John will command that boat. C.G. and Vince will go with them. Mary Ann and Dr. Persons will travel in that boat. I'm sorry, Dr. Persons, but you'll have to try to keep Mary Ann under control," Jim grinned at Dr. Persons, and he winked in return.

"Team Four will take Gwyneth's Voyager. Papa Andrea will be at the wheel. Sean Oxton is in command of that boat. Phil, Chance, and Lee Roy will be on that boat with Heidi and Ferenc.

"Each person will carry a pack of supplies. The ladies will carry thirty-pound packs of staples and medical supplies. The men of the research team will carry forty-pound packs of chemicals, staples, weapons, and ammunition. Team members will carry their usual eighty-pound packs."

There were the usual groans from the team. Marching through the jungle in this heat with eighty pounds on your back was going to be pretty miserable. They all hoped that their journeys would all be by boat. Every one of them knew better. Jim listened to the comments with a patient smile. Every soldier complained, but the good ones went ahead and did their duty. In fact, he would have been concerned had he not heard the usual complaints. Once on the trail, he knew none would offer a complaint except in jest.

"We have to stay out of sight and move carefully. Researchers will stay with their assigned groups when moving through the jungle and take orders from their commanders. Out here, you can die in a heartbeat, so listen and do what you're told," Jim said this with a smile, but his voice also said there would be no room for anything else. Cecilia heard the iron in his voice and nodded in agreement. Safety came first.

Later that night, he met with the separate commanders of the boats to brief them on how to handle the researchers. His men were good leaders and knew how to handle "packages" or people who needed to be rescued or transferred to safety. Jim wondered if they could even look at the research team as "packages." He doubted it, and that made it a little more complicated. When you aren't involved with someone, you can stay detached and do what is needed without confusion or complications. Relationships lead to complications.

Zeke and Smitty were confident that their tracking systems could keep them on course, even if the river changed course some-where, which rivers in this area did regularly. They took the time to explain to each operator how to follow the GPS directions. When they were confident that the operators understood, should they become separated for any reason, they nodded. The night would be short for some, especially those with guard duty. Jim dismissed them and went to his cabin to rest.

Before dawn, the team was assembled and, in the boats, stowed away gear in the most advantageous locations. After a hasty breakfast, they led the groggy research team to their separate boats and began their journey up the Juami River. Driver kept them at a steady pace of twenty-five knots, keeping a close eye out for any dangers floating in the river ahead. Any threat beneath the surface would trip an alarm and flash a yellow or red light on his control center. One would warn him to slow down and the other to stop completely.

Commanders on the boats ensured everyone hydrated properly, wore their hats, sprayed their repellent, and used adequate protection against the equatorial sun. No one resented this attention, even the seasoned soldiers, though most didn't need to be reminded. Every one of them had learned hard lessons in the field and remembered.

Regular stops were made to allow people to use hastily prepared latrines. Most of the women didn't want to use the devices but bowed to necessity and found them functional if not comfortable. In this way, the day passed slowly, and for the researchers, at least, it seemed dull. Jim understood. Getting to an insertion point or reaching an objective was always the most challenging part of the journey. Still, the jungle was amazing, and plenty of exciting sightings of animals and birds broke the monotony.

Dr. Gregg's team initially found the MREs unusual and, therefore, interesting. Later, Jim knew they would come to accept them for what they were. Squeezing food out of packages, warming food without a stove, and tasting these meals for the first time was full of discovery. His soldiers were so used to them that they dug into their packages, pulled out everything, and traded with each other those items they disliked for items they wanted.

Lunch was eaten on the river as they traveled, but Jim hoped they could eat supper on the shore at the next stela. Steadily, they approached their target, following the GPS tracking system and carefully checking with the ship's computer system and satellite feeds to be sure they were on target. Smitty was satisfied; if he thought they were where they should be, it was good enough for Jim.

At three that afternoon, they came to the spot where the Purui River fed into the Juami. Dr. Gregg, shouting and pointing from the lead boat, let everyone know they had reached their objective. Jim grinned as the little man gestured. He made far too much noise but quickly quieted when Dorf touched him. The marker was in place, as he suspected it would be.

"Those Mayans were pretty good at navigation," Smitty said, looking at the GPS. The instrument indicated that the marker was very close to where it should have been. "They were only off by about twenty feet!"

This time, the studies went much more quickly. Prepared for this stone, Cecilia and the professor deciphered it before nightfall. A few lines of new text gave them pause, but they had nothing to do with directions, so they left them to study further the next day. It would provide them with something to do on the trip.

After feeding the information into the computers to the third and last stela on their journey, they settled down to eat their MRE dinner and drink their water. Jim went through the camp, ensuring everyone had finished at least two quarts of water, refilled their canteens, and used the water purification tablets.

Abe packed tablets that turned their water into sports drinks, adding electrolytes and necessary nutrients to their systems. The tablets made the water taste a little like one of the popular flavors of a sports drink all the men were familiar with. It also left an after-taste one had to endure. Some of the researchers didn't like it, but most of the team knew the value of the electrolytes and accepted the taste, even developing a liking for the drink. In the bush, one puts up with many things for the sake of safety and energy. If the jungle could do one thing effectively, it would be to sap energy with dehydration. Salt tablets were also part of their staple diet to replace that lost by sweat. So far, most of the explorers followed the rules, though Lisle hadn't emptied her water container.

"I'll have to pee if I drink all this!" Lisle argued with Sean when he noticed she still had water in her canteen. Her petulant expression on her pretty face made many of the men smile.

"That's the spirit, missy," he said with a grin. "If you don't have to pee, you're not drinking enough liquids."

"I hate the jungle!" Lisle snarled with some heat, finishing the water. "Not yet," Sean replied, his face suddenly very serious. "But you will. We all will," he said ominously.

"And when I get up in the middle of the night, who will escort me to the latrine?" she asked.

"Whoever is on guard will assist you," Sean said with a grin. "I guess that didn't come out quite right," he sputtered, his face coloring as the men around the camp roared with laughter.

"If a snake eats me on the way to the latrine, I'm going to hold it against you," Lisle said, laughing.

"The snake, or the fact that it ate you?" Sean retorted.

That night, the guards turned off all the lights and waited until their eyes were accustomed to the dark before taking their positions. Light ruined your night vision, a fact that few appreciated until they'd been in the field. Using NV goggles, they scanned the jungle constantly, guns ready. Nothing came close that night, even when Lisle had to take a trip to the latrine. Heidi and Cecilia went with her.

Striking camp early in the morning, the team packed the boats and ate a quick breakfast. Once again, they set off up an unknown river. The Purui was narrow in places but deeper than the Juami. As before, travel went at a steady pace of twenty-five knots while Dr. Gregg and his people worked on the lines from the stone yet to be deciphered.

At noon, they stopped for lunch and to care for their physical needs. Jim took latrine duty and dug the pit, erected the triangular wooden seat above it, and put a can of lye next to the seat. When he was finished, he was the first to use it. That was the only benefit of having latrine duty. Covering it later, after everyone had used it, was an unpleasant but necessary duty. They needed to be unseen in the jungle, their presence unmarked, so the job was serious.

No one said anything if anyone found it odd that the group leader should take this responsibility. His men understood. Jim never shirked duty and was willing to put his hand to anything necessary. They appreciated him the more for that, even if some thought such jobs were beneath his station. Over the years, none ever won an argument against his pulling his weight, and they were convinced they never would. Over the last year the men gave up and accepted his efforts for what they were.

Dr. Gregg pulled him aside before they set off after lunch. His face was serious as they stepped a little apart from the others. Jim kept his rifle ready, watching the jungle around them as the little man spoke.

"I've deciphered those lines. They are a warning to anyone who would follow this map. It seems the Mayans took protecting their treasures seriously. Traps have been set for the unwary," his face showed deep concern as he spoke.

"I take it these traps are a very real danger to everyone," Jim said flatly. Glancing at the professor, he returned to watching the jungle.

"I've read about expeditions where everyone was lost in Mayan ruins, though none in the last century," Dr. Gregg said, his eyes furrowed as he looked at the warnings again. "I'll have to read up on what information we have. They could have used certain traps, and we'll know about them because of those lost expeditions."

"It will give you something to do on the trip," Jim said with a smile. Dr. Gregg didn't value long, boring trips where nothing happened, but Jim hoped for them.

CHAPTER 19

T HIS TIME, THE stela was within six feet of the GPS marking, and according to Dr. Gregg, this was the last map. Following the information on this stone would take them to the hidden city. This was higher ground, with better drainage and the stela was in better shape, actually still receiving some sun. If the sun ever shines in this part of the world! Dr. Gregg wasn't sure about that, having spent the last several weeks in a steady downpour.

Smitty discussed the river's changes, and Cecilia explained that even though the river switched beds at times, it usually returned to its regular course after the rainy season. Various topographical maps of the area shot through satellite imagery over the past fifty years determined that to be true. With the satellite imagery to help, they plotted the river's course for future cartography efforts. However, changes could be noted, and Zeke expressed the thoughts of all of them.

"Thank God we can find our way back to the riverboats!" he said with a grin.

"At least as long as your computer doesn't crap out on us!" Phillip Eustus said sarcastically.

"Come on!" Zeke exclaimed indignantly. "This is a Mac, not one of those cheap imitation computers."

"I take it you don't like IBM or clones of that ilk," Phillip said.

"You'd have to put a gun to my head to make me use one of them!" Zeke said emphatically. "Think about it. Every Tom, Dick, and Harry can write programs for the IBM or a clone, and those programs don't have to work together. You can load one of those into your computer and kiss the thing goodbye just because some idiot couldn't check if his idea would work with others or, worse, didn't care. On a Mac, that can't happen! Every program has to work perfectly with the system and all other criteria. Have you ever compared the instruction manuals for IBM and Mac? Those for the IBM are usually two or three times thicker.

"Macs have twice the power, too. Why do you think sound, DVD, and movie studios insist on Macs? Or why does the entire engineering department of any aircraft design company insist on using Macs? They have so much more power than any other computers out there. That's why. And they're twice as reliable, too. I've never had a serious virus on my Mac. Ever have one on your IBM? Comparing a Mac to anything else is like comparing a blueberry to a pumpkin!"

"Cripes! Can't anyone shut him up?" Phillip asked, throwing up his hands. "Okay! I give in. You're the expert, and if you say Macs are better, I'm okay with that!"

"Alright then!" Zeke said with a grin. "No more sacrilege in this camp!" Everyone laughed.

No studies on the stela were done that night because of the late hour and getting the camp established. Tents were set up in a tight circle, all entrances facing the fire pit, and smaller fires on the perimeter roared and crackled with bright orange and yellow flames. Every man on the team knew how to go into a wet wood and find dry tinder to burn. A large pile of it lay beneath a tarp. The guards would keep the fire high at night, keeping predators at bay.

Bright spotlights were ready around the stelae and beneath the tarp covering that area. Tarps also protected the latrines. When all was in readiness, the tired campers gathered around the fire under sloped tarps that stretched out four ways, covering the tents and camping area against the rain. There, they sat on fallen logs or folding camp stools and ate MREs before turning in for the night. Conversations were few and far between because everyone was tired.

In the darkness, early in the morning, FM spotted a panther creeping up a limb toward his guard position. He didn't want the cat to get the idea to come closer, so he aimed his Mossberg 590 at the branch about two feet in front of the cat. He'd chosen a slug round for his gun that night instead of the usual shot. The weapon roared in his hands and bucked up, but the slug slammed into the branch, shattering it. The roar of the gun and the branch splintering in front of the panther's face chased it into the jungle.

Jim was the first out of his tent, his MP5/10SD in his hands, looking toward FM. He could see Frank peering off into the jungle and silently made his way to him. The other Team members held back, taking up a defensive position. Noting all that as he moved, Jim listened to the retreating animal.

"Panther," FM said when Jim touched his shoulder. He'd been listening, but Jim made no noise. "Good thing I knew it was you coming up behind me, boss. I might have peed all over myself, thinking it was the Panther's mate. Saw you coming, so I waited and kept an eye out for our hunter."

Jim patted FM's shoulder and returned to the camp, waving the men to lower their weapons. That was when he saw the snake.

It had to be as big around as his thigh and twenty-five feet long if it was an inch! It was hanging in a tree above Vince, who was on guard on that side. Vince had his shotgun pointed at the head of the snake, and he was standing completely still.

Everyone picked up the change in Jim's attitude on the Team, and as one, they turned to see the snake drop out of the tree. Vince's shotgun roared, and the snake's head exploded, but the heavy coils fell on top of him, burying him beneath a struggling mass. Part of that mass began to constrict around his chest. It was as if the snake, in death, was seeking revenge!

Dorf reached him first, and instead of trying to pull those powerful coils away, he dragged out his KA-BAR knife and began slicing the thing. C.G. was on the other side, doing the same. The coils dropped away as the razor-sharp knives cut through the body quickly, and Vince drew in a long, shuddering breath.

"Get me out of here!" he croaked. This snake stinks!" He grabbed Dorf by the hand and laid another hand on C.G.'s shoulder. "Thanks!" The two men nodded to him and helped him step away from the still-writhing coils.

"Quick thinking, guys," Jim said, adding his brand of thanks.

During the night, no further attacks came, and though everyone was wide awake immediately after the attacks, none had trouble going back to sleep afterward. Jim was satisfied when he checked the tents to be sure none of the Gregg team was suffering any night frights. They were all sound asleep, mute testimony to their trust in the guards who watched over them. After one last visual check around the camp to see that everything was as it should have been, he turned in and slept until morning.

Dr. Gregg and Cecilia worked most of the morning on the stela, deciphering the Mayan symbols carefully and comparing their notes with what they learned at the previous stelae. This map was much more detailed, making it challenging to instruct Smitty and Zeke to input the information. Both knew how the jungle could obliterate any old trails. It would be tough going all the way.

Once again, lines of symbols warned anyone of the dangers of attempting to enter the hidden city. One of those lines puzzled Dr. Gregg, who spent the entire afternoon trying to decipher its meaning. When supper came, he ate his MRE like an automaton, unaware of what he was stuffing in his mouth as he puzzled over the lines. Sitting next to Jim, Cecilia smiled and nodded her chin toward the preoccupied professor.

"What's got him so puzzled?" Jim asked, watching the strange little man he had come to like and respect.

"Two lines at the end of the text basically say that the secret is the city within," Cecilia said, her face dimpling prettily as she smiled. "He can't figure out what that means, and it's bugging him."

"The secret is the city within. Those are the exact lines?" Jim asked. "Yes, why?" Cecilia asked.

"Because I have the distinct impression that those words will unlock all the secrets for us," Jim replied, his green eyes suddenly thoughtful. She loved the way he looked when he was thinking deeply and sighed with pleasure, leaning against him.

"What about the map? Do we know where to go and where to look for this hidden city?" Jim asked next.

"Absolutely. We're in for about sixty miles of trekking through this infernal jungle. I hope everyone is up to it," Cecilia added. She looked at Dr. Persons, who was sitting by Heidi and Lisle. Jim followed her gaze.

"Dick is tougher than he looks," Jim said with a grin. "He's a former jarhead, which means he can walk your legs off, young lady, so beware!" he grinned.

"Really?" Cecilia inquired, sitting up straight and looking at the man. "He seems fit. But did he stay in shape during his years in the classroom?"

"He runs two miles daily, and he works out in the gym three times a week just to stay fit," Jim answered. "He hasn't lost much of his skill with weapons either," He added. Dick Persons had indeed demonstrated his ability with his Remington.306 and a spare Five-seveN.

"Well, that's good. What about the girls?" Cecilia asked. Some of them, she knew, were not into physical fitness.

"They'll make it. The men will help them." Jim replied, his mind back on his food as he unwrapped a peach pie dessert.

"Still, sixty miles through the jungle won't be simple for us," Cecilia commented. Jim could hear the stiffness of her voice. He looked at her.

"Are you worried about how you'll do?" Jim asked, suddenly seeing through what she had been doing.

"A little," she admitted.

"You've been training with us for months. Don't underestimate yourself, young lady. You're tough enough to endure just about anything." Jim said with some heat.

Secretly, she was pleased. To have his approval meant more to her than she realized. She watched him eat his pie, his eyes scanning the camp's perimeter, never still, always watching. He didn't miss much, she decided. If he thought she could do it, she might as well quit worrying. I might as well tell myself to stem the tide. I'm worried and scared! She sighed and stood, preparing to clean up her dinner wrappings.

After dinner, the men worked hard at dismantling the rigid raiders, pulling them to high ground, tying them securely to trees, and then covering them with deadfall. Once one moved a few feet away, the area looked like any other piled deadfall after a flood. The boats would be safe enough.

CHAPTER 20

Trekking through jungle growth was not exactly what Ferenc, Heidi, and Lisle pictured. Dr. Gregg had been in the jungles of Africa with hunters and had some idea, but even that did not prepare him for the way this group of soldiers took them through the thick growth or the intense energy-sapping heat and closeness of growth. It seemed to everyone that they had to fight for every step.

C.G. had point, and he left ten minutes before anyone else. He moved with purpose, slowly to minimize noise, and carefully to make sure they weren't walking into any danger. Jim led the units, which were divided into their boat teams, with Vince bringing up the rear. All the men moved now as though they expected an attack at any time, and their attitude communicated to the explorers. The only noise anyone heard from that cautious advance was the constant chopping of the machetes clearing a path.

Ferenc had a tendency to wander off the trail to identify fauna, especially some of the more appealing orchids that seemed to thrive in this dense jungle. He was repeatedly warned that this was dangerous, but he only learned his lesson late that afternoon when a fifteen-foot Anaconda dropped from a tree branch and began to wrap around him. His horrified scream was cut off as his chest constricted.

Sean, tired of warning him, burst through the undergrowth, assessed the situation immediately, and called for help. Lee Roy was there immediately, and the two wrestled with the snake. Sean held its head tightly and tried to unwrap it from the top while Lee Roy, Chance, and Phil joined the wrestling match. It took nearly three minutes until they finally had the thing off Ferinc, who lay in a heap, panting for breath and hurting.

"Damn it, Ferenc!" Sean swore, bending down to check him out. "How many times did I tell you to stay on the trail?" the anger in his voice was tangible, but Ferinc was too sore at the moment to say anything.

"If it was more than once, it was too many times!" Jim said in his sternest voice, and he came close after watching and absorbing the situation. Phil and Lee Roy moved the snake along, unwilling to kill it.

"Six times I warned him," Sean snarled. The heat in his voice was obvious, and he was frightened and angry. Jim grimaced, his face suddenly fierce and his green eyes hard, boring into Ferinc's terrified eyes.

"Beat the living daylights out of him the next time he steps out of line! He put every one of you in danger! You see to it, he doesn't do that again!" Jim announced harshly, spinning and leaving the little clearing.

Ferenc watched the men around him in fear. It had been foolish to ignore their warnings. Now, they had been forced to risk their lives to save him, and suddenly he understood their anger. He had placed everyone in danger. They because they had to wrestle with that snake, and the others, because they were not there to protect them. He rolled onto his knees, vomited, and shakily rose to his feet.

"You won't have to beat me, Lieutenant," he croaked to Sean. "I won't wander again."

"Idiot!" Sean breathed, pushing the man ahead of him back to the trail. He said it loud enough for Ferinc to hear and hoped the man would be warned now. Ferenc was more than warned. He was terrified, and thereafter, he did everything he was told without comment. For days, his whole body was bruised and sore from being squeezed by that snake.

Heidi and Lisle were another problem. They insisted on talking. Jim took care of the problem within the first hour. He wrapped his hard hand around their mouths and chins, nearly lifting them off the ground, his stormy green eyes boring into theirs with a fierceness that frightened and fascinated them simultaneously. Like iron, his hands held them in place, actually hurting more than a little. He would only look at them for a second, and then his eyes scanned the surrounding jungle. His voice was as stern as his eyes.

"You keep that pretty little mouth of yours closed, or I'll tape it shut!" he warned. Ten minutes later, he slapped six inches of duct tape over their mouths despite the hatred that showed in their eyes. They stayed quiet after he ripped the tape off the first time. Cecilia watched the whole thing with some amusement and refused to comfort the silly girls when they stopped for lunch. Barbara and Mary Ann, who understood the need for silence, refused to listen to or comfort them.

Pouting for the next two days, the girls kept quiet when they were walking. When they stopped, they didn't talk above a low murmur and only when someone from the Team said it was safe. On the third day of their march, the reason for their silence became very clear to them.

Sean Oxton was on point. At the moment, he held something in his hand that looked very much like a GPS tracker but was instead an instrument that could find and pinpoint the location of human hearts with a range of up to a thousand feet. As he walked, his head constantly turning from side to side, his eyes scanning the ground in front of him, pushing leaves and branches away that might make noise if he stepped on or snapped them; he would glance at the unit.

Something told him there were people nearby and that these people were somehow a threat. He'd been a soldier long enough to trust his instincts and was not disappointed. Suddenly, small triangles appeared on his screen, and he counted them anxiously. Eighteen heartbeats were walking toward them, moving almost as slowly and carefully as he was. That they were moving so slowly indicated they were hostile. He keyed his microphone.

"We have company. Eighteen, I say again, eighteen unfriendlies, coming toward us. They are moving with extreme caution, Shep. I don't have eyes on yet. I'm going up a tree to look."

"Roger that, Ox. Use caution," Jim replied.

His hand went up with four fingers and waved left and right. Then he keyed his microphone. "Four Team Three, you have forward position," he said tersely.

John clicked his microphone twice to let Jim know he heard the whispered command. He led Wade, C.G., and Vince forward to find Ox. Like ghosts, they disappeared into the bush. Jim took the research team aside, found a hollow to hide them, and told them to make no sound and stay perfectly still, no matter what. All this he did while clearing away any threat to them. They mutely nodded in agreement. The girls huddled together in the center of the hollow, and the men took up defensive positions around the edges with their Remington.306 rifles at ready. No one knew what was out there yet, but the danger was real, and everyone felt it.

Sean saw the first one. The man was small, carrying what looked like a blow gun to shoot darts; a bow was slung over his back, and a quiver of arrows rode at his waist. He held a spear in his left hand, and his head turned from side to side, carefully searching the jungle. Although his skin was dark, it seemed as though he was covered with some gray powder. His face was painted grotesquely in a mask that would leave grandmothers fainting in fear.

He saw several more now, all of them small, all of them painted and powdered gray. Suddenly, three clicks sounded in his ear, and he looked down to see John and his team looking up at him. Climbing down carefully, keeping the tree between him and the oncoming natives, he joined them on the ground.

"They know we're here, and they're hunting us," Sean whispered.

"Team 1, copy," Dorf whispered. "We're sixty feet north of your position. "Team 2, copy," Jim whispered. "We're about forty feet south of your position.

"Team 4, copy, LT," Chance was talking quietly. "We've flanked them to the north and will come in behind."

"I think their darts may be poisoned," Sean warned.

"Use the bean-bag shot. We don't want to kill them if we don't have to," Jim ordered quietly.

MP5/10SD weapons were shunted to the back, and the shotguns, already loaded with the beanbag shot, were brought forward. Sean went with John's team in the front. There was a small stream ahead that the natives would have to cross. Each team took up a position where they could get a good shot at the natives if there were trouble.

When the first native came out of the bush, Jim stepped forward, his hand raised in peace. The native took one startled look at him, raised his blowgun to his lips, and then fell back unconscious as John's shot hit him just below the left ear. The roar of the shotgun brought the other natives forward with a cry. That sound they recognized, apparently, and it made them very angry.

Perhaps they were expecting only a small party, but sixteen shotguns roared, and sixteen natives went down with grunts and cries. The last stared across the stream with a snarl on his face, his spear ready, but he could see no one. His arm went back to hurl the spear, and two shotguns roared again.

Carefully, the men used their plastic restraint ties to bind their captives once they were disarmed. Every weapon was collected and cataloged, then broken. Jim kept one dart and a stone jar of some sticky-looking substance that seemed to be on the end of the dart.

When their captives regained consciousness, they were amazed to be alive and enraged to be held captive. They struggled until their wrists and feet bled to no avail. The sixteen men standing over them watched them with blank stares, showing no expression. One of the men tried to spring at Mark; his teeth bared as though he would bite. It was totally unexpected. The quick move was more animal than human and downright vicious.

Mark's instinctive kick hurled the man back five feet through the air to land in a flaccid heap on the ground. At that, the captives grew quiet and still. Mark spoke in fluent Spanish, asking them why they had attacked. No one answered. He tried Portuguese, but still, no one answered. Then, one of the men, perhaps the chief, spoke in halting Portuguese.

"Our medicine man saw you coming in a vision and ordered us to hunt you and to kill all of you," Mark translated.

"Tell him we did not come here against his tribe, and we will leave them in peace if they agree to leave us alone," Jim suggested. Mark spoke slowly, watching to see if the chief understood.

"If you turn back now, we will let you go. If you do not, we will hunt and kill all of you," the chief threatened, his eyes hard.

"Always nice to know where we stand," Chance said sarcastically.

"Tell him if his tribe comes against us, we will kill them. We will not use shots that only render a man unconscious. We will use bullets that kill," Jim said.

Again, Mark spoke slowly and saw that the man understood. Dorf walked to the group of prisoners and began to cut away their bonds. One tried to bite him as soon as his hands were free. Dorf clamped a massive hand around the man's neck and lifted him off the ground easily. The man struggled, scratched, and tried to kick Dorf but could not. When his struggles weakened to the point of losing consciousness, Dorf put him down on the ground and turned and released the other prisoners. That prisoner fell to his knees, gasping for air and rubbing his throat. None of them tried to attack Dorf again.

The tallest of them could not have been more than five feet tall. Hunched over in defeat and shame, they shuffled off into the bush, the chief promising that they would return to kill them. Back at the hollow, Zeke opened his laptop and began to scan satellite photographs of the region through which they were traveling. He found the village from which the natives must have originated. Carefully considering the size of the village, he turned to Jim.

"If they come back, they'll come in numbers," Zeke surmised. "I estimate their strength to be sixty or so able-bodied warriors, maybe more. It will take them about five or six hours to return, even if they run, so we have a little time. Either way, they know this jungle, and we don't, so they have the advantage."

"Team three," Jim barked. John and his team stepped forward. "Take point; find us a defensible position, high ground if possible." John saluted and led his team into the bush at a trot. Once they reached the stream they slowed to a walk and moved with great caution.

After ten minutes, the groups followed, with Team Four taking the rear position. They walked through the jungle for three hours until they finally came to a hill. John and his team were already building a low fortress wall at the top of the hill from which they could defend themselves. The rest of the teams positioned tarps so that they could crouch behind the trees out of the rain.

"Any thoughts?" Jim asked when all was in readiness.

"We need to keep an eye on the trees. If I were attacking this position, I'd try to get a sniper up in one of the trees, high enough to take a shot," Wade mentioned, scanning the trees around.

"Good point. Team four, you have the tree perimeter. I want four of you up in those trees to clear the other trees. You'll have a good field of fire from up there, too," Jim replied. "Just don't fall out of the tree when you shoot!" The men laughed. Something like that hadn't happened since basic training, but they all remembered experiencing the kick of a military weapon while holding precariously to a branch or tree.

Ox nodded, not bothering to salute, and led his men out. Scaling wet trees in the rain was a messy business. Still, the men quickly dispatched that duty, taking positions approximately thirty feet from the ground in four trees that gave them an excellent view.

Jim stood, his head turning from side to side, his senses on alert, but his mind pondered something else. The medicine man had seen them in a vision and sent men to kill them. That could only mean one thing. The medicine man had a familiar spirit, a demon controlling him, though he probably thought the opposite. Jim knew a little about demons, not enough yet, but enough to know that they hated everything God created and loved. It was sobering to realize that such an evil presence had chosen to attack his group. *Lord, I don't know much about the demon world, only that the powers that follow Satan hate us and hate You and Your world. Send your angels to help us, Lord, and keep our hearts from evil.* With his silent prayer spoken, he suddenly felt an awareness, almost a tangible presence of something, and sighed with deep emotion, tears filling his eyes for a moment. He felt as if the Holy Spirit had let him know He was there, with him, watching over him.

The words of Psalm 23 flooded into his head, and he suddenly understood how David must have felt when he wrote those words. When God let a man know He was close, there was a deep sense of peace, a removal of fear, and an awareness of purpose. Jim knew God loved him deeply, but he rarely felt the depth of that love as he did now. Silently, he thanked the Lord.

They slept uncomfortably that night, with rain pelting the tarps and predators roaring around them. Soon after dawn, everyone was awake, and breakfast was served and cleaned up. An hour passed as the men patiently waited. Then Sean caught a glimpse of movement on the ground following the trail they had used to climb the hill.

"Smart buggers," he said into his microphone. "They picked up our trail and are trying to catch us by surprise from behind."

"Can you estimate their strength?" Jim asked.

"Well, there's about forty coming along smartly this way," Sean replied. "And about forty coming along nicely from the opposite side," Lunch Box said from his tree. "They're spreading out now so they can come up from three sides," he added. "I guess they've done this before, especially with larger groups, because they seem pretty confident."

"Let them get into range and then hit them hard. If they break and run, let them," Jim ordered sadly.

"Sir, this wasn't in the books," Ox said in a low voice.

"I know it stinks, LT," Jim whispered back. "We have to protect our researchers. We have to protect the women."

"Roger that, Shep. I won't let you down."

"I never thought you would," Jim replied.

One thing every soldier knew and hated was that sometimes, he had to do unpleasant things to protect innocent people. Killing these natives would take a cold, calculated hand and a will of steel. The toll it would take on the spirit of every soldier was heavy, and some men never recovered from having to do something so repugnant. Those coming against them were simple savages with simple weapons, not at all prepared to face the firestorm of Jim's team.

Jim was glad that Cecilia could not look into his eyes now. He knew they had grown empty and as dark and cold as an open grave. At first, he thought they might break and run after sixteen of their number went down, their faces and heads ruined by the three burst shots from the 10-mm bullets. The diopter sights made it almost impossible to miss. Then the village magician, witch doctor, or medicine man appeared out of the jungle, urging them on, ranting and raving like a madman. His screams were almost maniacal, and Jim sensed a wave of evil emanating from the man.

Dick Persons knew what he had to do. He had a Remington.306 with a great scope. Patiently waiting, he zeroed in on the medicine man, then fired one shot. It struck the man's center chest, and for a moment, he just looked down at the hole in his chest, and then he fell. Dr. Persons sighed.

At that point, the natives turned, startled at the silence from their great medicine man. But an older version of the first appeared in the jungle, his face visible around a tree. He screamed for the natives to attack. It was obvious he held great power over them. As one, they turned and rushed the fortress.

Vince had the Barrett M82A1, and he could clearly see the medicine man's head from his position. That the man was protecting himself and risking the lives of those he claimed to serve was obvious, and Vince hated such cowards with a passion. He tested the wind, took a measurement, and slowly let out all his air, sighting down the scope and centering the crosshairs. The medicine man thought he was out of range, but a two-hundred-yard shot was no challenge for a marksman like Vince Hall. Carefully centering the crosshairs to allow for about a sixteenth-inch drop, he depressed the first trigger and moved his finger forward. The 12.7 mm bullet entered the medicine man's face just below his right eye, right next to his nose, and destroyed the entire back of his head as it exited.

Now, there were just twelve warriors left. They turned when their medicine man grew silent. They could see him lying there on the ground, his dead eye staring up at the sky. Like a mist driven by the wind, they turned and disappeared into the tall grass. From the trees, Team Four could see some of them scampering back toward their village.

"Clear!" Ox yelled from his position. "Clear!" Sounded from three more voices.

"I didn't see all of them running for home, boss," Sean announced quietly when he rejoined the others on the ground.

CHAPTER 21

"PACK IT UP and move, now!" Jim ordered.

Scrambling into their gear, the men formed up, and the procession moved into the jungle, following a route that would take them around the village.

"Will they follow us?" Lisle asked, just a little too loud.

Ox swore, leaped at her, and drove her to the ground. The thump of a dart hitting the tree just behind where she'd been standing was audible. She looked at it, and her face turned deathly pale. Putting a finger to his mouth Ox motioned for her to stay down and stay quiet. Now, at last, she understood the need for silence. Wide eyes looked at the quivering dart, and she wanted to vomit. Ox knew the look and hoped she would do that quietly.

An MP5/10's suppressed barrel clacked as three shots found their way to the native who had been stalking them. The little man never uttered a cry. He simply dropped where he stood, most of his head mangled by the 10-mm bullets.

C.G., who now had point, located the remaining villagers with his instrument that found human hearts. There were two more out there. He raised his hand carefully, held up two fingers, and then pointed toward the hiding villagers. Vince caught movement from behind two bushes. Without thought, he raised his H&K G36 and lobbed a 40-mm grenade between the bushes. Screaming in agony, the two men fell, both of them wounded beyond saving.

Cautiously, they moved on, C.G. keeping an eye out for any extra heartbeats appearing on his screen. None did. Once past the village, they maintained their pace for about ten kilometers before allowing a bedraggled and frightened group of researchers and soldiers a much-needed rest. Ten miles through the jungle was like forty on open land.

Lisle finally understood the importance of following orders and keeping quiet and spent much of her rest time thinking. When they ate a snack before moving on, she went to Captain Shepherd and Ox and apologized humbly for her foolishness. Both men accepted her apology without much comment.

It was Lunch Box who broke the somber mood. He looked at Lisle and cocked an eyebrow. "The LT's going to be put out with your compliance, little lady," he said flippantly.

"Why is that?" she asked.

"I think he had some fun throwing you to the ground. If you feel the need to be reminded, I'll be glad to throw you down a few times myself," he grinned. "Us black fellers are always up for throwing you white ladies down," he added with a wink.

"I'll volunteer!" Barbara said, putting her arms around Lunch Box and kissing him noisily on the cheek. "You could do with a shave, though. A bath might help, too," she added, wrinkling her nose. "I've heard that bathing is something you know at least the rudiments of, so I'll expect that next time!" she added. "A bath and a shave if you want any more attention from this Sheila!

"It's the story of my life!" Lunch Box complained in mock despair. "Here, I could be having fun, but the captain makes me run about in this muck until I smell like a wallaby."

"Isn't a wallaby sort of a cross between a large rodent and a small kangaroo?" Phillip Eustus quipped.

"Keep your comments to yourself, you cheeky pelican!" Lunch Box laughed.

The troop moved on in a much lighter mood, now pushing cautiously through an unknown country, heading for the hidden city. Jim chose to push on after dark for a few hours to put distance between them and the village behind. No one argued or complained. Still fresh in their memories were the maniacal faces of the strange warriors. Yet the dark hid menace as well. Snakes were a real danger, and the grunts of jungle cats could be heard as if they were far too close for comfort. Jim trusted the size of his group to discourage an attack and hoped he was right.

When he did stop, it was because he sensed danger ahead. While others set up camp, he went to the edge of the small clearing he'd chosen and stood silently, staring into the darkness, listening. Whatever was out there seemed to be watching them with malicious intent, so he kept the safety off his MP and kept his eyes moving. If anything disturbed the undergrowth or a tree branch in that direction, he was going to spray the jungle in a hail of fire. Nothing did. Only when he silently offered up a prayer did the feeling leave him.

Arriving at the designated location of the hidden city without further mishap in the early evening of the following day, Jim chose to camp on a lonely knoll surrounded by damp rocks. Once camp was erected and arranged to his satisfaction, he stood on one of the rocks and looked through his binoculars at the place where the hidden city was supposed to lie. Only ruins greeted him, thrusting up among trees that had slowly overgrown the buildings. Ruins always looked so bleak and defeated in the jungle, like broken teeth of a rotting jawbone protruding through the ground.

At one time, the city was a marvel of construction, busy with life and activity. Now, it was incongruous, looking out of place in the undergrowth, as though something foreign had somehow inflicted itself upon nature and left a scar that nature was desperately attempting to erase, to hide, so that none would see the spectacle of such loneliness.

He moved among the men, complimenting them on their improvements in moving through the jungle. They had, he noted, quickly become one with their surroundings. Most could distinguish noises that threatened from the usual racket produced by myriad birds, mammals, reptiles, and amphibians. Everyone had noticed a danger, pointed it out, and kept anyone from venturing too near.

"I'm glad you stopped last night when you did," John shared, coming to stand beside him and speaking so low only Jim would hear. "Whatever was out there felt... heinously evil," John breathed out those last two words, and Jim turned to look at him.

"You felt it, too?" he inquired. John nodded. "Do you know what it was?" "None of my team came across any tracks of signs. I've asked the other teams, including yours. Nothing," John sighed, looking around. "I wondered if it might be the familiar demon of that witch doctor. It felt like that kind of evil!"

Jim nodded slowly. He'd also thought that, and when he'd faced whatever was out there, he'd prayed fervently.

"Best not speak of it to anyone else," Jim suggested quietly. John nodded. Night on the hilltop proved to be a mixed blessing. There was a slight breeze, but that caused the rain to find its way under the tarps. Jim didn't mind because the humidity in the jungle made everything feel wet anyway. He could tell some researchers didn't like the invading showers. The soldiers, he noted, seemed immune to the wet. None had hunched shoulders or ducked heads and looked irritated like the researchers. All of them slept well, snug and dry in their tents.

Filled with anticipation and excitement, the research team descended on the city once the soldiers had checked it and began their meticulous search. By noon of the first day, they had covered only a third of the city and had found nothing of the entrance to or suggestion of a hidden city. Everyone passed the lunch hour seated in the shade of a broken wall covered in vines that would eventually break into tiny pieces.

Conversations ranged from memories of their trek to the city they now searched to the air-conditioned boats they missed. One or two amethyst crystals had been unearthed, and a very pretty microcline feldspar, often called Amazonstone. Lisle held a chunk of Hemimorphite, silvery gray and white crystals seeming to jut out at all angles. Dr. Gregg had uncovered a pretty, white crystal called Danburite.

Later that evening, they sat around their camp on the knoll, tired from their afternoon search and anxious to get on with it the next day. The Aussies spent the evening teaching everyone some of the funnier songs from their homeland. As night settled over them like a slowly descending blanket of darkness, they sought their beds quietly. Jim noted that though they still had to find the entrance to the hidden city, enthusiasm was high.

The following morning, they finished searching the city, only to discover nothing of the hidden city. Despondently, they sat at the far edge of the ruined city and discussed various possibilities. Jim waited patiently, knowing that eventually, they would arrive at the truth and be able to continue. It was not one of Dr. Gregg's team members but Cecilia who remembered the lines that had puzzled Dr. Gregg.

"The secret lies in the city within!" she exclaimed suddenly, her voice filled with excitement.

"I say, what?" Dr. Gregg said. Then his eyebrows rose, and he leaped to his feet, spilling his food wrappings in the process. Barbara picked them up without comment. The look of excitement on his face was almost comical.

"Yes! Of course!" he exclaimed. "We're looking in the wrong place!"

"There's another city we have to search for?" Lunch Box asked, not quite grasping the truth.

"Yes, in a way. But not in another place," Dr. Gregg answered. "We need to find an entrance to a city beneath this one. That is what those words mean! I've been so obtuse!"

"Wouldn't anything under the ground be filled with water?" Smitty asked, raising his hands to indicate the heavy pouring rain outside their tarp's protection.

"Not if it's a cave system. This ground is higher than anywhere we've been. I believe there is a cave system beneath us, and in one of those caves, a hidden city lies," Dr. Gregg explained. "Mayan architecture often included underground facilities, cleverly hidden and difficult to discover. They were amazing architectural engineers for their time!"

"So, where do we look?" Dorf asked.

"My first guess would be the temple ruins," Dr. Gregg said, looking back toward the city's center. They searched that ruin with particular care, hoping to find what they sought.

Jim thought about that for a few minutes, remembering everything from the search, and his mind suddenly focused on a memory. He rose quickly to his feet, towering over Dr. Gregg, and seized the little man's shoulder.

"Do you remember the base of the altar?" he asked.

"Yes," Dr. Gregg said, his eyes suddenly unfocused as he recalled the memory. Something about it had seemed almost out of place. "There was something about it that caught our attention. You could be right, Captain! Come, we will search together!"

Leading the way, practically running, Dr. Gregg never looked back to see if anyone was following him. He didn't need to. Everyone was once again filled with excitement and hope. Jim kept pace with him, easily calling out orders behind as they went.

"We'll need the shovels for this one! Make sure you have your packs and gear. If we find the entrance, we'll probably have to break camp and make a new one in the cave system. Remember to watch for snakes. We've seen about half a dozen different kinds that were poisonous. Now would not be a good time to be bitten!"

Dr. Gregg slowed down enough to watch where he was stepping. Reaching the temple ruins, they came once more to the grizzly altar, blackened with dried blood on the top where nothing grew except lichen. It was as if the memories of the horrors that took place on this altar repelled all but the most destructive forms of life. Mark, Jack, and Frank stepped up with shovels and began clearing away the grass, small plants, and dirt that built up around the base over the years. Others joined them, working carefully, while others stood by with machetes in case a snake appeared. No one knew quite what to expect, what dangers might lurk beneath the ground, but those thoughts were held at bay for the moment.

Once all the dirt was cleared away from the temple floor, Dr. Gregg knelt and studied the base. Wade, who loved engineering, looked critically at the solid structure and almost immediately found the answer. With a huge smile, he stepped forward and grasped one of the small square stones near the ridge of the altar. He wiggled it until it suddenly came away in his hands. Dr. Gregg rose on his knees to look into the empty space. Studying it carefully, he felt the stirrings of excitement.

"Good heavens!" he breathed, shining a flashlight that Barbara handed him into the opening. "I believe there is a mechanism here, turned by a key of some sort!"

Wade knelt beside him and looked into the opening. A diamond-shaped indention in the center of a small five-inch circular stone was visible. For several minutes, he studied it from every possible angle, scratching his chin once or twice and finally sighing, and then he rose to his feet.

"I'll need some of that hardwood we found on the knoll, the stuff that was hard to split. Bring me three pieces, no more than three inches in diameter, please," he requested. Vince headed off to pick up three branches from the wood they'd cut earlier for the campfire. He made sure it was the hard stuff, a fruit tree of some kind, growing a strange nut. Whatever it was, it dulled hatchets quickly. It might even be a Brazil nut. He didn't know.

Wade used his knife to form the diamond shape at the end of the stoutest piece, sticking it into the opening and checking the fit every few minutes. When satisfied it fit tightly enough, he began working at the other end, making it square. Using his Mini Tac because of its double edge and razor point, he cut a square from the center of another piece and fit the two together. Then, carefully inserting the makeshift key into the opening, he tried to turn it to the left.

Nothing happened. Straining against the stone, he jerked the key a few times until he decided to try the other direction. With amazing ease, the key turned to the right one-half turn and stopped. Beneath his feet, he could feel some vibration. To everyone's astonishment, the altar suddenly rolled away from Wade, exposing a five-foot square opening leading down into the beckoning darkness! He stared at the hole in the ground with his mouth open, his face delighted.

"Now I know how Indiana Jones felt!" Wade said with a laugh. "I have to see what's down there!"

"I volunteer to be the woman he kisses!" Mary Anne quipped, raising her hand.

"Not me?" Wade asked, his face a study of disappointment.

"It has to be Harrison Ford, love. Sorry!" Mary Anne shook her head.

"Way to go, Wade!" John said, slapping his back enthusiastically.

Everyone cheered as the altar came to a halt. Wade and Dr. Gregg could feel the cold air rushing out of the cave. It felt wonderful. Jim broke three light sticks and tossed them into the darkness. They landed at different levels on the steps, and as far as they could see, they continued into the darkness. As he studied the carefully cut steps, hewn from solid rock, he saw that the entryway had also been cut out, probably from a very small hole in the ground that revealed the cave system below. Idly, he wondered how the Mayans found the hole in the first place and knew it led to caves. Someone very brave had to explore that opening. Or, perhaps, it was one of the slaves forced to go in and explore.

"Okay, people!" he said, getting instant quiet. "We break camp, move everything into the cave, and set up a new camp. Tomorrow, we'll explore. Dr. Gregg will lead the way with Wade to ensure there are no traps."

Trooping together to the knoll, the camp was packed up in an orderly fashion, hearts light even in the intense heat, driving rain, and humidity. Dr. Gregg picked his flashlight up and looked at it quizzically. It was different from anything he'd seen before.

"What is this?" he asked.

"It's a new type of flashlight. No batteries are required, and the bulb should last a lifetime. You shake it, and its energy causes a chemical reaction with some crystals in there. Wade could probably explain it better than I can, but the thing shines brightly," John replied.

"Nifty!" Dr. Gregg said, trying it. "What will they think of next? We save a lot of weight not having to carry extra batteries!" he added.

Once every pack was checked, the explorers made their way into the ruined temple and began the journey into darkness. Every third person had a flashlight, and the two between carried light sticks. Jim was taking no chances on accidents or unseen dangers. Wade, FM, and Driver carried Franchi PA3/345 shotguns, shorter than the Mossberg and suitable for quick action against snakes or other dangerous creatures that might be found in caves. The men carrying those weapons took places scattered evenly throughout the group so that maximum safety was guaranteed. Protecting the scientists was essential to each of them.

Behind Wade, John walked, carrying his Trimble Scout M+GPS. His task was to record every inch of their journey so that they could use the instrument to find their way back. At the rear, just in front of Driver, Smitty carried a similar unit for the same purpose. Redundant backup systems added safety.

According to the Trimble Scout, their descent into the caves down wide stone steps chiseled out of the hard granite rock took them seven hundred and twenty-five feet beneath the earth's surface. It was amazing how uniform the steps were despite the time it must have taken to cut them out of the solid rock! At the bottom, they paused to take their bearings.

"Look!" Dr. Gregg's voice was tight with the excitement of discovery. "They began these steps here, at the bottom! See these marks here!" The marks did not look like anything recognizable to most looking at the wall before them. But Wade and a few others, including Jim, saw what he meant. They looked up to the top.

"They measured exactly to form the steps," Dr. Gregg said breathlessly. "Good Lord, they were amazing builders!"

"That they were," Wade agreed quietly. "They measured in spans, did they not?" he turned to Dr. Gregg.

"Yes," Alistair said softly, nodding. "They must have measured the depth and then figured how far out they had to go to make the steps uniform. One of them knew at least the rudiments of trigonometry! Imagine cutting away this section of the wall with the rough tools of that day!"

Beyond the steps, the wall extended about twelve feet, neatly cut into a corridor for the steps and passage into the cavern. A small, deep stream on the opposite wall flowed swiftly deeper into the system.

"At one time, I imagine this river filled this entire cavern, pushing out the top and leaving that entrance. Sometime in the distant past, it pushed through another wall and formed a waterfall or perhaps found a deeper fissure into the earth itself. We will have to see," Alistair looked into the darkness. He began to rummage through his backpack for his sweatshirt. It was cold down here!

CHAPTER 22

WADE MOVED TO one side of the steps when his light caught something else man-made. To his surprise, it was another stela. He called Dr. Gregg over to study the stone monument. Cecilia and Jim joined them, and within an hour, Dr. Gregg had dictated the markings to Mary Ann for their record. Barbara snapped pictures from different angles.

"Another map!" Dr. Gregg said with glee. "This system of caves was discovered during a mining expedition nearly fourteen hundred years ago!" he informed them, shaking his head in admiration. "Where the alter was, only a small chimney existed to lead them down here. They spent twenty- eight years cutting out the steps and tunneling down! During that time, they explored and made a map of the caves, which they inscribed on this stone. It doesn't give the city's location, but I can guess which caves to search. There are only three large enough to contain a city; one of those is the largest, and that's probably a good place to start. The first exploration seems to have been specifically for mining gold."

"Did you say gold?" FM asked quietly. "I wouldn't mind finding some gold." Several others nodded and murmured in the affirmative.

"Yes, see here!" Dr. Gregg pointed to a line on the stelae. "This stream disappears underground about half a mile from where we are. Oh! Dear Jesus, have mercy!" Alistair looked up at those gathered around with eyes filled with sadness and shock. "They threw a slave into the stream to see if they could find his body where it exited the cave system. His body was never found."

"How many slaves died in the making of this city?" Dr. Persons mused. "If one believed in the existence of ghosts, one would imagine the caverns would be haunted by the spirits of all those who died here. But we know that to be absent from the body is to be present with the Lord. I hope they knew Him." He looked sad, thinking of people dying without knowing the Savior. Jim nodded his agreement and thought, not for the first time, that God surely must be tired of man's inhumanity to his fellow man.

Smitty and Zeke, working at Zeke's laptop with the information, soon had a working map of the cave system to download to the Trimble Scouts. Once this was accomplished, the group moved carefully into the corridor that would ultimately lead them to their goal. Each woman had taken advantage of the pause to pull sweatshirts from their packs. It was very cool beneath the earth, and to them, it felt wonderful after the wet heat of the jungle above.

After a trek of about three hundred yards, the roof of the corridor slanted down until everyone was bent double. After another fifty yards of dodging stalagmites and stalactites, some of which had formed columns, they arrived in a domed cavern. For Dorf, it was a very tight squeeze at one point, where he had to remove his pack and guns before scraping through and grunting with the effort.

Three passages were visible. Dr. Gregg and Smitty studied the map and chose to explore the left passage first. Once they entered that cave, everyone stopped to stare in wonder at the deposits of Precious Opal, Wood Opal, and Fire Opal. Some of it had been mined, but the deposits remaining were considerable. In the glow from the explorer's flashlights, the walls literally glittered with a myriad of colors. Such beauty was rare, and everyone paused to enjoy it fully. Awe was the emotion that almost everyone felt, and in the midst of it, Jim made an observation that many would remember.

"Isn't it interesting that in the middle of rock, beneath the ground, where only those who explore such depths can enjoy, God has left such beauty for us to share?" he asked. "It is as if He wishes to remind us, even in the depths of the earth, that He is present!" Cecilia took his hand and leaned against him with a sigh. Jim had a real relationship with God that she appreciated, and his words, at that moment, had reminded everyone that God was there with them.

Soon, they passed into a corridor whose walls were Granite Gneiss with white quartz veins. Exploring a small side tunnel, they discovered a vein of gold, some of which had been mined, while most of the deposit remained untouched.

"We're stopping here on the way out!" Ox said as he ran his hands over the softer, precious metal.

"You get to carry whatever you mine," Jim said with a grin.

"I thought that's why we brought Dorf," Mark snickered. "He's as big as a horse!"

"Where are Abe and Sturdy when you need them?" Dorf said, throwing up his hands.

"Gentlemen! We are the only people who know this is here!" John said quietly. "And we have a CH-53D!" he added.

"You know, boss. We could retire after this!" FM remarked.

"You'd be bored in a month!" Jim replied, clapping him on the shoulder. "Besides, what will our next treasure hunt be like? How could you pass up the opportunity for another adventure? We may find records of other such cities to explore! Just think about that!" Jim could see his words' effect on the group as they paused momentarily to consider the possibilities. The thrill of the hunt called to them more than anything else.

"You're tiring me out, boss! Just thinkin' about it is sappin' my energy. You see it sloppin' on the floor at my feet, boss?" FM complained sarcastically. "Somebody, please carry my stuff!" he whined with a moan.

"Here, I'll help!" Heidi said. Her tiny frame was already dwarfed by the pack she carried.

"On second thought, let me help you!" FM said, picking the girl up in his arms. She laughed, and he put her back on her feet.

Entering another cavern, the left section of the caves came to an end. There were arched niches carved into the walls at regular intervals and in each niche, a statue. Ferenc exclaimed in pleasure as he approached a small golden statue of the Mayan sun god. Something about the room bothered Jim. As Ferenc reached out to touch the statue, Jim yelled a warning.

"Don't touch that!" he snapped, a moment too late. Standing close enough to Ferenc, Jack heard the warning and pushed the young man aside. From a hole above the statue, a dart sprang with a thump from within the rock. The dart, made entirely of stone, penetrated Adley's shoulder. If Jack had hesitated, the dart would have transfixed Ferenc in the center of his chest.

Ferenc screamed in pain as he went down, with Jack still holding him to help him down gently. Ox was struggling out of his pack and making his way quickly to their side. About an inch of the dart was protruding from Adley's back, and another three inches stuck out of his shoulder. Jack was holding his hand in a tight grip while Ferenc grimaced in pain and bit back his screams.

"You're lucky, mate!" Ox said, kneeling and examining the wound. "This bit rammed right under your clavicle and punched through the scapula. It missed your lungs. Now, Ferenc, I'm going to give you a local so I can work on this. Hold on for a few minutes till it takes effect," Ox said, pulling fluid from a small jar into a hypodermic needle. He jabbed the needle into Adley's shoulder and gave him several shots. Ferenc felt the hot sting, but it was nothing compared to what his body was already suffering. His body began to relax three minutes later, and the pain slowly abated. Ox had been studying the dart carefully.

"I don't dare pull this out from the front," Ox said to Ferenc, his eyes sober. "I'm going to have to punch it through. Pulling it could catch on something important if it has a barb on it. You shouldn't feel too much pain when I do this," he added.

Ferenc nodded, his face covered in sweat, and watched while Ox pushed the dart deeper into his shoulder. It stopped, an inch still sticking out of the front. Ox reached around, grabbed the pointed part with one hand, and with the heel of his hand, struck the end, and it punched the rest of the way through the clavicle so that the medic could pull it out. He did it quickly, knowing it would be difficult for his patient. Adley fainted, which made it a little easier for Ox to pull it out.

Ox held it up for everyone to see. The bloody stone dart was barbed in the middle, the pieces of rock thin enough to catch and slice through anything. He laid the dart aside carefully and then began the task of cleaning the wound with a surgical bath solution. He stapled both openings once he was satisfied that no pieces were left inside the wound and that the dirt had been cleansed away.

Ferenc came around as he was putting the bandages on. His face was pale. Ox sat him up slowly and gave him some water from his canteen. When some color returned to his face, Ox smiled and gently patted his uninjured shoulder. The man would feel tremendous pain for several days, but at least he was alive.

"All patched up, mate. I've put the arm in a sling and want you to leave it there. We'll carry your pack for a while."

"Merci!" Ferenc said with meaning.

"Je vous en prie," Ox replied. His French was excellent, and Ferenc smiled.

"Not bad Frog for an Aussie!" Phillip said with a grin.

"How would you know? You don't even speak English!" Ox replied good-naturedly.

"Ouch! I retire worsted!" Phil replied. Adley was helped to his feet and tightly grasped Jack's hand with his free left hand.

"Thanks. If not for you, I would have fallen here, no?" he admitted.

"Just don't let your enthusiasm run away with you again!" Jack said. "I don't want to make a habit of saving your butt!" It was said half in jest and half in seriousness. Ferenc nodded his head, chagrinned. Foolish didn't begin to describe how he felt for falling for such an obvious trick.

"Okay, everybody. We know there are dangers. Let's be smart about this from now on," Jim said. "I realized that something was wrong. Why those niches and statues in a bare cavern? It didn't make sense. Let's clean this dart and keep it for the museum," he nodded at the dart. FM cleaned it carefully, noting how sharp the pieces of stone were, packaged it in an evidence bag, wrote down its description and location in the cave, and stowed it in his pack. He finished by adding photos of the niches and describing how the traps were sprung.

Dorf stooped, picked up Ferenc's pack in his huge right hand, and nodded for the Frenchman to move on. Everyone trooped back through the cave corridors to begin a trek down the center opening.

Shortly after entering that corridor, Heidi was drawn to a set of ropes that glittered like gold. When she touched them, she discovered they were indeed woven of gold, certainly not strong enough for anything but decoration. She ran her hand up one and screamed when something slammed through her hand, two barbs springing out with an audible ring, and beneath her, with a wild rumbling sound, suddenly disappeared as blocks of stone fell away with loud crashes! She hung there, screaming, impaled, and helpless.

Wade was the first to reach her and realized that her hand would be cut through because the blade impaling it was sharp. Throwing himself down, he looked beneath the hole and then stood and straddled the fissure. He grasped her around the waist with both hands and held her fast against the wall. She was shaking and sobbing hysterically, and blood flowed freely from her hand.

"This blade will cut her hand in half!" he shouted as Ox, Jim, and Dorf arrived simultaneously. Dorf looked at the situation, and, putting his guns and packs aside, he laid down and slid beneath her until her feet were firmly planted on his massive muscled back. Wade stayed close, keeping her upright, afraid she might pass out from the pain. Everyone watched, praying and afraid, alarmed by the amount of blood.

Mark reached into his pack, pulled out a collapsible bolt cutter, put it together swiftly, and snapped off the end of the blade where the barbs kept it from being removed. Ox didn't even wait to give the girl a local. He grabbed her wrist and pulled the hand off the blade in one quick motion. She bit back a yelp of pain as tears streamed down her face.

Once she was safe, Ox took the time to treat her wound, putting stitches inside and on the surface and wrapping the hand. Dorf and Wade shone lights down the fissure at four-foot-long spikes, about eighteen feet beneath the floor. They looked at one another and stood guard over the hole, keeping everyone away.

"Nothing in here is safe, people!" Jim growled tersely. "I want all of you to refrain from touching anything until we've had a chance to examine it. Understood?" Everyone nodded. He wondered if the students would heed his warnings. Two were now injured, and both could have died except for the quick thinking of his men. He looked over at Wade, who understood and nodded. He studied the other ropes for a moment, his eyes taking in every detail.

Wade ran his KA-BAR knife behind the gold chords to show the danger, and two more blades sprang out of the wall. The engineer in him demanded to know how those things worked, so he dug at the stones in the wall until he had unearthed the mechanism. Those Mayans had been advanced enough to spring load the blades, use a counterweight to release the spring and build it well enough that it still worked.

"Jim," he said while Ox worked on Heidi, and Lisle held the poor child, stroking her soft blond hair.

Jim stepped over and waited. "We have to assume that the floor could be rigged, too," he pointed to the hole beneath his feet. It's time to put someone with really sharp eyes on point, but keeping them close enough for all of us to come to the rescue if needed." Wade looked the men over as he spoke. "Mark's probably the best man for that job," he added after some thought.

"Mark, front and center, please!" Jim commanded. Mark hurried over. His face was set as it always was when he knew he would receive important orders. Jim almost smiled. "You have point. Wade thinks the floor may be rigged to drop out from under someone. You've got sharp eyes and gymnast moves. Stay sharp and stay alive! Use your feet carefully! We'll be about six feet behind you, so if you need help, it's near enough to be viable."

"Okay, Shep," Mark agreed quietly. "May I suggest we only use green light sticks so I can use my NV glasses? Down here, that might make all the difference. A rope would also be a good safety precaution, don't you think?"

"Good suggestions!" Jim admitted. With the NV glasses, any white light was enough to confuse the wearer's sight. Green light sticks would give them enough light to see where to put their feet and would not interfere with the NV sight. Mark took his NV goggles out, pulled out the batteries, and put them in his meter. They showed a full charge, and he put them back in, perching the goggles over his head until they would be needed.

In that fashion, the group moved onward, with every other person carrying a lighted stick. In contrast, Mark moved ahead about six feet, his NV glasses showing him everything in a strange greenish glow that he was very familiar with. His head moved back and forth as he searched ahead of his feet carefully. Traps set by others were rarely easily detected, and he knew this. Trusting more upon his intuition, he moved carefully.

Pausing before a pattern of tiles on the floor, he raised a hand for everyone to stop. Dorf stepped forward to within two feet of his tiny friend, dropping guns and packs. Mark was testing the knot of the nylon climbing rope around his waist and climbing harness, and he handed his pack back to Dorf. Wade joined Dorf, and the two became his anchor. Jim watched silently, knowing his men would protect their friend as he worked out the puzzle.

CHAPTER 23

PEOPLE CROWDED FORWARD to watch as Mark reached out with the butt of his Franchi PA 3/345 and tapped on the first tile. Nothing happened. He put pressure on the tile, but still nothing happened. He squatted and waited for a count of thirty seconds before stepping carefully on that tile.

He put his shotgun down on the second tile, and a dart flew from the wall to his right, clanging against the stone of the wall on the opposite side. It was iron, about six inches long, barbed, and aimed at what would have been chest height for a Mayan. Carefully, Mark tapped the tile again, but no dart flew. He put pressure on it and then waited for a count of thirty seconds before carefully moving to that tile. Feeling the threat more than seeing any, he was careful, moving slowly.

This time, the tile he touched shattered and dropped, with two on either side and nine more in front. A man would have pitched forward, found nothing to catch hold of, and plummeted into an abyss. Mark cautiously peered over the edge and whistled. There were sharpened wooden stakes pointing up from the floor, spaced out enough so that only one or two might have impaled a man.

One might not die from the fall, but the stakes were barbed to keep anyone from getting away. Death would come very slowly for the unwary, slowly bleeding, starving, and lacking water.

Mark backed up and looked at the first tile. Each tile had a different figure carved into its surface. Locating a tile with a similar figure, he carefully tapped it, put pressure on it, and then moved onto it after another count of thirty seconds. Nothing happened. Standing up, he carefully stepped on another properly marked tile. He was about to take another step when he paused, his foot only inches above the tile. Something about the figure caught his attention. Instinctively, he knew there was something wrong with it.

He looked beneath his left foot, solidly planted on a proper tile, and saw that the figure in this one was smiling. The figure was not smiling in the next one. Drawing his foot back carefully, he squatted and again tapped the tile. Darts from both sides flew across before him, traveling fast enough for him to feel their deadly draft.

Slowly, painstakingly, he crossed the tiles to solid flooring. He had given a quiet commentary of his actions so the troops would know which tiles to choose. Dorf went next, carrying Mark's other guns, his own, and three packs because he still had Ferenc's to-tote.

Jim marveled at the catlike movements of the giant as he made his way across the stones easily, joining his friend on the other side. Now, they had a rope stretched all the way across. Jim sent Ferenc over first and then Heidi. Both carefully made their way across, the ropes tied to them in case they fell. Their steps were steady, and they made it without incident. Each time, Dorf threw the rope back, and Wade caught it before it landed on any of the tiles. He handed the rope to Jim, who tied it around the next traveler. Everyone was concentrating on making sure nothing else happened.

The rest of the explorers crossed, Dr. Gregg coming last, and Jim sent his men over. He tied the rope around his waist and made his way across last. Sighing, when he reached the other side safely, he untied the rope and returned it to Mark, who was already looping it in his pack.

At this point, several caverns opened on the sides, and they explored them, finding that they ended quickly. One led them into a room where gems gleamed from the walls and ceiling. Crystal formations were abundant, and it was one of the most beautiful sights they had ever seen. They rested in that room, content to sit and wonder at the various colors around them. Only a privileged few would ever see such a sight, and they appreciated it thoroughly.

Other side caverns contained living quarters, rough wooden furniture, and rotted hammocks, which remained as mute testimony of their use. These rooms were scrutinized, unearthing chisels, hammers, picks, and shovels with dried handles still in place. These tools were worn and well-used. Dr. Gregg studied them carefully for some time before speaking.

"What might these people have done if they had discovered gunpowder or a liquid explosive like nitro-glycerin?" Dr. Gregg asked no one in particular. He carefully examined one of the chisels in his hands, turning it slowly. It was carefully tooled by a craftsman who obviously took great pride in his work.

"How many lives did they use up mining these caves?" Barbara wondered aloud, hard on his heels.

In the final chamber, they found a room that had been cut, almost a perfect square, and in the center, another altar, like the one that had opened to bring them down here. Dr. Gregg stood at the entrance for a long time, looking around. Something about the room bothered him. At last, he worked it out.

"Why would they cut out a square room and then put blocks on all four walls?" He mused. "I don't like this. It smells like another trap." His eyes moved over everything, but he could not see what it was that bothered him so much.

After the discussion, Mark moved into the room, looking at the floor, which was smooth but not tiled or broken anywhere. He moved right up to the altar, and finding the proper stone, he wiggled it out of its place and saw the same key space as before. He returned to the door to talk with Wade, and the two discussed possibilities quietly.

Wade sent men back to the living quarters to gather bamboo poles stacked by the walls. Using binder twine to make a pole long enough, he tied two ropes to the two handles of the key and had Mark insert the key. A hushed silence fell as the two worked, so only their efforts broke the silence. Once Mark had the key in place, he moved slowly out of the room.

With Mark safely outside the door, using the long pole and rope to turn the key, Dorf held the whole thing off the floor; Wade twisted the key. There was an audible click, and the altar moved back as the one above moved. Dr. Gregg waited patiently, and when nothing happened, he was about to enter the room when Jim grabbed his shoulder and halted him.

"Wait!" He commanded. He didn't know why and would later attribute it to the Holy Spirit, but he knew no one should enter that room.

After about forty-five seconds, without any warning, the block walls, halfway up, suddenly fell in with horrifying speed. Anyone in that room would have been crushed to death or trapped in the pit beneath the altar. Once the dust cleared, Dr. Gregg stared at the bamboo pole beneath his feet, which was smashed flat by the huge square blocks. The entire doorway was blocked off! He instantly realized that the room was nothing more than a deadly trap!

"Struth!" he said softly. "Whatever is down here was of great importance to these Mayans."

"They certainly didn't value human life very much," Jim said quietly. He was still holding Dr. Gregg by the shoulder. That realization and the prompting of the Holy Spirit had made him ask the good doctor to wait. He understood that now and even began to understand why. The firm grasp became an encouraging pat.

"Why do you say that?" Dr. Gregg asked, looking up at the captain. "Anyone who would go to the lengths these people went to kill intruders in horrible ways can't value life. And look at their altars and the sacrifices. They killed their own people, probably family members, all in the name of religion. Somewhere along the line, they lost sight of the worth of human life and dignity," Jim said. "You can't argue that point."

"No. I would say you are correct. And you should know. I have seen how reluctant you are to take a life, even when that is the only option you have," Dr. Gregg said, patting Jim's shoulder. "I sometimes forget what dead cultures did to destroy themselves. In each, without exception, they committed unspeakable atrocities against innocent people. Well!" he said, squaring his shoulders. "Let us tackle the last cave system. But first, I think we should rest," Dr. Gregg said.

"That's not a bad idea. We've had many adventures, and we're all a little tired. We'll camp back in the main cavern at the bottom of the steps," Jim replied. We know it is safe there, and we have everything in place. In the morning, we can come back for the final exploration.

Returning to that place took longer than everyone expected because they had to cross the tile section again, and many were exhausted. Jim got everyone across safely and after returning to camp and wolfing down their MREs the explorers stretched out on the cold rock floor.

Their evening Bible Study seemed to cheer everyone up. That was one thing that Jim appreciated now that he was a believer. One could be in the darkest situations and still find the light of truth to buck up wilting spirits. The darkness weighed heavily on everyone. In that heavy darkness, the light of the Word of God came as a blessed respite and gave strength. Yet, when the study was over, the weight of the darkness seemed to settle in just as heavily.

Jim noted that the women tended to huddle together, even though their sleeping bags would keep them warm enough. He lay in the darkness for a long time, listening to his sleeping companions' steady rhythmic breathing and snores. Very conscious of Cecilia's proximity, he lay quietly, pondering the next day's exploration and the journey up the river to take care of the terrorists. Darkness, he decided wryly, was a good place for such thoughts. Before he closed his eyes in sleep, he offered up a prayer, seeking God's presence and guidance, and felt much better after his communion with the Lord.

Sparks woke him, and he knew instinctively that he had not slept long and that it was not time to rise yet. Instantly awake, he sat up slowly, his head turning, knowing something was wrong. Then he heard the bats.

"There must be thousands of the little buggers!" Sparks said softly. "Do you think we should wake everyone and warn them?"

Jim saw the shadow of thousands of bats overhead and knew they were following an age-old instinctive pattern: leaving the cave for the night and hunting for food. These were giant bats, but he knew they would leave the humans alone. He shook his head.

"No. Let them sleep. If any wake up and get frightened, keep them quiet," Jim said. I think they're all tired enough to sleep through this anyway," he yawned and saw Sparks grinning at him. His grin was almost feral.

They hadn't seen bats in the caves explored thus far. That meant that tomorrow, they would have that to contend with. Guano would be a problem and a health risk. He decided to talk to Ox about it in the morning before they set out. Indeed, they were making a racket, and then he realized they had discovered the altar opening.   That discovery was being communicated to the rest of the flock. Hoping they wouldn't get too stirred up, he watched until the flock was finally gone and went back to sleep. In the morning, they devoured breakfast and prepared for the final series of caves.   Heidi's hand was giving her trouble, and Ox treated it carefully. The pain showed in her fingers and thumb movements, eyes, and body language. Ferenc's shoulder was mending nicely, and he seemed eager to move. Jim was glad to see both of them submit to Sean's careful medical care with equal confidence. After treating them, Sean reported that both were able to continue.

Dorf once again took Ferenc's pack without comment, and Mark took the point as before. Jim noted that the Mayans respected the natural beauty of the caves, changing little in their quest for the perfect location of their hidden city. Drainage in a few spots kept the passage clear of stalagmites rising from the floor, and stalactites had once been cut back to allow passage in an upright position.

This corridor yielded the most precious metals and stones. Once barely passable, several caverns were opened wide enough for man and beast to enter. Jim wondered how much they had taken from those caves. What remained was enough to inspire thoughts of mining the wealth of dreams. Wealth, he knew, could corrupt. *Don't let our success corrupt us! Please, God.* The dangers of this were genuine, and he knew instinctively that rich men tended to trust in their wealth rather than in God. In the second vaulted cavern, they found the bats.   Long before they reached the cavern, they could smell the foul stench of the flying rodents. Jim wondered how long the creatures had inhabited that particular place. The guano was several feet thick and, in some areas, almost liquid.

Ox suggested wearing their dust masks and soon wished he had brought gas masks along. Some bats moved around and chittered as they passed, but none approached the humans. It was probably the first time a human had passed this way in a thousand years.

That cavern was the only one inhabited by bats, and Jim soon saw why. The stone was almost perfect for perching, nesting, and caring for young. What he hadn't counted on was the presence of venomous snakes. He supposed the plethora of insects drawn by the guano gave them ample food supply. Also, they probably ate bats when they could catch one.

The Aussies proved good company when it came to venomous snakes. Lee Roy Brown had very quick hands, often catching a Cobra, calming it, and releasing it away from the group. Chance Edwards also seemed fearless in the presence of the deadly reptiles, grabbing them by their tails and examining them before moving them along.

"Have a lash at the colors on this one!" he said, holding a Coral Snake for everyone to admire. Jim guessed that the phrase "have a lash" meant to look at the snake. "You don't want to get bit by this little beauty!" Chance said, showing the fangs leaking venom as he pressed the head. "You'd be in Barney if that happened."

"What did you just say?" Zeke asked. "What the heck does "in Barney" mean?"

"Barney Rubble, the cartoon character! Trouble!" Chance said as if that explained everything.

"Why didn't we see any snakes in the other caves?" Cecilia asked, wincing away from a Cobra that Lunch Box showed everyone.

"Do you feel that cool touch of air?" Frank Miller said. "There's no exit from the other caves. This one has some vents somewhere. I think that's why they're all in here. They can move in and out at will, though hunting here must be good. An inexhaustible food supply, places to hide in wait, all give them exactly what they want."

"I think you may be correct, young sir!" Dr. Gregg said. "In the pyramids, snakes only inhabit rooms with more than one exit. That is, an exit they can use. Sometimes, it's not much more than a loose stone with a gap they can barely squeeze through."

"I always thought these kinds of snakes would be more aggressive toward humans," C.G. said.

"Usually, snakes will go out of their way to avoid a confrontation with humans," Lee Roy said. "We don't really represent food to them, but we do represent danger. They'll avoid us if they can or attack to defend themselves."

"Have you ever been bitten?" Cecilia asked, intrigued.

"Got tagged by a King Brown once and nearly bought the farm on that one. My whole hand turned black and was swollen for six months. It was so sore I couldn't touch it against anything, either. I was eighteen," he replied. "Australia's got some nasty creepy crawlies, don't you know?" he added. "They inhabit most of Australia and make people's lives miserable whenever possible."

"Four less, now!" Cecilia said with a smile.

"Oh, she's quick, she is!" Chance said with a grin.

CHAPTER 24

LISLE AND DR. Persons were the next two injured. They were exploring one of the side caverns filled with crystals, mostly Celestite with Calcite and a few sections of Willemite. Along one section, Wulfenite fascinated everyone, forming arches of crystal that reflected various colors in a wonderful array of beauty. Some Axinite had formed along the floor, and both cut open their ankles on the sharp orange-yellow stone crystals.

Although the wounds were not serious or life-threatening, they were painful and slowed the two down. Ox treated them just as carefully as he had the other injuries and checked them often. Lisle took some Tylenol for the pain, but Dr. Persons didn't feel it was bad enough for that. Ankles were tender places for injuries and he did limp for the rest of the journey. The cut was in a tough spot that moved with every step.

Mark stopped everyone in the main corridor and motioned for Jim to come forward. Wade joined them as they looked at the obstacle in their path. It was a square opening, the entire width of the corridor, and twelve feet across. Below, the sound of a rushing underground stream could be heard. Black tarantulas with orange stripes slowly traversed the walls, but they weren't what stopped Mark.

"There used to be a bridge across this," he explained, pointing to the wood beams that stretched from side to side. Whatever planks once provided safe passage were long rotted away. The beams were tree trunks. "I wouldn't trust walking across one of those at all," Mark added unnecessarily.

Above the opening, stretching from wall to wall, a squared stone beam had been carved out of the cavern. Wade looked at it. "They must have used that to rig the bridge," he said, pointing. "See the worn spots where ropes were used? Someone in their midst was an amazing engineer!"

Mark took out his climbing rope, uncoiled some of it, and tossed it expertly over the square beam. He'd attached a chock with a wire sling on the end, and as it sailed over, the momentum and weight of the chock brought it back toward him. He caught it easily, passed the rope through the wire sling, and drew it tight.

Pulling on his climbing harness, he passed the rope through the proper carabiners and looped it through his descender. He leaped out over the opening, swung down and across, and let the rope out through the descender to easily reach the other side. He landed with his chest against the far wall and then pulled himself up on the other side. Spiders scurried away from the sudden movement of something so large.

"I think a rope bridge will work," he said across the opening, casually brushing a tarantula from his arm. It was a Baboon Spider, primarily black, and the huge King Baboon Spiders were among them, reddish in color, as big as his hand.

Dorf pulled his rope out of his pack and then tossed one end to Mark. Mark took out three pitons and his hammer ax and began to drive them into the stone floor. Following his friend's example,

Dorf did the same on his side, waiting until Mark had fastened his rope through the eyes of the three pitons before pulling it taught and fastening it on his end.

Dorf crossed the bridge with all his gear, using Mark's rope to steady himself. He came back and, lifting Heidi to his back, took her across. She buried her head in his neck, refusing to look, and sighed with relief when he lifted her gently to the floor. Ferenc said he could do it one-handed as long as the climbing harness was in place, and he knew he wouldn't fall to his death if he slipped.

The group passed over the bridge one by one. Some went in fear, but most of them accepted the means as safe and practical. Dr. Gregg pointed out that if ropes were attached properly, the bridge could be raised from this side, keeping unwanted visitors out. Wade looked at the arrangement and nodded.

It was late, and they had walked over ten miles, including their side trips into caverns. Smitty guessed they were five miles from the steps when they came to the entrance of the hidden city. No one suggested exploring it immediately. They were tired and sore and ready to rest.

To protect everyone from the spiders, snakes, and bats, they erected dome tents that seemed to spring into existence, large enough for two people in each one. They were inflated with foot pumps, weighed six ounces, and provided ample insulation and protection. These could be zipped closed to keep the dangers of arachnids, insects, and snakes at bay, much to the relief of everyone. The mattress at the bottom of the tent provided some protection against the hard rock floor.

Cecilia surprised Jim yet again when she offered a suggestion that had every woman nodding in agreement. "I think that there should be a man in each tent with the women tonight," she pleaded.

"We'll all sleep better knowing we have a knight protector with us," she added.

Jim considered its propriety, but the nods and pleading expressions swayed him. No one thought it odd that Cecilia should crawl into his tent. He looked over at John, who was helping Lisle into his tent and got a huge grin from his brother.

"It's good to be a knight protector!" John joked, winking at Jim.

Shaking his head Jim crawled in after Cecilia, zipped the tent closed, and sat down on his sleeping bag. When his gear was arranged to his liking, he turned toward her. She reached up with both hands, kissed him with an impish grin, and then slid into her nylon cocoon. Of course, their shadows could be seen through the tent's nylon, and there were catcalls from some of the men. Jim's face burned beat red as he slid into his sleeping bag. Lingering in his memory was the feel of her soft lips on his and the scent of her in his nostrils.

He pulled out his well-worn pocket New Testament and read from the book of James. Cecilia watched him, that mischievous grin still mocking him. He couldn't say that he minded her eyes on him. Somehow, he felt more confident with her close.

"Ah ha!" he said suddenly. "I am to consider it all joy when I encounter various trials and temptations!" He raised his eyebrows at her. "I shall be obedient to Scripture tonight and enjoy this!"

"That's rather a loose interpretation!" Cecilia said, laughing. "I hope I'm a temptation rather than a trial!" she added.

"It's the temptation that's the trial, dearie!" That was Ox speaking from the tent right next to theirs. Everyone laughed. Jim kissed her forehead lightly and put his Bible under his pack, which served him as a pillow. Contentedly, he closed his eyes and slept deeply and peacefully.

To his delight, when he woke up after seven hours of sleep, he found Cecilia curled against him, snuggled with his arm beneath her head. For a long time, he lay there listening to her steady breathing, ultra-aware of her shapely body pressed against him. Yet his thoughts, without considerable effort, were chaste. In the darkness, he quietly waited.

She awoke slowly, opening her eyes in the darkness and sensing her surroundings. Aware that she was tightly pressed against Jim and his arm was around her, she sighed with contentment. When she moved, he lifted his arm, and she realized he was awake. He didn't move away, and she smiled slightly, knowing that in the not-too-distant past, he would have recoiled from her. Feeling his strength filled her with delight.

"Can we have some light?" she asked. "I need to get dressed so I can go out and pee!"

Once a light stick had been cracked, she sat up, her hair a tangled mess. While she brushed it out, she looked around the tent. There were spiders resting on the outside of the tent walls, probably because they were warmer than the rocks. One suddenly leaped away, and there was a squeak of terror from a mouse.

Deep within the mountain, the constant struggle for life within nature went on despite the presence of strangers. Everything ate something alive in that cave system. She looked over at Jim, who was running his hand over his three-day growth.

"Best mouse trap ever!" she commented.

"I'll take some back to the ship, shall I?" Jim asked. "They will keep the roaches at bay as well."

They grinned at each other as they listened to the sleepy sounds of others waking up, the muted conversations, and other sounds. As they opened the zipper of their tent, the cool air from the cave came rushing in, and Cecilia realized how insulated these tents were. She shivered in the cool air, and, with Jim, made her way to the latrine, where behind a privacy curtain, she went first after Jim made sure there was no creepy crawlies waiting for either of them.

One had to be careful where one stepped in the camp area because the insects were all drawn to the light, and the snakes were drawn to the insects. Cecilia decided the best tactic was to ignore them unless they invaded her personal space. She actually kicked a large tarantula away and watched it as it lumbered off in another direction, surprised that it did not rise in an attack pose. Seeing no snakes, she asked why, and Chance explained that they were nocturnal hunters and were probably resting in seclusion, digesting last night's dinner.

Eventually, breakfast was finished, and plans were made to explore the inner city. Jim elected to keep the team together in the darkness, adding the comfort of close bodies to the meager lights they used. It was a wise decision.

CHAPTER 25

SITTING BESIDE JIM, Cecilia ate her breakfast in silence. One of the tarantulas crawled across her hiking boot, and she watched it with a mixture of revulsion and interest. John was holding one in his hand and peering at it. The spider seemed content with the warmth of his hand and sat still, staring back at John with a multitude of black eyes nearly hidden beneath the coarse hairs.

"How can you stand to hold that thing?" Lisle exclaimed as she made her way out of their tent.

"It's not dangerous to us. I put my hand in front of it and it crawled up. I think it likes the warmth," John replied. "Say hello to our new mascot!" he added, slowly extending his hand. The spider remained still, unaffected by the movement.

She drew back with a look of disgust on her face and wandered off to the girl's latrine. When she returned, she crawled back into the tent, zipped it closed, and went back to sleep. Jim let everyone sleep late that morning. He sat in a circle with those habitually early to rise and talk to pass the time.

It was a pleasant couple of hours with Cecilia holding his left hand in both hers, her arm linked with his, her head resting on his shoulder. She didn't seem to mind that he was dirty from all their exploring. If the constant fifty-four-degree temperature in the cave bothered her, she didn't show it. Wearing a light jacket beneath her sweatshirt seemed enough for her.

Mark, Dorf, Wade, and John moved off to search for a safe passage into the city. From what they could see, it was an extensive city modeled like those of the Classic Period. A single stela carved out of sandstone stood at the vast cavern entrance as a silent guardian. After a few minutes of careful movements and checking, they let Dr. Gregg and Cecilia decipher the stela. There didn't seem to be any danger here, and the stela might give them valuable information about what dangers they might face.

Like their books and codices, the figures in the stela's designs seemed too elaborate to be written language. Dr. Gregg explained the symbols as word pictures, though some of them were numerical and astrological notations. After Dr. Gregg examined it for an entire day, this stela seemed almost entirely numerical. One side had a word picture he was able to decipher, and it held the key to the numerical and mathematical notations.

"Not much is known about the Mayan language, even today," he said when explaining what he and Cecilia had uncovered in their study. "Russian scholars claimed to have deciphered the approximately 720 signs, one of them claiming that 80 were syllable signs. We've built on that since 1961, though Dr. Persons and I are two of the few scholars still working on the project of Mayan writings.

"This stela describes storing their most precious religious and historical artifacts in this hidden city. I believe the mathematical and numerical signs indicate locations and a log of what is stored within the city. An entire side of this stela is dedicated to their four gods, the Bacabs, whom they believed held up the sky. I have deciphered the usual nine underworld signs and the thirteen horizontal layers or steps into which they divide the dimensions above the earth.

"If I understand the word picture, each storage chamber is guarded by one of the underworld's demons. I'm guessing there are traps to send intruders to a horrible death and an eternity in one of the nine underworlds. Following Mayan culture and their architectural advancement, we're going to have to be very careful," he sighed as he looked at his notes.

"Each stela we saw on the way here had the face of the current ruler on the front, with figures of the four gods above his head. This stela is dedicated to the gods, and no faces are present. From what we can see from here, the city is built on thirteen layers. Each layer will be six cubits or 18 spans, approximately nine feet high. They were quite clever when it came to building, I must say.

"At the top level, we will be one hundred and seventeen feet above the cave floor. I don't know how high the temple will go, but it will be on the fourth level. If this city follows the usual Classical Period pattern, we'll find stelae on the second level depicting the history of the building of the city and the culture that accomplished the task. On the top level, there will be a palace or throne room. It should rise to about the same level as the top of the temple," he paused while everyone gathered around to listen to his final statement.

"We are about to embark on an historic exploration of a city that human eyes have not seen for over a thousand years. Once we turn this site over to the government, they will assign specialists to explore, map, photograph, and record. But we are the first to see it. See it for what it is. Here is a culture that literally set in place its own destruction, a common factor in every culture on earth because of sin. Despite the cleverness of the people, they destroyed themselves from within. To me, this is the saddest part of archaeology, the unlearned lesson of the history of man and his sin condition," he sighed.

Once again, Mark took the lead, with Dr. Gregg, Dorf, Jim, and Cecilia close behind. Mark was patient, carefully searching the floor of the cave. He came unhindered to the first set of steps, which climbed three levels of the city to a long building with nine dark, observable openings in the light of his flashlight. The openings reminded him of a row of raised parking spaces or garage doors.

Each step was made of squared blocks of granite joined end to end without mortar. The end of one stone was recessed at the top, while the stone to which it was affixed was recessed at the bottom, each recess having a slightly angled lip to lock them in position. The steps were six inches high and about eighteen inches across, and there were thirty-nine of them from the cave's floor to the third level.

At the center of the steps, a twelve-foot wide section remained untouched. To either side, a low drainage ditch, about eighteen inches wide and six inches deep, had been cut into the floor, and it appeared to go all the way around the city. It was filled with a dark fluid, and Mark put his fingers in it and raised them carefully to his nose. Jim watched his eyebrows rise and already knew the answer. He could smell the petrol or oil. The ditch was filled with some oil.

Taking off his NV glasses, Mark bent down, employed his lighter, and drew his hand back sharply as the liquid roared into flame, racing away from him. He kept time with his watch. It took the flames about eighteen seconds to reach the other side of the section the group stood on in front of the steps. And then something happened that made everyone gasp.

With an audible whoosh, flames appeared on the second level, then the third, fourth, and up to the thirteenth level. Inside and outside the buildings, a dazzling display of light burst into the darkness, pushing it away at a speed the eye could not follow. Light smoke, rising from the flames, wafted off above somewhere.

Off to the right they could see steps leading to the first level, where a platform extended to allow for people to walk around the steps and make their way around the entire city. In the light of the flames, they could see ancient civilizations' fantastic designs and artwork. Another set of steps led to the second level, where they could all see the stelae, varying in height from six feet to almost twenty-seven feet.

"Why is the city white?" Cecilia asked breathlessly.

"They coated the walls and floors with a white plaster to achieve this pristine look. Here in the cave, where the sun doesn't shine, and no wind blows, it remained intact!" Dr. Gregg said, awe still in his voice.

Pyramids and platforms grouped around large open courts, comprising the buildings of the city proper. Each pyramid was crowned with small temples, and the low platforms supported large, many-roomed buildings. Impressive flights of steps led to the temple and palace, which appeared to be on the same level. A few buildings and terraces were decorated with huge portrait-masks of the four gods and intricate geometric designs in the stucco-covered stone. Long sweeps of smooth surface occupied all the remaining space. Every surface and floor was covered with the creamy-white stucco, which in sunlight must have been dazzling. In the firelight, it appeared almost golden in color.

Mark put his NV glasses away, and with a piece of bamboo he now carried as a walking stick, he tapped the stone block in front of him. Nothing happened, so he stepped onto that block and tapped the next. Immediately, he could feel a difference, and he leaped backward, landing lightly on his feet on the stone in front of the steps. A spear came from the wall on his right, thrust hard enough from its secret hiding place to drop only about an inch to the other side. That was thirty-six feet of distance.

Stepping back on the first stone, Mark tried the blocks to either side and found them solid. Dorf, following behind, marked each stone with a grease pencil used for painting black stripes on faces for camouflage. Spears sprang from the walls, leaving holes plastered over lightly to conceal them. At one point, about halfway up, four stones dipped, hanging from the stones above by ropes, which broke because they were rotted with age.

Below, everyone could see the sharpened wooden stakes that might have impaled any unsuspecting explorer.

Eventually, a pattern developed, and Mark could pick the steps that would be safe. He came back down the steps, and they moved over to the set on the right, leading to the second level and Stelae. To everyone's surprise, those steps were free of any traps. They led directly to the steps to the temple perched on top of the fourth level.

Each section of the pyramid was terraced so that it rose nine levels to equal the top level where the palace perched in the city's center. This was only one of many temples, and to get to it, one had to walk up to a height of ninety-nine feet. There were one hundred and ninety-eight steps from the second level to the temple.

To the left was an area large enough for everyone and all their gear. Most of the group sat with their backs to the third-level wall and talked quietly while Dr. Gregg, Cecilia, Barbara, and Mary Ann crowded around a stela. Dr. Persons, Ferenc, Heidi, and Lisle crowded close behind them, notebooks out and pens wiggling madly as they kept up with Dr. Gregg's deciphering.

Heidi, who had an eye for such things, stepped back and then walked down the steps to the cave floor to begin drawing the city from the front. She used a drawing pad and charcoal pencils for her drawings and they were quite good. Several men walked down to watch her work, standing respectfully behind her, craning their necks to see her delicate hands at work on the paper, watching the city take shape on the page. If she minded their presence her work did not slow or falter, nor did she say anything. Her concentration on her task was total.

Mark, Dorf, Jim, John, and Wade made their way up the center steps to the building with nine openings, carefully going inside. Each doorway measured nine feet wide and seven feet high. Square columns separated the doors to a vast, open space inside, interspaced with columns for support. This was, they discovered, a barracks for soldiers. On either side of the openings, sleeping quarters with rotting rope hammocks stood empty and silent, like waiting tombs. Weapons were carefully stacked at the far wall.

Weapons, modern or ancient, always seemed to fascinate soldiers. Spears made with kiln-dried hafts and sharpened stone heads were set upright in wooden racks, easily pulled free. Wooden shields with long rotted hides stretched across them were neatly placed behind the spears. At one time, the hides had been painted bright colors depicting various animals, fish, and birds.

All their bows were small, and the strings snapped, leaving them in disarray as they sprang apart. On the other hand, the arrows were well made with tips that had been sharpened in a fire, chipping off the pieces until they were razor sharp. Fletchings were rotted away, so none of them were balanced. Because of the arrows' length and the bows' span, the soldiers decided these people got very close to whatever they were hunting, mute testimony to their skills.

Pottery and some carved jade pieces were everywhere. Moving around the city on the third level, they discovered three more military barracks with similar weapons and artifacts. Each barracks appeared to have a central theme animal carved into the pillars that spanned the entrance. They laughed at the last, the image of a tortoise still visible. Most of the other central themes had been built around predators of one kind or another.

"I don't know," Jim said pensively. "The tortoise was strong and fortified and didn't have many natural enemies once it reached maturity."

"I just hope they weren't as slow as their namesake," Mark snickered. "Judging from some of the artwork, I'd say some of those soldiers looked like a tortoise." He was speaking of a pottery figure they'd discovered in one of the rooms depicting a soldier with a spear, bow over his shoulder, a quiver of arrows at his belt, and a rotund frame on which to hang it all.

"Yes, well!" Jim laughed with the rest. "That was a stout fellow, for sure. Perhaps the soldiers didn't have to work as hard as others, or they thought the size would give them an advantage."

They returned to the second level at lunchtime to eat with the rest of the explorers and hear what Dr. Gregg had deciphered thus far. He was excited, they could see, as they approached, gesturing to his students and talking too fast for them to keep up. His dialogue cut off as he spotted Jim, and he gestured wildly for Jim to come closer.

"Jim! We were wrong!" were the first words he said, and grabbing Jim's sleeve, he pulled the bemused Captain over to the group.

"I assumed, as did everyone who heard the stories, that this city was built to protect the treasures and history from Spanish conquerors. The Zapotec, Olmec, and Teotihuacán civilizations banded together and defeated the El Tajin people. Fearing they were next, the Mayan people chose leaders among them, all from the temple priests, to rule over them and protect them from this threat.

"From among them, one rose as the ultimate ruler, and we saw his picture on the stelae along the rivers. He sent this delegation to build this city and house their most valuable treasures and artifacts. He sent four units of temple guards, all commanded by men completely loyal to him. He also enslaved and sent six entire villages as workers and promised to send stores of food each season while the building went on. Men, women, and children from those villages were forced to leave everything and travel here! That was the reason for the stelae. Many perished on the journey, especially the children, and it seems Malaria was rampant among those who made the trip here."

CHAPTER 26

"I T T O O K F I F T Y - S I X years to finish this project, and during that time, mule trains traveled back and forth, bringing food, treasures, books, maps, fresh people to work on the city, tools, and engineers. Here, the priests had a stranglehold on the people, who were treated as slaves. When the city was finished, they were all put to death: men, women, and male children. The young females were made slaves of the priests and served in the temple in fertilization rites, I imagine.

"No one was allowed to visit this city unless sent by the rulers of the Mayans. The last stela, the smallest one, records that no visitors came to the city for ten years. Those who traveled outside the caves encountered savages and cannibals, fearsome warriors who took drastic tolls on their soldiers.

"Eventually, fearing that all their people were dead, the high priest ordered everyone out of the city to return to the Mayan city of Piedras Negras, near the Usumacinta River in Guatemala, I believe. According to the last stela, they found the city deserted, and none of their people lived there. Disheartened, they returned to the hidden city.

"A pestilence wiped out most of them on the way back, and only twelve men survived to return to the city. The last survivor recorded this stela! He claims we will find his bones in the temple, where he chooses to die beneath the stern eye of his favorite god," he paused to take a breath and gather his thoughts. Barbara asked a question.

"Why was Piedras Negras deserted, I wonder?"

"Ah ha!" Dr. Gregg said, his agile mind fixing on the question. "There are many theories about that. Between A.D. 800 and 900, great cities of the central area were deserted and abandoned; no more stelae were erected; buildings were left uncompleted. Some think soil exhaustion, pestilence, and grass spread over arable land produced a turf that the Mayans could not break up with their digging sticks. I think that's just a bunch of balderdash!

"Others suggest they moved away to new homes in the north, such as the Yucatán. Even an average historian and archaeologist can raise serious objections to such dribble. There is a fair body of supporting evidence that the common people revolted and massacred or drove out the ruling caste and that, lacking leadership, the peasant communities under their village headmen reverted to the simple life of farmers.

"Architecture, sculptural art, astronomy, hieroglyphic writing, and mathematics, which had never been part of their lives, died when the priest-rulers were thrown out or killed. I'm sure they kept up the simpler ceremonies in the great cities, but forest and time destroyed the untended buildings one by one. Simple peasant life continued on a reduced scale until it was swept away by disease.

"The Spanish certainly brought in smallpox, malaria, and hookworm. It's no wonder these people were swept away by time and disease," he said, his eyes filled with sadness for a lost civilization. "Discovery is often a violent and invasive act," his voice when he added the last was matter-of-fact.

"What else did you glean from the stelae you've looked at?" Jim asked quietly into the pause.

"Jim!" Dr. Gregg's eyes lit up as he spoke. "There's a reference on one of the larger stones of ships bringing these people from afar! They used stars to guide them!"

"Well, that's interesting!" Jim mused. "Do they say where they came from?"

"No, but their cities suggest they might have come from Babylon or Egypt. I believe it was Babylon because of the type of buildings," Dr. Gregg replied. His mind was again racing. "I've had photographs taken of all the stelae; we'll decipher them. Perhaps they hold the clue to that long-debated question. A panel from the Carnegie Institution of Washington, Peabody Museum of Harvard University, Chicago University, and Tulane University are working on some indications from a new city some oil explorers unearthed a few years back. It's definitely Mayan, and also of the Classic Period, so the stelae are important since they record some of the Formative Period history."

"So, now that we've learned that much let's eat lunch and then rest for a bit before tackling the temple!" John interjected. His stomach was rumbling with hunger. "After some good grub, I'll be ready to start on the work at hand," he added.

"What good grub?" Smitty asked. "We're eating MREs!"

"Of course, of course!" Dr. Gregg said with expansive gestures. He waved them on toward the packs.

Later, Mark looked at the steps leading up to the temple. Each step had thirteen blocks interlocked together, each a span high (six inches) and a cubit in width and depth (eighteen inches). That made the steps nineteen and a half feet wide. Thinking about the number, he began at the far left and, using his pole, tested each step to the right of the one he stood on, making his way thirteen steps to the right.

Repeating this process he now went to his left thirteen steps. Thirteen levels of heaven, thirteen steps, thirteen levels up. The third tier was not arranged this way. The step to the right sent darts in front of his face. Two steps over collapsed a large hole. The step next to him was safe, so he tried the next, and so on, until he was back on the right side. Now, the step above him was safe, but not the one a level up and to the left. Following a hunch, he tried the next step and found it safe. Thirteen steps later, he had to walk back to the left side of the steps to begin the zigzag pattern all over again. He felt he was beginning to understand the mind of the builders.

That pattern continued up fifteen times until the last three steps, which appeared normal. He didn't test them all, but made his way up, with Dorf marking the steps, as the others followed slowly behind. Three openings with square columns, much like the barracks, faced him, and inside, he could see the altar and the walls carved into figures and glyphs.

Dr. Gregg, who stepped up beside him, looked through the openings with interest. Dates were recorded on the walls, reckoned from a starting point nearly four thousand years earlier, together with information on the moon's age and calculations to show the difference between the Maya formal year and the true length of the year. He scanned through the now familiar glyphs intricately carved into the wall plaster.

Sprawled on the floor, beneath one of the carvings of one of the four gods, lay a skeleton, a tattered breach cloth its only attire.

Dr. Gregg would have run into the temple had Mark not physically constrained him.

"Wait! There may be traps, Doc!" Mark warned, holding him back.

Using his pole again, Mark tested the floor. It was smooth plaster and showed no joints. Not four feet into the temple, his pole went through the plaster. Poking around, he discovered a six-foot square section of the floor where plaster had been laid on thin branches and leaves to form a false floor. This time, it was not a trap but an opening that led down to the temple's lower floors. Still, a man falling through might have been seriously injured falling down the stone steps. They all studied the narrow steps and wondered why they had been hidden.

Mark, Dorf, and Jim explored the lower temple floors while Dr. Gregg and the rest waited. The former read the glyphs on the walls, deciphering what he could and photographing what he would have to work through. No one was bored since he talked his way through almost every process.

Beneath the temple were nine layers or stories, each nine feet on the outside. Inside, they barely measured six feet six inches, and Dorf had to hunch over to keep from bumping his head on the ceilings. It was uncomfortable, but he was too interested in their discoveries to complain or even take much notice of the discomfort. Mark teased him often by stretching his arms over his head with ease.

Stelae lined the walls of the first layer they explored. Some along one wall were blank, but all the rest were carved, each six feet in height, set on a base so that one could walk around the stone and read each side. Mayan hieroglyphic writing covered many of them; some seemed to be monuments to a god or priest leader. Still others appeared to be a historical record of the abundant animal life.

Unable to read the stelae, they still looked them over carefully, drawn to study them because of their irrepressible desire to know more about this strange culture. One section had recognizable images carved into the plaster covering the upright stone shafts. Accurate drawings of plants were clearly decipherable. Maize, cotton, beans, squash, chili, avocado, papaya, banana, pear, and cacao, the source of chocolate, were all given a place of prominence on the stelae.

Without which civilization is impossible, agriculture appeared to be fully developed at this site, as at most other centers. Later, they would learn that the few remaining priests and soldiers who made it back knew nothing of farming, a task allocated to the slave classes or peons. Many civilizations were like that, considering the growing of food beneath them, until there were no farmers to grow food. The last years were hard years for them, forced to hunt for wild food and constantly being hunted by the cannibals roaming the area.

Making their way down the steps to the next level, they paused in the steady flickering light of the oil fire to stare in wonder. Gems and precious stones filled pots, once brightly painted, now dull and worn by years of moisture. Uncut diamonds, rubies, emeralds, garnet, amazonite, tourmaline, turquoise, chalcedony, and jade filled every available space. Along another wall, all the pots were filled with opal. Sapphire, aquamarine, and spinel occupied another wall. Each pot was carefully placed, some on the floor and some on a stone counter above.

"Holy Mary, Mother of God!" Wade breathed, his Catholic heritage giving vent to a statement of awe.

"Yipes!" Jim breathed, picking up a handful of opals.

"Too bad we don't get to keep all this," Mark said, picking up a handful of dull diamonds and letting them fall back in the bucket.

"I think it would be appropriate for each of us to carry off two or three of these precious stones or gems as a finder's fee," Dorf said quietly.

"Just two or three?" Mark asked, holding a handful.

"Only on one trip!" Jim said with a grin. "I think the Brazilian government will want to hoard all this."

"How right you are!" Dorf grinned.

On the next floor, refined gold, molded into ingots, was stacked against one wall, while silver ingots of the same size were stacked along the opposite wall. Where the silver came from was a mystery, for none in the caves led to this city. Jim guessed that the silver had been carried here. Unrefined nuggets of both metals filled pots on the other two walls. Jim held one of the gold ingots and studied it.

"I think this is one palm wide and a span in length, or about three inches by six inches." He said, putting the ingot back on the stack. The ingots were about two inches thick and heavy. No carvings on the precious metal marred the beautiful soft surface.

"Maybe we should offer to buy this land and the mineral rights from the Brazilian government before we announce our discoveries!" Dorf said with a grin. He was joking, of course. No such option would be open once news of the discovery reached the outside world.

"I'm going to ask for a one percent finder's fee," Jim said thoughtfully. "I imagine the Brazilian government would accept that figure easily."

"There are literally billions of dollars worth of treasures here!" Mark breathed. "Treasure hunters eat your hearts out!" he added. He grinned as he looked around at his friends.

Moving down, they encountered a room full of books and, on the next level, pottery figures, almost full-sized, probably of priest leaders. Next, they came to intricate gold and silver carvings and amazing jewelry.

Another level was filled with skulls, stacked neatly along the walls from floor to ceiling. None of the skulls had the lower jawbone, and no other bones were visible. Finally, they came to the burial chambers, where the bones rested in niches carved into the wall and then on wooden biers in front of the niches.

Recording the finds, using photos and drawings, and cataloging most of their discoveries took time. At least, with the flames burning in the cavern, it wasn't dark enough to weigh so heavily upon them. Twice a day, they rested; on Sundays, they worshiped together and relaxed. Many, in small groups, walked about the city to view everything at least once before they left.

Fourteen days later, a tired but satisfied team marched out of the caves and into the hot jungle air. Above ground, they were able to contact the riverboats to report a successful completion of their mission. Jim consented to allow each explorer five precious stones of their choice, and he assigned John and Wade the task of choosing five for each crew still at the boats. Returning to the rigid raider airfoils and then going downriver to the riverboats seemed to take less time than expected.

After long showers, changing into clean clothing, and eating a dinner cooked by Abe in celebration of their safe return, the team slept like the dead, most resting until late morning before rising. In the afternoon, their CH-53D Sea Stallion appeared in the sky and landed in the river. At the controls, a crew of Air Force personnel sighed with pleasure as they switched everything off and exited the craft. Flying that aircraft had been an amazing journey for men who were used to military aircraft and lacked comfort. This helicopter was the most comfortable they'd flown.

"Well, howdy!" A man about six feet four inches tall, barrel-chested, and wearing the silver eagles that marked him as a full colonel greeted them. "I'm Tom Reynolds, your confused and somewhat concerned Air Force Colonel."

"I'm Jim Shepherd, Colonel. Why confused and concerned?"

"Some Admiral rousted my boss, a three-star puke, who stirred my bones up from a well-deserved rest and ordered me to fly this floating tub halfway across South America. On the way, I stopped at some village and dropped medical and staple supplies for some Red Cross and missionary types who seemed very worried about your group. I was told not to come back without you! Who the heck are you guys, and how do you rate an Admiral pulling strings for you?" he added.

"Well, Tom, we're a deep sea salvage, search, and rescue operation, strictly non-military, escorting the good Dr. Alistair Gregg and his researchers in search of a hidden Mayan city filled with amazing treasures. I'm guessing that the Admiral, whoever he is, sees an opportunity to kiss up to some Brazilian dignitaries and, through our discovery, bully them into something he wants. That would be my guess," Jim replied.

Tom threw his head back and laughed. "I know who you are. You were a SEAL Team Captain once upon a time. Everyone calls me Reynold's Wrap, by the way. Did you really find an amazing treasure?" he added.

"A treasure beyond your imagination!" Dr. Gregg said, rocking back and forth on his heels, his thumbs thrust into his belt. "We found a hidden city, deep in a cave, filled with enough treasure to have the Captains of the Spanish armada crapping in their coffins right now! I certainly think I hear a few of them trying to claw their way out, outraged that they missed this chance!" he laughed at the thought.

"So there's no danger of being shot at? We're not going into battle?" Reynolds asked.

"We did have trouble with one of the tribes, but I doubt they will return for more," Jim assured him. "This is an easy one. You fly these researchers to the city and then transport everything to Buenaventura, where a ship will be waiting."

"Heavy work, I take it," Tom said, glancing back at the six John Deere four-wheel drive farm RVs. They were brand new and would take the brunt of moving things from the city to the exit. A motorized light but strong conveyor belt stacked in pieces would take everything from the bottom to the chopper.

"Gold does tend to weigh a great deal," Jim said nonchalantly. "One favor though, Colonel," Jim added. "Don't let your crew touch anything Dr. Gregg doesn't approve. Ferenc, Heidi! Front and center, please!" he called.

They came forward, showed the Colonel their wounds, and explained how they got them. Both scars were still ugly enough to make the point. He listened with mounting interest and decided that as unusual as this trip might be, it would be fun. Opportunities like this came along a few times in a soldier's career, and he decided he'd pulled a lucky assignment this time. He grinned at Jim.

"This is the Air Force, not the Marines. I don't know how good they are at obeying orders. I'll ask them, though," he said.

Air Force pilots had saved his life on more than one occasion, and Jim knew they were disciplined troops. Still, he laughed with Reynolds. This easy-going banter was only used by commanders who had full confidence in their people. Jim guessed the Colonel kept tight control over his crew, and they respected him as much as he respected them.

Looking critically at the crew with Colonel Reynolds, Jim decided they were a top-notch bunch with a great deal of experience behind them. He liked what he saw and greeted each crewmember warmly, thanking them for their help. Some of them knew who he was or had been in the service. To be honored in such a way by Captain Shepherd was heady stuff to them, though Jim would have been surprised to know it.

CHAPTER 27

"I'M WONDERING, CAPTAIN, why you are not accompanying us to the city to retrieve the treasures," Reynolds said the next morning. He was picking his teeth after a sumptuous breakfast buffet.

"I'm doing a favor for the Admiral, Tom. I can't say what it is. Our military can't perform certain duties. Occasionally, the Admiral asks my team to look into something for him," Jim replied carefully.

"Ah!" Tom said with a world of understanding in his tone. "If it's druggies, give 'em hell," he added, winking at Jim, his voice barely above a whisper. "We never saw you leave, and we didn't know you were not with us!" he added with another wink. "You know how flyboys never see anything while on the ground!" he laughed.

"I know you guys are used to keeping quiet about things. Thanks for not mentioning the fact that we weren't around to help load the artifacts and treasures," Jim said after a moment of thought.

"Tell me about it sometime. If anybody asks, you were all here helping," Reynolds commented, shaking hands and walking away. Jim watched him, sad that he would never be able to diverge what actually happened on this mission and grateful that Reynolds would understand.

Once the helicopter was away, Jim got his team on the riverboat. Running silently, they traveled down the Purui and then turned upriver on the Japurá. Once on the Japurá, they traveled by night, slipping silently and unnoticed to the Columbian border. An inlet provided adequate cover for them to remain unseen from the river, and from there, they began covert thrusts up the Caquetä.

Every man realized that he was now in deadly danger. In enemy territory, a covert force that any government did not recognize because it didn't exist on paper would have no backup, no air patrol to keep it out of trouble or provide cover for a quick retreat. This river was deadly because it was patrolled by an aggressive force that employed a military solution to any intruders, determined to keep people away. And yet, each man on the team accepted that risk. There was a job to be done, and Omega Force accepted it, embraced it, and knew it was the right thing to do.

Jim took John, Wade, and Sean on the first recon across the border. Satellite photos, provided by Zeke, showed a patrol boat cruising the river and patrols camped along the way. Master Chief Warner and Inchworm exchanged the airfoils for the quieter 290-horsepower outboard motor. It was equipped to run quietly, using a noise suppression system that allowed it to creep within thirty feet of an enemy without being detected. Now that they were in harm's way, they needed every advantage.

The Rigid Raider had a range of two hundred and thirty miles and could move at a steady speed of thirty-six knots for a quick thrust at an enemy or a speedy retreat. John was at the wheel, and the boat was moving at a steady twenty knots toward the estimated position where they would intercept the river patrol.

An old hand at this kind of reconnaissance, John kept the Rigid Raider close to the shore, giving them ample time to make a run for cover if necessary. He kept his eyes on the river in front and on the shore, leaving the search for the patrol to Jim in the bow. With binoculars pressed to his eyes, he scanned the river ahead.

Afternoon faded into evening and then into night, the transitions from light to shadow to darkness, each presenting unique challenges to reconnoitering. Switching to NV after dark, Jim continued his relentless sweep of the river ahead, rewarded at last by the running lights flaring in his vision.

"Enemy patrol about two hundred yards and closing," he whispered into his headset. "Let's get under cover and assess our options," he put his eyes back to the binoculars and studied the boat approaching.

"Acknowledged," John replied, turning the boat to the shore and slipping under some overhanging branches of a giant willow. He slowed to a stop perfectly, leaving the engine idling for their next move. Constant practice gave them the edge they needed, and John's maneuver had been flawless.

Silently, the four men watched the patrol boat approach. It was a wooden boat that looked like it might have been on the river since before World War II. Six men could be seen, five sitting together around a small table playing cards and a sixth at the wheel. Careless and bored, the men smoked cigarettes, drank beer from clear bottles, and spoke animatedly amongst themselves.

They spoke Spanish, and Jim recognized their accent and colloquialisms as Columbian. Sean, who spoke Spanish fluently but didn't know about the local speech patterns, made a mental note. Next time, he would recognize a Columbian speaking. Military training in intelligence taught men to listen carefully to such things so they could fit in and pass as natives. By the end of this mission, Sean knew he would be able to do just that.

Sounding like a native Columbian, Jim yelled across the water, berating the men for their noise and telling them in no uncertain terms to shut their mouths. As expected, the boat turned and headed toward the sound of his voice. Carefully, he lifted his Mossberg 590 Tactical shotgun, moving his finger to the safety to be sure it was in the off position, and waited. They were using the beanbag shots again to take these men alive.

One of them began asking where he was, and Jim taunted him, much like a native of Columbia would. Machismo was essential to these people, and none wanted to lose face. Curses and taunts were exchanged until, suddenly, four shotguns opened fire. Wade and Sean were assigned the second shots. Wade took out his man, then turned the shotgun on the pilot, putting him down as he was reaching for his pistol. Sean hit both of his men in the forehead, knocking them unconscious. No shots were fired from the patrol boat.

John gunned the motor to get out of the way, reversing as the patrol boat unchecked rammed the willow's roots. Sean leaped over the patrol boat's gunwale with practiced ease and cut the engine. He hurried forward to check for damage. The old boat was made sturdily, and he could detect no leaks. Inside the boat, it was a mess, obviously not respected by its passengers. Wrinkling his nose at the smell from the men on the boat, he joined his team.

John and Wade began trussing their prisoners with plastic restraint ties while Jim stood guard, ready to send a prisoner into oblivion if one moved. None did. Once all six were securely tied, Wade tossed them across to the Rigid Raider. John was back in the boat but didn't try to catch any of the bodies. He made sure none rolled into the water or damaged any of their equipment, but other than that caution, let them take their lumps as they landed. They would wake up bruised and sore.

Towing the patrol boat behind them, they returned to the riverboat. When the river patrol began to stir, Sean held a plastic mask to their nose and mouth, effectively anesthetizing them. Some tried to struggle, but the drug worked fast. There was absolute terror in their eyes as they lost consciousness. This particular anesthetic was useful because when a patient began to awaken, he would answer questions without knowing what he was doing.

Sean monitored their return to conscience while other team members questioned the men individually. Preparing the questions ahead of time, each man knew what to ask, and once the patrol came fully awake, they compared their answers. It was clear that nearly two hundred soldiers were employed in the compound, training regularly, often going out on jobs for cartel members. They were an efficient army for that part of the country. None of these men, however, would survive boot camp or make it into the American military if the prisoners were any indication of their worth. With plenty of machismo but little motivation and almost no discipline, the latter made them lazy and careless.

Zeke entered Jim's office with a crisp knock and a smart salute. He held a piece of computer paper in his hand, which he immediately referred to.

"I intercepted a message to the patrol boat. When they didn't respond, whoever was talking said he was sending a platoon to check out what happened."

"He actually gave that away?" Jim's voice was incredulous.

"He gave away names, locations, and radio frequencies," Zeke announced with a grin. "They're lambs in the woods, Shep," he added with a grin.

"Better for us." Jim agreed. He thought about it and decided that although these men trained as soldiers and fought occasionally, they were not called upon to fight serious troops. They didn't see the dangers or feel the need to train any more than for what they faced. It was a grave mistake that would, in the end, cost them. That was all to the good, as far as he was concerned, because it ensured his team had advantages, and every advantage was valuable, especially against overwhelming odds.

On the other hand, he did not underestimate his adversary. Every good soldier learned to expect the unexpected, train for any and every possibility, and plan for contingencies. Adaptability in the field was paramount to survival. Jim was part of a group of sixteen men that he was responsible for protecting.

Long before the platoon strength unit arrived, Jim and his Team arranged the patrol boat artistically. Finding a rock to bash in the hull was child's play, running at it at full speed and then letting the boat drift and sink even easier. They ensured the craft sank in shallow enough water for the searchers to find it. Jim's team stripped the boat of all weapons as though the men had gone ashore and were trying to make their way back. Dorf even arranged a few false tracks in the mud near the sunken boat to make it look like men had stepped ashore there, using shoes taken from the prisoners. Looking at his work, he studied it carefully and then nodded. It was sufficient.

All that remained now was waiting for the platoon-strength unit to arrive. He wanted to see what this group of soldiers considered platoon strength. A platoon was usually a group of sixty or more soldiers under a lieutenant. Companies were generally divided into two platoons. Depending on the type of unit and its purpose, company strength differed in numbers.

Jim kept his men hidden very well along the river, keeping watch. Using satellite imagery to aid them, Zeke decided that six boats of ten men were coming down the river to investigate. Their riverboats were no newer or better than the one captured. Some of them were in even worse condition, obviously not well maintained. That was something else a wise military leader would never allow.

As he guessed, a lieutenant led this platoon of sixty men. He divided them into twelve squads, and after discovering the boat, he set the squads to track the lost men. Alone in one of the boats, the lieutenant radioed the base with the news of discovering the boat wrecked along the shore. He also reported that the men were on foot and attempting to return to the base. Zeke, of course, listened to the radio transmission as a matter of course.

Stomping through the jungle, smoking, and talking constantly, the squads did not attempt to travel off the trail or deeper into the jungle. Nor did they expend much energy in their search. No groups split off and went into the actual jungle growth away from the river. An hour into their trek up the trail, they turned around and headed back together, still making enough noise for an entire company. They would have been easy prey for an ambush.

There was a heated debate on locating the missing men, and finally, the lieutenant ordered the men back on their boats, and they all headed up the river, calling out from time to time to try to attract the lost unit's attention. Jim and his men watched them go with hard, flat eyes. Had they lost a unit of any kind, they would have scoured the area until they either found them or decided they had been captured or killed. American soldiers were firm believers in leaving no man behind. Also, the lieutenant had chosen the easiest solution, which was not guaranteed success. Officers like that didn't deserve to lead men!

No military unit worth its salt liked losing or leaving people behind. Every effort was made to find them when they were shot down or lost. That was one of the things that gave every soldier hope. He knew his fellow soldiers would be out there, risking their lives, looking. And he knew they wouldn't stop looking until he was found and returned safely or his body recovered and returned respectfully. Silently, Jim's team moved out of the jungle and back to their riverboats.

A radio call brought the CH-53D away from moving cargo from the hidden city to pick up the six terrorists. They would be questioned by Navy Intelligence personnel and then released to their government for prosecution. Admiral Runion would get any critical information out of them before he released them. Of that, Jim was confident.

He gathered his men together for one last planning session. After looking at the latest Satellite feeds, they discussed their options and the plan for infiltrating the terrorist base and extracting any information. Covering the actions they might need to take took the most time as they assessed what they might discover. As the men talked, Jim looked them over, noting how they had changed.

Their jungle trek to the hidden city had hardened them if that were possible, and they now moved through the jungle as a part of it. Using the natural cover, they even changed the way they camouflaged their faces, using more greens and browns and less black. Jungle heat was accepted stoically, and to fight against the smell, they used extra deodorant and washed three times a day when possible. Enemies had noses, and every soldier knew that he endangered not only himself but also others if detected.

When everything had been discussed and memorized, the team sat back quietly around the tables, looking at each other soberly.

This was the most dangerous mission they had been on since leaving the military. They would be on their own, and returning to the riverboat was a deadly and perilous journey. Some of them could be wounded, and the chance that some might not return was very real. Yet Jim knew, as he knew inside his heart, that all of these men would give his all for the team. He was proud of them and told them so before dismissing them for their last night's sleep in air-conditioned comfort.

CHAPTER 28

JIM KNEW THAT the enemy thought their patrol had been careless, and that was why their boat sank. Whoever was in charge knew that the river must be guarded against intruders and, as a result, left three squads of twelve men behind. One squad patrolled the river by boat while the other two took up positions on either side of the river at established camps.

Getting the raiders past those patrols would take careful planning. Ox came up with the master plan. He suggested it at breakfast the following day as they discussed their options. Although his plan contained risk, it was a calculated risk, and the men all thought it was worth the effort. Jim nodded when he raised a hand, still holding his fork.

"Hey, boss!" he said, around a mouthful of sausage. "We don't want this patrol to disappear, right?" he asked.

"That's correct," Jim replied, dipping his fork into scrambled eggs. "But then we have to deal with them on the way back," Ox replied.

"Yes. But no alert will be given if they don't know we've passed them.

We can deal with them as necessary on the way out," Jim said.

"Okay. That makes sense," Ox replied after a moment of thought. "So why don't we use the night to our advantage?" he asked. Without waiting, he continued. "If we can neutralize the patrol boat, we can slip by the camps at night without them spotting us. Should be easy enough!"

"I take it you have an idea?" Jim asked, chewing thoughtfully.

"It would be child's play to put the blokes asleep on the patrol boat," Ox commented. "We've done it once or twice. They wake up and think nothing of it if it's done right."

"What's to keep them from returning upriver and finding us?" Jim asked. He was curious now. He also trusted this interesting Australian and was sure the answer would be good.

"Timing," Ox replied with a grin. "They always stop for a snack about mid-afternoon and eat dinner around eight in the evening. When they stop for their snack, everyone leaves the bloody boat to relieve himself in the bush. Being the proper wallies they are, they don't even dig a latrine. While they're busy with that, we slip in, doctor up dinner, and presto! Bob's your uncle! They're in a world of Barney!"

"So we follow them on the river trail, wait until they head into the bush, and do the deed!" Jim said. "I'm impressed, Ox. I like it."

Ox accepted the mission and took Lee Roy, Chance, and Phillip. Watching the patrol boat from the satellite feed, Zeke picked the drop-off point, and Smitty operated the Inertial Guidance System. No sooner had Captain Rob turned a bend in the river than the patrol boat appeared. Smitty put on speed, quickly outrunning the patrol boat's five-knot pace, and was safely around the next bend before there was danger of discovery.

On the jungle trail, Ox and his men kept pace with the patrol boat, running behind at a distance of about thirty yards, keeping it in sight and maintaining their cover without much difficulty. Watching the patrol, Ox realized that someone looked to either side about once an hour, and only briefly, before returning to the card, dominoes, or dice game going on at the time. Dominoes seemed to be the game the men enjoyed the most. That they played games while on patrol was to his advantage and proved once more that these were not professional soldiers.

Lazy sods! These buggers deserve to get a Mickey Finn slipped into their dinner. Despite the lack of danger, he didn't allow his men to become careless. That was how men got killed. Carelessness could never be tolerated in a soldier, and his men maintained discipline without comment. They were in great shape, used to the jungle now, and paced the boat easily, working up a sweat that helped to cool them down as they trotted along.

No one snapped a twig or made a noise that could be heard more than five feet away. Ox was proud of his boys and their skills. Lee Roy had the rear guard, and he kept his attention on the back trail, the river behind them, and the trail he followed. His job was to be sure no one crept up behind them. Ox had point, while Chance and PU followed about five to six yards behind.

CHAPTER 29

As predicted, the patrol boat pulled into the shore, where the men could step off the boat onto dry land. Multiple keel scrapes in the mud indicated this spot was used often, another indication that the men were careless. Jim would never allow them to stop in the same place for such an activity, and he would post a guard at the boat and the latrine. Hess troops didn't leave a guard with the ship or send out a point man to be sure all was safe for the rest of the unit. They had been drinking their local beer and needed to hurry into the bush. Ox slipped into their boat almost before the last man disappeared, splashed the liquid he'd chosen for the job over their slowly cooking refried beans, and was back up the trail before the first man came back, still zipping up his pants.

A man looked foolish that way, both his hands engaged, and Ox thought about taking him down for a moment. He discarded the thought quickly and shook his head ruefully. Somewhere in their training, the SAS had drilled into him the importance of keeping one hand on your weapon at all times and learning to zip up one-handed as well. He grinned at the thought. Being taken down at that precise moment would be embarrassing in the extreme!

As predicted, the patrol boat turned to go upriver at sunset, and Captain Rob came close enough for the four Aussies to leap aboard without slowing. Smitty let the IGS keep them at a safe distance, and the computer made the adjustments as necessary. The only change he made in the program was to get close enough to shore to pick up the four men. After that, he let the computer have the helm.

Zeke, sitting in the computer room, watched the maneuver with interest. Smitty, like Zeke, had been denied promotion in the Navy because they were smart enough to know what was necessary and bold enough to criticize their superiors when they didn't make the adjustments. Right now, the Navy had nothing like the guidance system Smitty had designed and Zeke programmed.

Using an E6B computer, usually found in aircraft, Omega, a radio navigation system that provides worldwide coverage from eight stations scattered around the globe, radar, and radio beacons (200 transmitting for marine use), was not enough for Smitty. He included VOR (VHF Omni directional range), laser gyro, compass, and GPS. The system was so accurate that it could guide a ship or boat to within inches of its target. Because the Navy hadn't had enough screw-ups with GPS, they refused to entertain Smitty's idea. Their loss!

Within the program, Zeke included sonar and underwater radar indicators to adjust the program when necessary to avoid sunken logs, rocks, and sandbars. Also included in the program was every geodetic survey from the National Oceanic and Atmospheric Administration that produced charts for all navigable coastal waters. Most of those were in the U.S., Great Lakes, and U.S. possessions. Some, however, were of foreign waters.

Even then, Smitty checked and rechecked their position to be sure the program was operating correctly. Error was possible, even with the best-designed programs. Sunspots and other phenomena could throw off any program's parameters. Although Zeke wrote the program and designed the computer system to run it, he didn't trust it entirely either. Always check. That was why he said that Uncle Zeke was always watching. He was because he was constantly checking to be sure the system had it right. Trusting himself first was something he'd developed in his process years ago.

Their window for success was narrow. The men on the boat would be asleep in less than fifteen minutes. Any more would be suspicious. As sometimes happens when drivers fall asleep, the boat's pilot slowly drifted to his left, the first indication that the drug was working. Watching for that change, Smitty punched in the command to go to full throttle.

Silently, their riverboat swept past the sleeping crew. It was close, but the patrol boat missed the shore and continued straight across the river instead of making the left turn for the bend. Captain Rob was beyond the next bend, safely out of sight, when the boat ran aground with a thump, waking the pilot in surprise.

He cut the engine quickly and, to cover falling asleep, announced that he was going to the bathroom. Some of the other men woke up and followed suit. If anyone thought it odd, they had all fallen asleep; none said anything. Shaking his head, the pilot avoided drinking more beer for the rest of his patrol. It wouldn't do to have something happen while he slept!

Running silent now, Captain Rob opened up a safe lead before dropping speed again to match the speed of the patrol boat, which was now following. Unaware that an enemy lay before them, the bored crew continued their patrol without incident. Regular radio checks kept the camps ahead, unwary of an approaching enemy. All lights were extinguished now, and the Team lined the rails on either side of the boat, their NV glasses engaged, weapons at the ready. They were shadows among the shadows, and if deadly force were necessary, they would have the advantage of surprise. In many battles, surprise was the turning point and key to success.

Jim saw two guards on a floating dock. They were talking quietly and, better yet, had a lantern lit on the table between them. Both sat in canvas chairs, playing a game of cards. Every few minutes, one or the other would look out over the water, but Jim knew they could see very little. They were arranged in their chairs so that they could look up and down the river, and neither, while he observed, looked across at the other shore. In their minds, they probably thought that was unnecessary. That was not a mistake any of his men would make.

Any light ruined night vision because the eyes didn't adjust quickly enough to allow them to see far into the darkness. Jim knew they could not see his boat as it slid past. But they could see the light from the dock on the other side of the river, and if a guard looked up at just the right moment, he might catch the silhouette of the riverboat coming between his vision and the light across the river.

His right hand came up, two fingers straight up, the others folded down, to let the men know there were two guards and to watch them. He pointed to his eyes and then to the guards. On the other side of the boat, John was doing the same with his group lining the rails. Now they knelt, still as the shadows in the darkest corners of a deep cave, their eyes locked on their targets. A silenced weapon would put him down if a guard looked or attempted to raise an alarm.

Silently, Jim prayed that the guards would not look at the moment the boat slid between the two lights. He didn't want to engage the enemy needlessly, and if the alarm were raised, this platoon would have to be neutralized, and that meant death. Not aware he had been holding his breath, he let it out slowly and quietly, breathing thanks to God as they slid past the danger undetected.

Yet even now, the danger to his team has doubled, and Jim sits with his back to the rail for a few minutes, thinking about that. There were enemies behind them now, to cut off their escape, and people to watch who could, at any time, choose to head back to camp and discover the Bring It Up Team. With an inward sigh, he hoisted himself to his feet and made the appropriate motions to put the men on guard but more relaxed now that the first and most immediate danger was past.

Later, in Zeke's center, Jim studied the pictures of the soldiers on the computer screen. They wore Columbian military uniforms and insignia, but like many masquerading as soldiers, they didn't know how to match the insignia properly. That told Jim two things. These men were posing as official soldiers, but their training was incomplete. Complete training would make them indistinguishable from the real thing.

One other thing became clear to all the men on the boat. The real Columbian military had little to do with this particular geographic area. These men were operating here with a free hand and little fear of interference from actual government troops. Either Marta Hess and her father bribed the military to stay away, a genuine possibility, or they were bribing someone high enough in government to keep the military away.

CHAPTER 30

Late the next afternoon, the team spent several hours camouflaging the boat in a deep cut of the riverbank, where floodwaters had cleared away. Thorough in their work, the men labored silently and carefully so that when finished, the presence of a boat could not be detected from three feet away, either from the river, the riverbank, or the air.

Once finished with that task the men ate dinner and rested for a few hours until just after midnight. Once the bewitching hour had passed, they readied themselves for an insertion into enemy territory. Serious work required serious skills; Jim knew his teams had the skills. Training had prepared them for this moment and would, with God's grace and exemplary leadership, keep them alive to return. He was confident the training his men had was enough.

Once ashore, they spread out in the jungle away from the main trail, moving with amazing skill and almost absolute silence. Slowly, for that was the only way one moved through the jungle quietly, they made their way the final two miles to the enemy camp. Mark, who had a point, clicked his microphone twice and then once after a pause to call Jim to the front.

Cautiously, Jim approached, using the infrared flash of Mark's helmet to guide him. Every few seconds, Mark turned his head and uncovered the ultraviolet display that only NV glasses would register to guide his boss forward. Listening for Jim Shepherd was useless, so he used his night vision to locate and follow Jim to his position. It didn't do to be startled when you had point, and Jim had done that many times in Mark's past, appearing out of nowhere, suddenly and menacingly there. He didn't know how a man as solidly built as Jim could move so silently, but he appreciated the skill.

Jim parted the leaves slowly in front of his face to peer out at the perimeter of the enemy camp. It covered five acres of space, cleared from the heart of the jungle, about a mile from the river to keep it hidden from any river traffic. Jim had seen camps like it in other places in South America. Another five acres inland also cleared from the jungle, housed the pharmaceutical laboratories.

There were no perimeter guards around the military camp, but the pharmaceutical laboratories were heavily guarded by more than men. Jim could see some faint outlines of laser beam-triggering devices through his NV glasses. Heavy diesel generators provided electricity for the camp and laboratory. All four were housed in a small area between the two separate entities, inside four concrete block units that effectively deadened the sound.

Someone had taken a great deal of trouble to run a waterline from the river to the laboratory. Jim could hear water rushing through the plastic pipes no more than ten feet away from the waterline. Just before the water entered the laboratory compound, it met up with about an acre of filtration. The first half of the filtration system was pretty basic, but the second half made Jim's hair stand on end. It was the kind of filtration he'd seen on heavy water systems for nuclear purposes. This was unexpected. His mind discarded one idea after another, racing over the possibilities until he hit upon the one that made the most sense.

Inside one of those buildings was at least one nuclear reactor, probably used for laboratory purposes. It didn't require much to transform such devices into service for producing atomic weapons of mass destruction. Jim carefully looked at the trees around the compound and chose several, sending his men scurrying into the high branches.

Where had they found the funding to build such a devise, and who had approved it? Did the Columbian government understand what they had? Jim didn't like these thoughts and knew he had to destroy the lab and reactor. That would mean contamination by radiation. While he worked on his section of the platform, he thought furiously.

Wade, with the help of Master Chief Warner and Inchworm, manufactured a lightweight aluminum alloy platform base that could be erected high up in a tree. When properly bolted together, it provided a five-foot wide walkway around the tree. During their training, Wade had enjoyed testing them in the bayou, and Jim knew they were sturdy and dependable. Cutting fresh bamboo shoots from a grove nearby and small branches from the tree and intertwining them between the aluminum spokes gave a fairly sturdy platform from which two men could easily work.

Jim was amazed that the whole thing weighed less than four pounds. Some creative packing made room for several of the platforms, and by morning, sixteen men lay comfortably concealed by branches high above both camps. To be sure, Jim and Mark walked all the way around to the opposite side of the compounds and searched the trees carefully. Even knowing where the platforms were didn't help. Both men found themselves searching where they knew their men were before catching a slow movement to indicate they were looking in the right place.

Grinning from ear to ear, they returned and climbed into their respective trees. Jim loved trees, and climbing sixty-two feet into the air in this huge, venerable jungle denizen gave him a fantastic sense of climbing into the sky. It was almost as if this great old occupant of this particular spot in the jungle wished to share the wondrous vistas of nature's beauty from its branches with him. Patting the tree kindly, he climbed onto the platform through a trap door, closed it softly, and stretched out on his side of the tree.

John was on the opposite side. He'd been studying the compounds, but when Jim arrived, he put down his glasses and grinned at his brother.

"Some adventure, huh?" he whispered. "I watched you when I could spot either of you, which wasn't often. I knew where you'd be and that you had to get close enough to the clearing to look up. We're invisible up here, aren't we?"

"From everywhere but the air," Jim replied with an answering grin. "And I don't think we'd be spotted unless they hovered close enough to the tree to spot us. The branches above provide adequate cover if they stay above the trees. We need to be ready for that contingency, but I doubt it will crop up," he added.

"Okay, men!" Jim's voice suddenly sounded in every ear as he keyed his COMLINK. "Here's the drill. We study the compounds today. Sleep when you can, stay hydrated, and eat. Please use the emergency packs for urination," Jim could hear a light snicker from a nearby tree. The emergency packs were literally sacks of disposable diaper material you could pee into, seal, and dispose of later.

When one didn't want to leave any traces behind, the packs made sense. They sealed completely and kept any odor from escaping. Still, the men found them humorous, and Jim wondered what Cecilia would make of them or the men's reaction to them.

Every soldier understood the need to remain as still as possible and, when moving, to move with guarded, ultra-slow, exaggerated motions. Although he kept a sharp eye on his men, Jim didn't notice anything that he could criticize. His men were the best, and even the Aussies, in their short time with the unit, had become one with the group.

Sean lashed his hammock to some branches above his platform, artfully stuck large leaves in it, and was sound asleep. Jim saw him through his glasses, missing the configuration the first time, then coming back when he noticed the toe of a boot hanging over the edge. He grinned. No one from the ground would recognize what that hanging lump was.

Days of observation did not pass slowly. Everything that happened in the compounds was interesting, important, and noteworthy. Men scribbled on their notebooks, drew diagrams, took photographs, and watched for anything they might use later. No one was bored, and those who had to sleep did so because they knew the importance of sleep to soldiers, not because they were tired or even ready to rest.

All that training would come into play later that night when they infiltrated enemy territory. They knew the risks, but here, the risks were even higher. They were a paramilitary unit with no official recognition. If any were captured, they would have to depend upon the rest of the team to rescue them. If they were killed, that was it—game over. The men prayed that didn't happen.

Jim knew this and appreciated his men all the more because of their loyalty and commitment. He remembered a movie he saw once about an impossible mission force. Grinning, he remembered the handsome actor, flying off a motorcycle and shooting his pistol with accuracy, surviving the crashes and falls with all the panache of Hollywood grandeur. Sighing, he wished he could pull some of those stunts off in the real world.

But in the real world, shots were taken carefully and with as little movement as possible. Men didn't rush into danger or survive crashes. Fights were never drawn out but ended quickly in bloodshed. Every true soldier knew there was only one way to fight. One fought to kill quickly, instantly, lethally, or one died at the hands of an enemy.

Lunch came, but the watchfulness did not take a break. The men ate as they watched. Each soldier picked the MRE he liked best to pack, avoiding any he didn't appreciate. There was no need for that anymore. NASA food packs were also available, so every man enjoyed his lunch, even though Abe and his crew didn't prepare it. Keeping one's strength up was paramount to success.

Jim preferred fruits and liquids in this heat, downing the necessary salts, vitamins, and minerals his body craved. His canteen was filled with a sports drink full of electrolytes and tasty enough after years of drinking it. Once he had carefully cleaned up his wrappers, he returned to watching the laboratory compound. It was there they needed to spend most of their energy.

Like him, his men were weighing ideas on how to enter the facility safely and how to disable and destroy it. Every moment spent studying the guards' routines, and the placement of defenses would be used to make the plan most successful. Adaptation would be necessary, and several options would be mapped out carefully. This was second nature to him as he studied the compounds below.

In the early afternoon heat, Dorf and Sparks climbed down carefully and disappeared into the jungle. When they returned an hour later, both had satisfied looks on their faces, but Jim noted that the first thing they did upon returning was use wipes to clean their hands and arms carefully. He wondered what the two had been up to but decided to wait and see rather than ask. He turned his mind back to figuring out how to get into the compound.

CHAPTER 31

STEALING UNIFORMS MIGHT work for two of the team, but Jim discarded that idea. Mark and Jack could pull it off since both were under five foot nine inches in height. Jack was just by an inch but twenty pounds lighter than the muscular Mark. Like many men his size, he was easy to underestimate. Stringy muscle and whipcord actions made him a dangerous fighter. Anyone who went through Marine boot camp, Navy SEAL training, and Delta schooling was doubly dangerous. Both men would still appear different, leaner, tougher, something to give them away. Every soldier Jim saw in the camp below had extra weight and ill-defined muscles.

Jim knew that every one of his men, including himself, were killing machines in many ways, so well trained it seemed natural to take life. He was working through the ethics and morality of all that, even now, with his newfound faith. Still, he didn't regret the training or the skills. Tonight, they would need all their skills.

After midnight, Dorf took Team 1 into the military compound to neutralize the guards. Team 1 consisted of Dorf, Jack, Mark, and Bill Kline. Jim knew Mark would do most of the neutralizing because he was the most deadly and quietest of the four. Bill Kline was practically a ghost himself. Jack backed him up with a silenced Beretta M92F 9-mm pistol. Dorf backed Mark up with his favorite, an H&K Mark 23 .45 caliber, silenced and adjusted for his colossal hand and trigger finger.

Jim led Team 2, which included Zeke Kline, Frank Miller, and Smitty. Even though Zeke and Smitty were lighter on their feet than Jim, none of them had his panache for moving silently. His job was to neutralize the guards at the entrance to the laboratory compound. FM went with him, backed by their trusty seconds with silenced weapons. Guards could not be taken alive in this instance and were dispatched silently. Deadweight was lowered silently to the ground and hidden from sight.

John, Wade, C.G., and Vince were the Marine unit, or Team 3. Their job was to take out the electricity for about twenty minutes and make it look like a natural outage. All day, Wade had been working on his special tool, cleaning the jawbone of a panther and attaching it to his sheers for strength. The natural bite marks would pass muster for an accidental outage. Dorf and Sparks supplied the panther, one they saw on the way to the compound not long dead, and even planned to fry it with the severed cables if he could.

The Aussie team, Team 4, followed Sean. Lee Roy, Chance, and Phillip stayed close to Jim's Team as they crept into the compound under the cover of darkness. There was too much to risk by taking the guards alive. Jim regretted the action, but the lives of his men were too valuable for him to attempt it any other way. With sadness, he broke two necks and used his Ontario Navy Knife, sliding it silently into the base of the skull of another. In each instance, he lowered the dead body to the ground and carefully concealed it.

FM carried out his assignment with the same ferocity and deadly force, taking down three guards, one with a garrote, one with a sleeper hold followed by snapping the neck, and a third with a thrown Mini Tac knife that dropped a guard with no more sound than a soft sigh of death. He caught the guard before the body fell to the floor, lowered him into a natural sleeping position, and left him with little thought about what he'd done. Thinking about it never helped. That only made the dreams worse.

All the teams waited patiently for the Jarhead team to take out the power. It happened within seconds of their estimated time. Wade found the jaws worked great, piercing the thick vinyl coating of the wire harness in several places, even causing a few sparks. Then, he used his cutters to cut through the wires where they were particularly chewed. C.G. had the dead carcass hooked up, and it cooked nicely for about thirty seconds before the breakers went off. Smoke rose from the dead animal, and its jaws were now locked around one end of the wires.

Quickly cleaning up, the team vacated the area of the break and sought cover. Not long after, in a surprisingly orderly fashion, a crew of electricians and soldiers appeared with lights, following the heavy chords on the ground from the generators outward. They found the break almost immediately, reported it and even described the dead carcass. No guards raised the alarm, and Jim's teams slipped into the laboratory compound like so many shadows.

Apparently, timeliness wasn't enforced here. Jim expected them to have the electricity up and running in twenty minutes, twenty-five at the most. It took the team forty-three minutes to fix the main feed and get everything up again. As the security systems came on, they detected nothing out of the ordinary because the intruders were already inside.

Zeke worked quickly and silently at the central console for the laboratory compound's security system to identify, hack, and control all the systems. He accomplished his work in under twenty-four minutes using a remote battery energy source, and from a hand-held unit, he now easily controlled doors and security codes. As he did that, he also downloaded everything from the Hess mainframe onto a remote hard disk. With that evidence gathered, he carefully stored the disk in his pack. His last keystrokes would register once power was back on, but they would be a mystery to any techs.

It was all there. The formulae for the viruses, the potency predictions, predictions on the number of deaths, and the antidote. Even the plan of how they intended to infect every major city in the U.S., Canada, Western European countries, Israel, and South America was included. Zeke had it all, every bit of evidence. Jim had seen it, and the look in his eyes was one that Zeke knew well. He knew his own eyes reflected the same rage.

To cover his tracks effectively, he inserted what he called a "killer" algorithm that would defy anyone discovering what he had done without a complete reboot of the system, which would effectively destroy the system. All computers would have to be replaced, and all data would be completely lost because the virus ate information exponentially.

"This military unit belongs to Hess Pharmaceuticals," Zeke said quietly to Jim as they watched Sean work in the laboratory. "They're an enforcement group our old friend Mr. Van Poole put together. That means they're going to be a sadistic bunch. I thought you ought to know what we'll be up against."

"Jim!" Sean, looking angry, motioned for him to come forward. "This is the virus they released in the water! They've been working on making it more virile. This is one bad chemical weapon!" Jim looked at the canisters in the room, and his mind wrapped around the amount of destructive material already prepared.

Looking into the microscope Sean was motioning him to, Jim saw several strange cellular-shaped figures attacking something big and blue. The blue turned to black almost immediately, shriveled, and seemed to die.

"What was that?" Jim asked.

"That was a red blood cell. The white blood cells were killed before you had time to look," Sean said quietly, his eyes suddenly dark pools. "We're destroying this!" he added. "This could kill billions of people! What kind of sadistic person thinks this stuff up and then plans to use it?" Sean didn't expect an answer. He already knew it. People just like him, sinful and twisted, following after the prince and power that ruled the world of sin.

"How will we destroy it?" Jim asked quietly, looking around at the huge laboratory. They hadn't brought enough explosives, he was sure, and he berated himself for that oversight.

"A vacuum and then an intense rush of heat," Sean said, nodding emphatically. "We'll use the nuclear reactor to accommodate for the spatial disproportionality. That will destroy the reactor as well. My boys and I know what to do. Can you give us about eleven minutes?" Jim looked at him with appreciation, realizing that the Aussies were indeed an effective addition to the team as a whole. He nodded without giving it more than a second of thought.

"Go!" Jim ordered, slapping Sean softly on the shoulder as Sean turned to take his team off. He alerted the rest of the men and moved them safely out to the guard station, still blessedly quiet. Exactly eleven minutes later, Sean appeared out of the dark, and the team made their way expertly out of the compounds. Zeke, controlling the laser system, turned it off momentarily to allow them to pass undetected and then turned it back on.

Smitty took the lead now, taking them directly to the boat. According to Sean, they needed to be at least two miles away before the explosives detonated. The presence of the nuclear reactor was just too tempting, and he'd made sure the explosion would include the machine and wipe out most of the compound. Moving silently on the trail, still taking great care, with a point and a rear guard for extra protection, they hiked the three miles to the boat.

Alarms went off just as they reached the boat. The dead guards had finally been discovered. Jim looked at his watch. Four o'clock in the morning, the number 0400, gleaming in the darkness, told him it was time to go.

Clearing away the camouflage took half an hour, but no one chaffed or worried at the time. Slowly, quietly, the boat crept out onto the river, heading downriver and picking up speed. Radar and Satellite images showed nothing moving their way from the three twelve-man units downriver—not yet, at least. They would come once the trouble was spotted at the lab.

In the lab, Marta Hess saw at once that her computer security had been breached, and when her technicians could get no answers, she berated them. Continuing to work, they could not break through whatever was happening. Angrily, she ordered a reboot, only to scream in frustration when the entire system went down in a way that told the techs they were being destroyed, signifying that she would have to travel to the coast, get the new computers, and reprogram everything.

Realizing they had been infiltrated, she thought quickly and then called her soldiers together. No one had come by air because the radar would have picked that up, which meant they were in the jungle or on the river. She divided her forces into two units of equal strength and sent them up and down the river, looking for intruders.

By then, Jim's Team had camouflaged the boat again on the opposite side of the river and ferried everyone back across with one of the rigid raiders. Dorf and Mark hid the raider carefully and arrived back at the rendezvous before anyone discovered they were there. While doing that, Sean took advantage of the nearly empty compound and flipped the switches to detonate the explosives.

Even three miles away, the thump of the explosion was impressive. Followed by an eerie silence that lasted seconds, and then a strange roar that seemed to grow in intensity flowed out over the jungle. Jim and his men kept their eyes down, not looking at the red sky that told everything they needed to know. Marta Hess, who had been at the docks to see her soldiers off, looked in horror at the red cloud rising above her precious laboratory. Everything was ruined! And then the pressure hit them, tossing them to the ground and into the river like rag dolls in a tornado. Eighteen men died, most of them her scientific staff.

Crawling out of the river, she looked around at the carnage, at her men slowly getting to their feet, knowing that all of them were now contaminated. Her jaw tightened as she looked at the scientists and shook her head. Someone would pay!

"Get them!" she hissed, holding herself rigidly as she watched all her hard work burn away. All her research, all her records, everything was gone. She leaped suddenly into one of the boats heading upriver. She wanted to see these men caught and killed, and the west coast was closest. She expected them to go that way.

Meanwhile, Jim prepared for the troops moving toward them on the trail. For their first assault, they used claymores, carefully hidden in the bush just off the trail. Claymores were horrible devices, with thousands of steel balls hurled suddenly by explosives that could literally rip a man in half. Needing to discourage further assault, Jim planned to make his first warning one the men would have difficulty ignoring.

Marta Hess lost sixty-two men in those first eight blasts. Some of them died instantly, while others lay screaming on the jungle floor, missing arms, legs, half their bodies, bleeding out. Jim didn't expect the jungle creatures that suddenly appeared, drawn by the blood, panthers that dragged screaming men off into the jungle. Even crocodiles came up on the trail from the river and dragged bleeding victims into the water.

The carnage was horrible, and the troops broke and ran screaming, returning to the destroyed compound in moral disarray. Hearing the explosions and screams, Marta ordered her men to return immediately. When she learned what had happened, she wanted them to set out after the culprits immediately. Ashamed of their fear, especially in the presence of a woman, the men foolishly seized their machismo and set off down the trail in hot pursuit of the enemy.

All day, they marched until they finally reached the unit guarding downriver. No one had passed them on the river or in the jungle. Disappointed, they camped there and returned the next day to report.

Hating the need, Jim used the last of his claymores on the trail in the same place as before. As expected, the men marched into it, unaware that they were about to die. Thirty-three died in that explosion. From across the river, Jim watched in horror as the forces melted into the jungle and the dying screamed for help. Again, the crocodiles and panthers were there swiftly. Even a huge anaconda appeared to scoop up a man missing his right leg and half his right arm. It was horrific.

Again, hunting an invisible enemy, the troops finally gave up when darkness fell and returned to the ruins of their compound. Jim got his team moving, removing the camouflage once Mark returned from that side of the river to report that no sentries had been posted. Their riverboat coasted out into the river and silently slipped away. So far, they remained unknown, and Jim knew that would eat at the forces in the compound, for an unknown enemy was one to be feared.

Half her troops were dead, and all her work destroyed. Marta Hess could only gather a force of one hundred and twenty soldiers. Satellite photos showed them making their way cautiously down the jungle trails on either side of the river. Jim didn't want them making their way to populated areas.

"Snipers and flankin' maneuvers, boss?" FM asked quietly, looking at the photos. "Hit 'em quick and get out. Harass 'em all the way down the river to the border."

"Some of us could be killed doing that," Jim said quietly. It was a risk but a calculated one.

"Yeah? Well, we could get killed just takin' a leak in this jungle, boss," FM said with a grin.

"Okay," Jim said with a sigh. "Teams two and four on the south side of the river. One and three on this side. One sniper from each team, three to draw them forward, and three to hit them from the sides. We split and rendezvous at agreed points as soon as we do damage. John has command of the north side. I have command of the south. Make sure you stay under cover as much as possible and move quickly once you've hit the enemy. Let's not get killed out there, men! You know the drill. Stay close to your second! Move!"

C.G. and Vince were the snipers for the north side of the river trail. They were using the heavier Barrett M82A1 sniper rifles with 12.7-mm rounds. Each man could fire off ten rounds per minute and hit a target with each round.

FM and Lee Roy were on the south side, each with the lighter Accuracy International L96A1 firing a 7.62-mm round. They could fire ten rounds per minute and take ten targets down. At a thousand yards, they would be safe from enemy weapons' return fire.

Soon, the troops came into view, and eight men died, seeming to simply melt to the ground, the pops of the rifles a thousand yards away coming seconds after the bullets killed. As expected, the troops melted into the jungle and sought cover while the snipers left their positions and moved ahead to set up for the next round.

Just ahead, Colt M16A2 fire and H&K SA80 fire, set on three round bursts, put ten more men down. The troops broke cover to attack while the team shooters melted into the jungle. From the side, a barrage of fire came, deadly fire that mowed troops down by the dozens before suddenly growing silent.

Angry now, the men forged ahead, sure they were almost upon their enemies, only to have eight more men drop as snipers picked them off. Again, the tactics worked: a frontal attack killing more, a frenzied run at the enemy, and a flanking attack mowing them down. One hundred and eight of one hundred and twenty men were dead in less than four hours of fighting, and they still hadn't seen one of the enemy forces. To them, it was as if a ghost force had attacked them.

From above, hidden in the trees, four men launched 40-mm grenades into the remaining troops, killing the rest of the men. Others would die later that day from their wounds. None would survive to tell the story of the ghost unit in the jungle. Jim didn't care that the story would never be told because it was a story of horror and death. His teams were lethal.

In the wild firing in that final attack, no one was hit by a stray bullet. Jim waited breathlessly until all his men checked in and told him they were okay. He bowed his head, and tears filled his eyes as he watched the carnage in the jungle before him. God had protected his team and given him a great victory.

Marta Hess, he knew, would not rest until she discovered who had been responsible for the attack upon her compound. What he didn't realize was that her biochemical team of scientists had been killed in the blast, leaving her quite alone on the compound. She would have to wait nearly three days for the supply helicopter to arrive before she could leave. For her, it would be a frightening time during the night because of the predators drawn by the dead bodies.

On Captain Rob, the men carefully cleaned their gear, stowed everything properly, took delicious showers, and gathered on the boat's bow to pray. No one suggested it or gathered them together; they just came, knowing that Divine protection was granted and thanksgiving was required. Jim felt closer to his Lord and Savior than ever before.

None boasted of what they had done. Most were sickened by the need for such bloodshed. Instead, they sat in chairs in a circle, and each man prayed, some awkwardly and shyly, others confidently, but every man offered thanks for the safety of the unit. In the end, Mark read through the account of David's mighty men in II Samuel to remind them all that God could do great things with men who were dedicated to Him.

After a meal, they moved back downriver to join the other riverboats. Again, the equipment Zeke and Smitty built protected them, so the thirty-six men ordered by Marta Hess to keep the unseen force from leaving the area were detected and avoided. Slipping past them this time had been even more stressful than before, but they managed it basically because the patrol boat was parked at one of the camps. Undetected, they rejoined their crew.

CHAPTER 32

Returning to Bring It Up Coral was like coming home for all of them. Abe and his crew disappeared into the galley area as soon as they set foot on the ship. Jim helped with the equipment and treasure storage before retiring to his cabin, taking a hot shower, and changing into his best dress uniform. They were having a celebration to commemorate a successful hunt and safe return.

A band was hired to provide music for entertainment, and a space was cleared in the dining room for couples to dance. Heidi, Lisle, Cecilia, and Millie often found themselves on the floor. Dredging up memories of dancing with his mother when he was fourteen, Jim managed to move around the floor twice with Cecilia and once with each of the other ladies. Dr. Gregg surprised everyone by being by far the best dancer among the men. Despite his age, he was spry on his feet and produced surprised giggles of enjoyment from the women in his arms.

One of the band members, an agent for the drug cartel, reported that no conversations regarding the river of death could be heard. No one on the ship appeared to know anything about the battle that took place on the Columbian side of the border. They were too excited about their discovery of the hidden Mayan city and a map showing an undiscovered Mayan city near the Guatemalan and Honduras border. His report satisfied the drug cartel that this group, at least, had nothing to do with the death of hundreds.

Marta Hess had spies, too. They were much more thorough and came away as empty. She was sure that the crew of Bring It Up Coral was somehow involved. Without evidence, she remained frustrated. During the next ten years, she spent most of her family's fortune trying to buy information on the river ghosts. Worse, she was watched constantly by agents, even made aware of their presence, because somehow her plan to kill billions with her biological weapon was leaked to American and British forces. Nor was she able to make drugs for the Cartel or any legal pharmaceuticals after her losses.

An untimely death in a plane crash would end her search. She would never know who had destroyed her plans or her empire. Those things would pale when she came face to face with Almighty God and was called to answer for her sins.

Bring It Up Coral set sail for Cairo to return Dr. Gregg and his museum artifacts and treasures, his students and notes, safely to port. Retired though they were, the guards who watched over the ship kept it in pretty good shape. Dr. Gregg was interested in noting that Jim and his men were not one hundred percent satisfied. Working hard for two weeks brought everything to Jim's and the crew's satisfaction. He saw in that dedication something that would ensure they would work together again.

Mark arranged for the riverboats to be returned to the docks on the Potomac River at the mansion. He kept in constant contact with the firm that towed and delivered the boats, reporting to Jim one afternoon that the boats had reached their destination safely.

Jim expressed his thanks and put that bill in his files, marked paid in full. Still, he didn't feel that he was finished. There was something yet he had to do.

He was restless, and he knew why. At last, on a calm day in the Mediterranean, he took action. As sunset approached, he asked Cecilia to join him on the observation deck. She had watched him carefully over the last few days and tried to determine his intent. She wore the dress she knew he liked best in honor of the occasion.

Standing there in his Captain's uniform, he looked as handsome as she had ever imagined he could. His smile was tentative and unsure, and his eyes were softer green than usual. As she came to him, he held out both his hands, taking hers, and turned to face the rose sky. After a moment, he leaned down and kissed her, and then, kneeling with old-fashioned grace, he finally found the courage to ask her to be his wife.

"Cecilia Merton, I think you know that I love you deeply. I believe God put us together and drew us to each other, and I would like to be your husband," he stated with tears in his eyes.

Misty-eyed, she stared at him, her hazel eyes first going blue, then almost green, and tears gently tumbled down her soft, smooth cheeks. His hard, calloused hands held hers gently, and she could feel the strength in them. Gently, she squeezed his hands, kissed him somewhere near his nose and eye, and spoke, laughing and crying.

"I would be happy to be your wife, James Shepherd!"

He lifted her off the deck and then drew her into his embrace, holding her tightly, kissing her eyes and mouth. Neither remembered what they said in those following moments, but Cecilia would never forget the rosy sky, the warm Mediterranean breeze, and the feel of her man's arms around her. A quiet voice brought them back to earth, red-faced and embarrassed.

"So we'll be having a wedding at sea, I take it," Millie said. She laughed merrily as they blushed, then reached for her husband, who was climbing the steps to join her.

"May I be the first to congratulate you?" Doc Wozniac said quietly, shaking hands with Jim and kissing Cecilia on a still salty cheek. Quietly, he handed her a clean handkerchief. "I must confess this is not quite the secret you hoped it would be," he added with a smile.

The blast of the diesel air horn split the evening, and suddenly, Cecilia and Jim were surrounded by people congratulating them as the crew rushed to the observation deck in celebration. His friends had been watching, too, and several of them had seen him with the ring, and one even heard him practicing his lines. But the wedding did not take place immediately. Jim knew his mother would never forgive him if she were not present.

Dr. Gregg and his team and cargo were dispatched with the promise of further adventure. Jim returned to Live Oaks to the mansion and married Cecilia Ann Merton on the sweeping lawn overlooking the Potomac. Admiral Runion was there, and Andrea walked Cecilia up the aisle in place of her father.

For a wedding present and reward to his crew, he booked an entire cruise ship for his men, their families, and friends who wished to accompany them to Alaska. He and Cecilia planned it together, and though it was expensive, both felt it was appropriate. They shared the best suite of rooms on the ship for their honeymoon, and everyone respected their privacy, allowing them to determine how much time they spent with friends and family. And in that suit, Jim and Cecilia began a lifetime relationship built upon trust in God and each other.

It was a merry journey, lasting twenty-one days and filled with the proper balance of relaxation and excitement. The vessel crew was quite pleased to have such a small group of people to serve and went out of their way to make the time enjoyable for all. Looking back, Jim decided the cost was well worth it.

Ken Worthington and his family attended the cruise as special guests. During the twenty-one days at sea, he found an opportunity to recoup the entire cost of the cruise and then some through an investment in gold shares and a new gold mine in Alaska. When he told Jim what he'd done, the captain threw his head back and laughed.

As a silent partner in the corporation, Worthington had increased the wealth of that worthy entity tenfold in the two years he'd been with them. Jim and Cecilia thanked him appropriately and reminded him he was supposed to be on vacation, enjoying the cruise. Ken grinned. His answer was typical.

"Finding investments like that is fun!" he laughed. "With the money I made personally on the deal, I'm taking my wife and daughter on a bicycle trip from Canada to Mexico on the West Coast," he added. An avid cyclist, he often took a month here or there for such a trip.

As all such things do, the trip drew to a close, and the families and friends returned to their homes while Jim took his team back to Live Oak Mansion to prepare to go to sea once again. After twenty-one days of relaxation, the team needed to get back into shape, and that would take at least thirty days of hard work to regain their edge.

Now, added to all his other responsibilities, Jim had a wife to balance in the works. He found the experience quite pleasant and frightening at the same time. Bad people still inhabited the world, and he and Cecilia had jobs to do. That they could face the challenge together was a new experience for both of them. Somehow, it felt right. Life is like that. Just when one thinks life is settling into a pattern, it provides amazing challenges.

Theirs was already waiting for them when they returned. But that is another story.